Secrets fro

By
Christopher Masterman

Dedication

To my wife, Elizabeth Horne, for all the encouragement you gave to me and for joining in our adventure to Arisaig.

With thanks also two my two daughters, Amanda and Stephanie, for their helpful comments and their contributions to the medical aspects of the story.

Also by Christopher Masterman

Non-Fiction
'An Average Pilot'
An affectionate history of Cedric Masterman OBE DFC

Fiction
Travelling to Tincup
Deathly Confessions
The Bridge at Braunau-am-Inn

Ian's Story

Chapter 1

My brother Ian and I were often taken to be identical twins, although I was a year younger. That lasted until our late twenties when I began to get fat and balding and he began to get thin and hirsute. Until then, and throughout our childhoods, we exactly matched each other in height, build, colouring, behaviour, interests and habits. We also looked just like our father, Colin; all three of us being just under six foot in height with fair hair. Ian was born in 1941 and died 42 years later.

Colin was an RAF Officer; he survived the Second World War but was killed in a pointless flying accident over Germany two months after that war had ended. Although he was a highly experienced pilot, he wasn't flying the aircraft when it crashed in cloud amid the Harz Mountains. None of the six occupants survived the mangled wreckage of the Avro Anson light transport aircraft. His body was swiftly returned to England and buried in the cemetery at RAF Manston airfield in East Kent, near to where his wife and two very young sons were living.

My mother, Mary, brought Ian and me up as a single parent. My first clear memories of my childhood date from

1946 when I was about 4 years old. We all lived in a house at Westgate-on-Sea on an estate called 'The Courts' – a horseshoe shaped crescent of white pebble-dashed, detached, late 1930's two-story houses and bungalows surrounding a large green space dominated by a large, very crooked and easy to climb tree. Ian and I called it 'The Old Oak' but on reflection it was probably an ancient, gnarled fir. The house belonged to my grandfather Byron, Mary's father, a retired London banker who lived with my grandmother, Joan, in an identical house facing us on the other side of the green. I believe that he had bought both houses at the outbreak of war as investments and boltholes away from the anticipated London Blitz.

Had he lived, I suppose that Colin might have wanted more children. Mary said that it would have been nice to have had a little girl to bring up as a counter to Ian and me and to be more of a companion for her but, as she never remarried or had any male lovers that I knew of, she poured her love into her two sons. I have no memories of Colin at all. I'm not even sure that he ever saw me after my birth as he was abroad for much of the war although he must, of course, have spent time with Mary when Ian was a baby for me to have been conceived. Ian claimed that he stayed with us for a while at the war's end and remembers going for walks along the sea front with him – that would have been just weeks or even days before he died.

Neither Ian nor I ever felt the lack of, or need for, a father; Byron took that role. He was only fifty or so years old when we were born and still less than sixty as we came to the ages when a father was needed as a male guide and mentor; effectively, he was our father and for most of our childhood Ian and I were either in his house or he in ours. He stopped work through ill health just after the war, the results of being attacked by poisonous gas during the preceding European conflict, before either Ian or I reached our fifth birthdays. We loved him and were devastated when he died at the age of seventy-two just as we were leaving our teens.

My other grandparents lived in London, about two hour's

journey from Westgate by car. I can't remember the grandfather as he died soon after his son Colin's death, and the grandmother was looked after by a spinster daughter, Colin's sister. I suppose I only met my Aunt and Grandmother about three times in my whole life, although they did send me and Ian cards with small sums of money at Christmas and for our birthdays. We, in turn, dutifully wrote them thankyou letters.

What might be considered an oddity in Mary's behaviour, certainly unusual at least, was her insistence when Ian and I became teenagers that we addressed her by her first name rather than 'Mummy, Mum, Ma' or similar. That request took some effort to comply with, but by the time we were adolescents our peers thought we were really cool to be on such familiar terms with our mother; what their mothers might have thought of it all I have no idea. And on reflection it was a request entirely consistent with her own experience for she called both Byron and Joan by their first names. The appellations 'Father, Daddy or Dad' were thus never heard in our house and that, I think, is another reason that neither Ian nor I ever missed having our real father.

My brother and I often played up the appearance of being twins. It wasn't hard. If I looked in a mirror my mind saw him; and as he was left-handed to my right handedness we really did seem like reflections of each other. We persuaded Mary that we wanted to dress alike; she acquiesced and came herself to treat us as twins. Although we had none of the talents that genuine identical twins seem often to have − knowing what each other is doing, thinking or about to say − we would sometimes rehearse behaviours and tricks to persuade our friends that we did possess a certain 'spookiness' in our relationship. We thought of ourselves as being the same age and sometimes quoted the others birthdate when asked for our own.

When we reached about five years old (I can't help but regard Ian and I as being the same age because that is always how we were treated) Mary resumed her interrupted career as a book illustrator − she had attended the Slade School of Art in

London before the war – and was able to work mainly from our home. The work brought in modest amounts of money at infrequent and unpredictable intervals and, even with her War Widows pension and no rent to pay, she would have found it hard to survive financially on her own with two growing boys. But she was Byron's only child and was doted upon, and Byron was a quite wealthy man with no expensive hobbies to indulge other than membership of the local golf club and an appetite for good Scotch whisky. Byron paid Mary a regular allowance which he rationalised as payment for Colin sacrificing his life for his country; thus we lived comfortably enough by the sea-side as post wartime rationing and other restrictions gradually eased throughout the 1950s and the near miracle of the National Health Service started and matured. Byron also helped with education expenses when Ian and I progressed through the local Grammar School and our colleges.

Mary was always a most caring parent and our childhoods were very happy. As we entered our teens and the old fashioned and very restricted attractions of Westgate-on-Sea (which could easily have doubled as the setting for the TV show 'Dad's Army' with its winter gardens, seafront tea rooms and crumbling Victorian salt water swimming pool set into the cliff face on the beach - absolutely the best place ever for boys to seek out crabs and star fish) we discovered the attractions of nearby Margate with its 'Dreamland' funfair complete with Big Dipper, its 'racy' reputation and visits by the 'Royal Eagle' paddle steamer with its cargo of carousing Londoners. We found pubs there that would serve us half-pints of beer despite us being clearly under the official drinking age of eighteen, but that was the nearest we ever came to getting into any real trouble.

Once Ian and I were safely established in our Grammar School, Mary threw herself whole heartedly into her publishing work. Her illustrating commissions became more frequent and more lucrative as the years passed and she often went to London by train to meet with her publishers – as she said. By the time Ian and I were in our late teens she had bought a spacious, two bedroomed flat in South London with money that Byron had given to her shortly before he died. She would stay there for two or three nights at a time, leaving us under the not too watchful eyes of Grandma Joan across the road. As salaciously inclined schoolboys, we speculated that she had a lover stashed away somewhere in London; and well she could have had, perhaps a succession of them. But I never saw her with any close man friend; she may not have had any because, when he went to live in the flat while at college, Ian told me that he saw her with women friends - one in particular sometimes shared her bedroom. We were pleased to know that she was living a happy and seemingly fulfilled life when we had fled the nest.

Mary was what might be described as a 'handsome' person; appearing tall for a woman in those days with a trim figure, who followed clothes fashions quite carefully and always seemed immaculate, even when engaged in household chores. Ian and I were proud to have her as our mother and in our young eyes she was a beauty, although later our more cynical eyes saw that it was her personal grooming that contributed greatly to her attractiveness. Nevertheless, when attending school functions and the like she seemed to us to put other mothers to shame. She never appeared flustered – always in control - yet love flowed copiously over her two sons.

Ian and my paths parted when we left school in 1960. I believe that Ian deliberately held back in academic work one year so that we could graduate at the same time. We both received sufficiently good exam results to enter our chosen professions.

Ian took up a place at the London School of Economics having decided to become a Civil Servant, while I studied marine engineering under a Merchant Navy cadetship; we both had to leave Mary and Westgate. Ian ended up in the London seat of British Government bureaucracy, Whitehall, while I joined my first ship, an oil tanker, as a very junior and green ships engineer

Thus, Colin didn't figure at all in the lives he left behind in Westgate. Ian and I didn't need to forget about him – there was nothing to remember; that is until many years later, when we read his war time diaries and discovered his role in the defence of Norway. A role that had repercussions right up until the end of Ian's short life and involved an extraordinary decision made by Mary right in the middle of the war, but that remained a secret for years afterwards. And looking back as I do now, I believe her sexual propensity may have influenced the genesis of her war-time secret.

What Mary did or didn't do in 1941 makes her and Ian the centre piece of the story, but the roles of a Norwegian partisan and her British manipulator were also pivotal. My beautiful partner, Fiona, worked out the solution to Mary's secret. My name is Martin, I was Ian's younger brother.

--///

Ian worked exclusively in London principally in helping to create and implement Government policy on the UK's defence procurement programmes, although he was never very forthcoming about what he did. He lived in the London flat and was occasionally joined for a few nights by Mary; most weekends he spent in Westgate keeping Mary and Joan company, and sometimes bringing a girlfriend down with him. My knowledge of his life during the 1960s is very sketchy because I was almost continually at sea and, with what land time I had, I took in the overseas countries to which my chosen career conveyed me. I had a fling or two during that time but nothing serious or sustained and I had absolutely no desire to settle down, marry and have children. I don't suppose I saw my brother, mother or grandmother more than once each year before my thirtieth birthday – but I did phone the Westgate house at least once a month.

During one such routine phone call in early 1971, Mary begged me to come 'home' as soon as possible as Ian had been taken ill. My ship then was a huge oil tanker operating mainly between the Persian Gulf, Holland and Japan; it had just docked in Dubai for a scheduled five days in port which gave the operating company enough time to replace me with another suitably qualified Deputy Chief Engineer. I flew directly back to London and boarded a train to Westgate where all of my family were waiting as I arrived by taxi from the station.

I suppose that I had half expected to see Ian in bed surrounded by anxious family, even a doctor or nurse judging by the distress in Mary's voice, but it was he that opened the door to me. I could see the others – just Mary and Joan - hovering behind him in the hallway. His handshake was firm as was his brotherly clasp of my shoulder. He looked me straight in the eye and thanked me for coming, then mouthed silently 'It really wasn't necessary, but it helps Mary'. I had no trouble understanding him because this 'silent talk' was how we used to communicate while pulling our fake twin tricks on our school mates.

Later that evening Ian told me about his illness.

"Do you think I'm any thinner since we saw each other here last Christmas?"

"Maybe a little," I replied. "I'm definitely fatter, it's the food on the ships – nearly always too good and too much. I guess we don't look so nearly identical now. Are you starting to grow a beard?"

"Yes, I thought I'd try. Not going too badly is it?

I nodded. Gazed into my whisky, and waited. 'It's coming now', I thought to myself. 'Cancer probably'. We never had to beat about the bush or be coy with one other. When we were very young our conversations were almost like two halves of the same brain talking back and forth. That facility had long since passed but the implicit frankness of our relationship had not.

"It's called Muscular Dystrophy," he began after the pause. "A complicated disease, apparently. It has various different forms I'm told. I've no idea what mine is. But it's supposedly not a common one like 'Duchenne's'. That one's named after a

French doctor who first diagnosed it in the latter half of the eighteen hundred's. Good job really otherwise I'd have been a sickly child and probably dead by now."

"Then what is it that you've got? I haven't heard of Muscular Dystrophy."

"Like I said, the quacks say it's some form of Muscular Dystrophy. MD I've learned to call it; no treatment known apparently. It's more of a progressively deteriorating physical condition than a disease such as, say, polio."

"Then how is it affecting you? How do you know that you are ill... you look okay to me."

"Basically, aches and pains over the top half of the body, the muscles of my shoulders and my pecs, and sometimes my thighs. I've had to give up playing squash. Shame, I was getting quite good, could probably have beaten you up to six months ago, and there is, I'm told, a rhythm abnormality of my heart. I got wired up to some fancy box of electronics in Harley Street. The quack looked solemn when he told me there was a problem, but then couldn't say if what his box had detected was serious, or new, or best ignored. Another Harley street doctor specialising in nerves, I gather they are called neurologists these days, made the diagnosis of MD. I'd complained about the stiffness and soreness to my local doctor about three months ago. He arranged all the referrals. But it's taken until just a week ago to get a good steer of what is going wrong."

"But if the heart thing isn't dangerous and you are just sore and stiff, why did you have to put the frighteners on Mary? Can't you just live with it?"

"Well, that's the nail whose head you have just hit. I can't live with it. It's going to get worse. The pain and stiffness... my muscles will disappear. I'll waste away in effect and eventually my respiratory muscles and probably my heart will be affected in the same way and I'll die of either asphyxia or a heart attack. But not yet Brother Dear. I could have anything between five and twenty years of life yet; although the last few years could be pretty grim and I'd have had to stop work well before then."

He got up and refilled my glass and his own. I felt as if I had been slugged with a bag of wet sand.

"But how did you catch it? How did it start?"

"There is really not a lot known about MD; it may even be a collection of similar diseases. There is some evidence, apparently, that some types of MD may be inherited while others just seem to occur spontaneously. So if I inherited it then I didn't catch it. It would have come from a parent; and if not inherited then I 'caught' it at about the time I started to get symptoms, about 6 months ago, as I said."

I couldn't help blurting out my next question. "But, if as you say you could have inherited this... this MD as you call it, then it must have come from either our father or Mary, so could I catch it too?"

"You wouldn't be 'catching' it, you'd have it already, although possibly not showing. But the doctor treating me, well, not actually prescribing any form of treatment bar gentle exercise and massages, says that from his experience I was very late in developing the symptoms, so if you do have it then it would be reasonable to expect it to have shown by now."

Because I'm a year younger than Ian, I wasn't much reassured; but he quickly went on.

"And in any case, assuming that it is inherited, some statistics come into the likelihood of it being passed on. My neurologist tried to explain the genetics of inheritance that may be involved, but I don't think he had a full grasp of the subject himself or otherwise was no good at explanations. However, he told me that statistically it's a one in four chance of inheriting it from a parent carrying whatever it is that initiates the disease. So if I'm one in two, that's you and me together, then your probability must now be much less than one in four."

I wasn't sure that his statistical analysis was correct, but it seemed believable and I had absolutely none of his symptoms. I grunted my agreement.

"I'm very glad you came to see me," Ian said, ending our conversation that evening. "Stay a few days to support Mary and Grandma then go back to sea. I've just taken a week's leave after which I'll return to my usual work. It's not at all physically demanding as you can guess, just office administration and meetings; I can continue doing that for years yet, I hope."

Chapter 2

Ian did keep going, fighting his debilitating disease for many more years. But, of course, I wasn't to know that as I stayed on in Westgate after Ian had gone back to London, and I had two concerns: Ian's unknown prognosis and the possibility that I, too, might develop Muscular Dystrophy. I concluded that I had to be in, or near, to England so as to provide support to both Ian and Mary, and to get medical support if needed.

I flew to Rotterdam and told my shipping company that I was taking extended leave from the sea which, we agreed, would be unpaid once I had used up all my accrued annual holiday entitlement of six weeks. I told the twenty-two year old girl, Sjoukje, who lived permanently in the small flat I rented as a base for when I was between ships, that I was giving up long sea voyages and in future would live somewhere in the UK. I suppose the simplest way to explain our relationship was as friends 'with benefits'. When I returned from a spell at sea, which often lasted as long as three months, she welcomed me into her arms and bed, usually after getting rather drunk together, but after a few nights the passions (in truth, neither of us were very passionate towards each other) waned and we lived a bit like brother and sister until I was off again. The arrangement suited both of us fine and we were happy in each other's company. I was well paid and she always seemed to have plenty of money so we lived the high life for the month or so that we spent together three or four times each year. I didn't know what she did for a living. She was never working while I was in Rotterdam and used to talk vaguely about being in the hospitality business, but never gave me any details. I had my suspicions that she was a high-class call girl. She was pretty, 'leggy' enough and harboured a very smart wardrobe. Years later a Dutch friend told me that temporary escorting had indeed been her first profession but that she had subsequently married a wealthy, much older businessman and settled into a life of comfortable respectabil-ity.

When I was leaving I asked Sjoukje if she wanted to move with me; it wasn't an idle offer, she was very good company, intelligent, smart and quite well educated and like so many Dutch she had perfect English, but she declined. I usually paid the rent on the flat and said that I would pay for a further six months in advance. She accepted that offer.

At the beginning of the 1970s the exploration and exploita-tion of the UK's North Sea oil was just getting into full stride. The companies involved were crying out for competent staff to work out of mainland Scotland, as well as the Orkney and Shetland Islands to the north and whilst Brent and Piper were the major oilfields then, many others were coming on line continually. My qualifications and experience as a marine engineer were readily transferable to the design, build or operation of oil rigs and pumping terminals, thus I quickly landed an excellent job as an oil rig pre-commissioning inspector based in Aberdeen. I was settled into that harbour city half way up the east coast of Scotland less than a month after my meeting with my ailing brother. My new company provided me with a flat spread over one whole floor of a large Victorian, slightly grim looking, terrace house constructed of sparkling grey granite (as was much of Aberdeen then). I had insisted during the recruitment interviews that I would not consider sharing this flat with any other employee because I half expected Sjoukie to change her mind (she didn't) and if not her, then perhaps some local lass would favour me (and so it later proved). My contract expected me to work, or at least be on call, for six days of each week that I was in Aberdeen but in compensation I could take one full week off every fifth week, with a return flight to London paid by the company, and in addition take up to six weeks of vacation each year.

These arrangements were ideal and enabled me to see Ian and Mary regularly. Effectively, we became a close family once again and it was made all the more complete by Joan, now well into her seventies yet still enjoying good health, who had sold the house opposite and moved in with Mary.

While I was settling into my new life I cast around for someone with a specialist knowledge of Muscular Dystrophy who could give me better advice than that which Ian had passed onto me. I found such a person in Edinburgh; Doctor McGregor and visited him there as a private patient in the spring of 1971 after a two week wait for an appointment. The doctor told me that what I had heard from Ian, and he from his Harley Street consultant, was basically right but not the whole story. McGregor started by giving me a thorough physical exam: reflexes, grip, arm strength, leg power and heart were all checked. When he had finished he pronounced me in robust health with absolutely no sign of incipient MD.

"That is not to say that you won't get MD, but I would regard it as extremely unlikely and, as you age, with each year that passes, the likelihood becomes smaller and smaller. If you have no symptoms by the time you are forty, so ten years or so, you definitely won't get it. It may seem easy for me to tell you not to worry because it is a terrible disease, but don't worry is my advice."

He went on, "A great deal of effort is being directed in many countries towards finding the true cause of MD and some progress is being made. Most importantly, perhaps, is the now general acceptance that it is hereditary and passed through the maternal line and to sons only, though there is a bit of a dispute about that, but it seems to be true that if women do display any MD like symptoms then they are very mild."

"But what does 'passing through the maternal line' really mean? Why can't it come from one's father also?" I asked.

"I can try to explain why it only affects men and also how it appears to be transferred from mother to son. What do you know about chromosomes and genes?" the Doctor replied with a question of his own.

"Absolutely nothing."

"Then I'll try to give you a five minute primer."

He took a sheet of paper and on it drew two symbols. "Do you know what these mean?" he asked.

"Yes," I replied. "They are the symbols for a woman and a man."

"Well, more accurately, they represent the female and male for all creatures. However, let us pretend that they represent a woman and a man who are about to procreate. Now let us bring in the chromosomes."

He drew two 'X's side by side under the woman and an 'X' and a 'Y' underneath the man.

"Now, a woman has two 'X' chromosomes and a man one 'X' and one 'Y' chromosome. That is the basic distinction between the two sexes. The chromosome is an incredibly complex piece of life which is only now starting to be unpicked. It includes the genes, bases pairs, enzymes and many more bits and pieces, thousands of components, millions more like. And this complexity is what makes us who we are, why we are all different. The children of this alliance, and all successive alliances, will also have the same pattern of chromosomes which are derived from both mother and father. The contents of these chromosomes determine the physical and psychological characters of the child at birth. They are extremely complex as I've said, so the girls could be very feminine or rather masculine with endless shades in between. It can also bring about a person who wants to be masculine although they are trapped in a female body, for which there are

14

remedies of course. The same logic applies to the boys. Now, let us identify the chromosomes."

He annotated the woman's chromosomes as 'X1' and 'X2'; the man's 'X' chromosome became 'X3'.

"Now," he said pointing in turn to each symbol. "This couple can produce four different types of children each of which has to have a combination of two of the four available chromosomes. One from each parent. So a girl may have 'X1' and 'X3', another girl of 'X2' and 'X3', a boy of 'X1' and 'Y', and finally a boy of 'X2' and 'Y'. There are four different choices. Do you think that you understand all that?"

I replied that I did.

"Right, now suppose that one of the woman's chromosomes contains a mutation that can produce Muscular Dystrophy in her offspring, let us say that this mutation is buried inside the 'X2' chromosome on this diagram. The 'X1, X3' girl will not carry the mutation. The 'X2, X3' girl will carry the mutation because of the 'X2' chromosome; the disease will, however, almost certainly not manifest itself in her because the 'good' 'X3' from her father will cover for the damaged 'X2', but she can pass that problem 'X2' onto some of her children. The 'X1, Y' boy will not get inherited MD, and cannot pass it on, but the 'X2, Y' boy will have the mutation, may develop MD, and will pass the faulty 'X2' chromosome on to his daughter because that is all he has. So there you are. There is one chance in four of the child of the woman bearing the mutated chromosome, and if a boy then one chance in two of having that chromosome and possibly developing the associated disease."

So, I realised that something within Mary had been passed onto Ian and developed into MD while I, although having theoretically the same odds as Ian, had probably escaped. Thus Doctor McGregor's advice did go a long way towards reassuring me, yet the possibility of developing MD didn't entirely leave my mind until I neared forty. I visited him three more times during those years. During the last he told me not to come back.

For about four years there was little visible change in Ian. He still worked and lived in London, his movements were a little slower perhaps and sometimes his face seemed drawn with pain; he said that he took pain killers when necessary but I had no idea how often that was. Mary was stoic and, I think, refrained from fussing over him or showing him special favours, in my presence at least, so as to maintain the sense of absolute equality between Ian and me. But in 1976 I had to go to America to attend some courses on the operation of deep sea oil rigs in bad weather. The extreme conditions experienced in extracting North Sea oil was taking a heavy toll on equipment and lives. I didn't get back to Westgate for about three months. As I approached the house having walked in good summer weather from the railway station, I saw Ian moving slowly around the garden. It was quite a large space with mainly roses and lawns and bounded by privet hedges. Ian was hobbling and using a walking stick with a tripod foot.

He waved at me as I drew near, pointed at the stick, shrugged his shoulders and tried to grin.

He admitted to me during my visit that, although life was certainly getting tougher for him, he intended to continue working for as long as he could still travel into his London office at St Giles Court. Mary's mask was off however. Her concern for Ian was palpable and compounded by a distinct ageing of Joan. I offered to move from Aberdeen down to Westgate, or London even, to be nearer and more able to help with Ian and to support her.

"Not yet, Martin, not yet," was her reply. "He's fighting on, he's stubborn. When he can no longer look after himself that's when we will need your help."

His deterioration was gradual and sporadic and was now being ascribed to 'Becker's Muscular Dystrophy' which apparently was a rare variant of the earlier diagnosis of Duchenne's MD. Becker's usually occurred rather later in life than most other forms of MD. For months at a time no change was detectable in his body or behaviour. Sometimes he seemed to go into remission and get a bit better, but he well knew that the general long-term trend was always downwards, as did his physicians.

By 1980, and already wheelchair bound, he had to stop work and move permanently down to Westgate to be looked after by Mary and a daily help. This was just after Joan had died peacefully in her sleep at the age of 85. Ian and I sometimes discussed the extraordinary times that she had lived through. The dawn of motoring and manned flight, voyages to the moon, computers, two world wars and many more minor conflicts, the collapse of colonialism and the rise of communism, nuclear weapons and amazing medical advances, although no promise of a treatment for Muscular Dystrophy.

Ian had long given up his car, and the one woman who might have become his wife in happier circumstances had moved to America with her bank three years earlier. But a Scottish woman had entered my life in Aberdeen. Fiona Buchanan and I had first met in Aberdeen in 1973 when I was 31 years of age. She was three years younger. Within a year I had forsaken the company flat and together we had purchased a similar looking house in the same street. Fiona was a corporate lawyer and was paid much the same as me, but oil had made Aberdeen an expensive place to live so there was a hefty joint mortgage on the property. We had an understanding that we would get married when I reached forty, the age that I would be absolutely clear of any chance of getting MD and then we'd start a family. She sometimes came down to Westgate to see Ian and Mary and became a firm favourite with both. As she was with me.

Fiona is, I suppose, not what one might regard as conventionally pretty, but startlingly attractive would be mine and most other of her many admirers' reaction on first seeing her. Her huge and bright blue eyes are set off by long, wavy, flaming red hair which can be quite hard to tame when it becomes her 'explosion in a mattress factory' look, as she puts it. Her fine boned and beautiful facial features are dotted with near orange freckles, freckles that continue over most of her full figure. In the beginning we sometimes played a game where I hunted for freckles around the erogenous parts of her body. These hunts invariably turned into passionate and satisfying sex for us both. We were well suited.

But she was not with me during one of my visits to Westgate in 1980, when Ian started to talk to me about our father, Colin.

"Do you ever think about him?"

"No," I replied truthfully. "No, I don't. I never knew him. I know nothing of him. I've seen two photos of him in Mary's bedroom, one in the uniform of a Royal Air Force Squadron Leader sporting half a dozen medals, so probably taken just before he was killed. The other shows the two of them together with you in their arms. Mary never speaks of him. What about you? Do you think about him?"

"Like you, not at all. Well... until that is a couple of weeks ago when Mary gave me a tin trunk that apparently belonged to him. It was returned full of his effects by the RAF shortly after he died. She said she had only ever opened it once, thirty-five years ago, and since then it has been under her bed; it's under mine now. It was a hell of struggle for the two of us to move it although it's not really that heavy, but she's not as strong as she used to be and I'm pretty useless. It's probably made of aluminium from old aircraft parts."

"What is in it? Have you looked?"

"Oh yes, I've opened it and rummaged around. Mary left my room when I did so. She said that as Colin's elder son she should have given it to me ages ago. I guess she thinks I've not got much longer before I join Colin, wherever he is, and ought to know more about him."

I tried, ineffectually, to ignore that last remark of his.

He went on, "His flying suit is in it, together with helmet, goggles and gloves. To begin with I couldn't figure that out as I assumed that he would have been wearing all that gear when he was killed, but then I remembered he had been a passenger in the crashed plane, rather than the pilot, so he had probably been wearing uniform rather than flying kit. His flying log book is there too. I haven't really studied it but it seems he flew in combat for most of the war in several different types of aircraft. Then there is a small box containing his medals and medal ribbons. There are several bits of RAF documentation, vaccination certificates and the like, so nothing that one might regard as unusual until I opened a small leather briefcase and found an exercise book inside. You know, the sort one might use for school work. It was almost full of hand writing. I thought that he might have been keeping some sort of journal, he has beautiful handwriting by the way, but only a few weeks in 1940 are covered. Do you know anything about the British efforts to stop the Germans invading Norway?"

"Absolutely nothing at all," I replied.

"Then you really ought to read this. Like I say, it's a sort of diary," Ian said, handing me the rather dog-eared exercise book.

I read the diary; more of a manuscript really, that night while in bed. It was suitable material for a good short story and told of a trip that Colin had made to Norway in 1940. I had no real knowledge of the geography of Norway. The places he mentioned meant nothing to me and I realised that I needed a map to fully understand the whole story. This I purchased the next morning from a book store in Westgate. With the map by my side, I settled down to reread the account of the two months he had spent in Norway. I reminded myself that he was just 26 years of age when his adventure had begun.

Colin's Story

Norway

- International boundary
- Province *(fylke)* boundary
- ★ National capital
- ◉ Province *(fylke)* capital
- Railroad
- Road

Akershus Fylke is administered from Oslo

0   50   100 Kilometers
0   50   100 Miles

Lambert Conformal Conic Projection, SP 47N/62N

RUSSIA

FINLAND

SWEDEN

ESTONIA

Norwegian
Sea

North
Sea

Gulf
of
Bothnia

Baltic
Sea

Gulf of Finland

ALAND ISLANDS

Nordkapp

Hammerfest
Vadsø
Vardø
Båtsfjord
Vadsø
Kirkenes
Alta
Lakselv
Tromsø
FINNMARK
Ivalo
TROMS
VESTERÅLEN
Narvik
LOFOTEN
Narvik
Kiruna
Bardufoss
Kemijärvi
Bodø
Bodø
Malmberget
Kolari
NORDLAND
Jokkmokk
Rovaniemi
Arctic Circle
Kemi
Mo
Sandnessjøen
Luleå
Oulu
Mosjøen
Namsos
Storuman
Skellefteå
Namsen
NORD-
Lycksele
TRØNDELAG
Umeå
Steinkjer
Kokkola
Kajaani
Trondheim
Östersund
Örnsköldsvik
Iisalmi
Ålesund
Molde
SØR-
Vaasa
MØRE OG
Åndalsnes
TRØNDELAG
Kuopio
ROMSDAL
Seinäjoki
Florø
Härnösand
Äänekoski
Jyväskylä
SOGN OG
Sundsvall
FJORDANE
Pori
Hermansverk
OPPLAND
Hudiksvall
Tampere
Mikkeli
Bergen
Bøverdal
Lillehammer
Rauma
Hämeenlinna
Lahti
Kouvola
HORDALAND
HEDMARK
Hamar
Mora
BUSKERUD
Gävle
Turku
Helsinki
AKERSHUS
Borlänge
Uppsala
Haugesund
Drammen
Oslo
Tallinn
Stavanger
TELEMARK
Moss
Karlstad
Västerås
Stockholm
ROGALAND
Skien
Tønsberg
Örebro
Södertälje
ESTONIA
VEST-
VESTFOLD
Vänern
Nyköping
Pärnu
AGDER
Egersund
AUST-
Arendal
Uddevalla
Motala
Norrköping
AGDER
Kristiansand
Skagerrak
Falköping
Linköping
Vättern

Chapter 3

Namsos

<u>22 April 1940</u>

Have now been at RAF Ickenham, a flight commander in No 325 Squadron, since October last year and not seeing much of the war from the cockpit of my Lysander: patrols up and down the Kent and Sussex coasts avoiding German aircraft, any of which could easily shoot me down, and army cooperation exercises that involve dropping messages or picking up messages from a wire suspended between two poles on the ground while flying the old girl as slowly as possible. The war in Europe appears to be picking up steam and I'm not sure that we or the French are doing too well. But here it's all too quiet. I've never seen a German or any enemy aircraft; most of the time I'm thoroughly bored and looking forward to escaping to a local pub or two in the evenings. But today things have changed.

It's a non-flying day for me and I'm sitting in the Officers' Mess anteroom enjoying a quiet beer when a Squadron Leader whom I've never seen before approaches me. I see he is going to talk so I start to get up as a courtesy to his more senior rank.

"Flight Lieutenant Colin Mitchel?" he enquires, motioning with his hand for me to stay seated.

"Yes," I reply

"I'm Noakes. Finding life busy?"

"Not at all, Sir."

"Would you like to go to Norway? Tomorrow?"

I can hardly believe my ears. Norway! The Germans had started an invasion a couple of weeks earlier I know; perhaps I would see some action at last. "Yes, yes of course. But what would I be doing?"

"I can't tell you that. Don't really know myself except you won't be flying anything. But if you get to this office at The Air Ministry," he handed me an envelope, "by ten tomorrow morning and ask for Wing Commander Sexton, then all will be revealed. Do you have your own car?"

"Yes."

"It's about a two hour drive from here to London. There are some extra petrol coupons in this envelope to help you on your way."

"But what about my Squadron Commander and the Station Groupy?"

"It's already fixed with them. They both said that you would jump at the chance. They reckon you're restless and getting a bit moody, so I think they're glad to be rid of you for a while. If anyone else asks you where you are going just say up to the 'Air Box' on detachment."

He waves good bye and turns to leave the mess.

"Will I see you again, up in London perhaps?

"Oh no, I'm just the messenger. Pack enough things for a couple of weeks at least, and take your pistol but don't wear it openly while still in Britain."

Why 'Britain' and not England, I wonder as I pack my kit bag in the evening?

23 April

My little open top Wolseley Hornet runs perfectly today; the intermittent firing of cylinders three and six seems to have cured itself after I had to retard the ignition so much to use this dreadful wartime 'Pool' petrol.

I park the car a hundred yards or so from the Air Ministry building in Whitehall, leave my kit and tin hat stashed away behind the dickey seat. My revolver is in the brief case I'm carrying and make my way up the steps of the building, gas mask slung over my shoulder. I have only been here once before and that was in peacetime. Now I see that the lower portion of the building is hidden behind a wall of sandbags and the windows of the upper stories are covered in criss-crossed sticky tape. A sentry salutes me and asks for identity papers; I show him the little card that I keep in the breast pocket of my uniform. He points me to an oldish man, Corps of Commissionaires I expect, who is acting as a receptionist and guide. I tell him that I'm there to see Wing Commander Sexton and that I'm expected at ten o'clock. He checks his watch. I'm ten minutes early. He consults a register, makes a phone call, tells me the room number (already forgotten) and says I can take the lift to the third floor. Instead, I walk up the large, marble finished staircase, find the room and knock on the oak panelled door. A voice tells me to enter. It's a small meeting room. Wing Commander Sexton walks towards me. I salute.

"Don't salute here. It's just not done in the Air Box and I can't respond as I haven't a hat on." But it's not a reproof, he is smiling, just advice.

He seems old, a lot older than me, but smart and fit. I look at his chest and see a medal or two from the First World War and an Air Force Cross. Perhaps he flew with the Royal Flying Corps which would make him at least forty-two I calculate.

The meeting is brief. He tells me that we, he, I, another officer and some non-commissioned airmen, are all going to Norway via Scotland, but he can't tell me the details of the mission until we are on our way. He tells me to drive up to RAF Hendon to spend the night, draw some cold weather clothing and a sleeping bag there, and be ready to fly out tomorrow afternoon, at 14:00 hours. I'm to be prepared for several weeks of very hard work.

I drive up the Edgeware road to Hendon. I book into the Officers' Transit Mess, have lunch and then find the clothing store where I'm issued with a down-filled bedroll complete with hood, a parka and fur lined gloves. 'Just how cold can it be In Norway in April?' I think. 'Perhaps we are all going to sit on top of some snow-covered mountain.' My fleece lined flying boots were probably going to get some use.

I have a beer or two in the Mess before turning in early for the night.

24 April

Read papers and magazines in the mess whiling away time until lunch then collect all of my kit and go towards the apron where I see a de-Havilland Flamingo is waiting. I've not seen one before. It's a nice looking medium sized twin engine transport. The two pilots are supervising its refuelling; they tell me we will have eleven men on board and can't take off with a full fuel load so will have to top up en-route. Our destination is to the north of Scotland near Inverness. The whole journey is about 500 miles they tell me. Sexton plus a Flying Officer Ball and five airmen wireless operators arrive in a crew bus and we all pile into the Flamingo. It looks like a conventional civil aircraft inside with comfortable seats and windows to look out of. The aircraft also has its own radio operator who doubles as a navigator. We take off promptly at 14:00 hours.

Into the cruise at about 200 mph heading approximately due North at 8,000 feet. I'm not used to being flown and I must say I don't like the feeling much. I want to be upfront past the radio operator where the co-pilot and captain are. The refuelling stop turns out to be Catterick in Yorkshire where we all get out while the bowser is pumping petrol into the wing tanks of the aircraft, then back in and airborne again after less than twenty minutes on the ground. I've been checking the map that the radio operator is using. By 17:30 hours we are over Inverness and the wide expanse of the Moray Firth; our descent starts and a little later we cross the smaller Cromarty Firth. I can see the seaside town of Invergordon with its long pier stretching into the sea and a small nearby airfield which the map says is called 'Novar' but the radio operator says is now RAF Evanton. We land there at 18:00 hours.

A crew bus takes all of us into Invergordon where I, Sexton and Ball are dropped at the little Officers' Club while the airmen are taken to the NAAFI. Sandwiches have been prepared in both places for our suppers. We are told that the next stage of our journey will not start until it is totally dark. We are far north now and the sun won't start to set until after 21:00 hours, so we have several hours to kill.

During this wait Sexton tells Ball and me the purpose of our trip.

"We are going to Namsos and there we will supervise Norwegian labour in the preparation of landing grounds for RAF aircraft that will soon be brought over by an aircraft carrier. We are flying there in a Sunderland which is already moored by the Invergordon pier."

I can hardly believe my ears. None of our party have any experience of building landing grounds on probably snow-covered terrain, and none of us speak Norwegian.

Sexton will brook very little discussion. An interpreter has been found he tells us, and the task will be completed he emphasises, although he adds the rider that things are not going well for the British and French expeditionary troops, known as 'X Force', that are trying to halt the German advance up Norway.

We approach the dark hulk of the Sunderland in a launch. I have never been so close to such a huge aircraft. In fact, I've never been near a flying boat before. Even in the gloom I can see the outline of its four great engines and the multitude of gun turrets. We gingerly climb out of the rocking launch and into the cavernous two-story interior of the aircraft. Big though the interior of the Sunderland is, there are very few creature comforts other than bunks and seats for resting crew members.

We will have a crew of just six we are told, although ten is a more usual complement. I find a free canvas bunk and after take-off, sit down to write up this diary. Although I managed to actually write little, as even with the aircraft being immensely noisy, I soon fell asleep using my tin helmet as a sort of pillow.

25 April

Sun shining through the windows awakens me at about 05:00 hours. I move up to the flight deck and look out as we fly for about twenty miles up a mist shrouded fiord flanked by high mountains. We approach Namsos, which is almost at the fiord's end.

As we descend towards the surface of the water, we fly over several quite large warships and a collection of fishing boats, some are moored to a long wharf while others seem to be stationary in the fiord. At first sight this small port of Namsos doesn't impress, but as we near I see that most of it has been flattened by bombs. A few buildings remaining intact. I've never seen such destruction before, this is my introduction to the true nature of war.

I return to the interior of the aircraft, Sexton tells us to prepare for alighting and that we are going to transfer onto the Royal Navy anti-aircraft cruiser HMS Calcutta. Once safely on the water the Sunderland taxies towards the stern of Calcutta but in doing so stoves in its port wing tip. Nevertheless, we get secured to the ship and scramble aboard through the front gun turret of the Sunderland and up a swaying rope ladder. Our whole party is then given a good breakfast in the ratings' mess. We hang around the ship while Sexton goes ashore to try to sort out accommodation for us. A Heinkel-III flies over at about 8,000 feet and the crew of the Calcutta immediately take up action stations, manning a multitude of anti-aircraft weapons, but the Heinkel drops no bombs and the Calcutta does not fire on it.

A sailor from the Calcutta climbs onto the wing of the Sunderland and repairs its damaged wing tip; the aircraft then takes off, presumably to return to Scotland.

I meet the two-man crew of a Fleet Air Arm (FAA) Blackburn Skua that, having run out of fuel, made a perfect forced landing on a mud bank at the fiord's edge. Unfortunately, they tell me, that while they were trying to taxi the aircraft onto dry land it got stuck in the mud and tipped on its nose leaving it irrecoverable.

Three German airman are brought aboard as prisoners; they come from their aircraft that was damaged by fire from the Calcutta and force landed further up the fiord. They look young and pleasant; I feel a sympathy for them until I look again at Namsos and see the damage wrought on it by the Luftwaffe.

In the afternoon we are ferried to shore by one of the ship's launches. Sexton has found a hut, which he calls a chalet, for him and me to sleep in, and another one for Ball and his radio operators. I explore the wharf and docks area which is full of military personnel, British, French and Norwegian and equipment. In the middle of all this melee are tented catering facilities and the GHQ from where all this confusion is supposedly controlled. I listen to several briefings, the German army is not as near as Sexton had earlier indicated to our party, but the Luftwaffe is very active and airfields for British fighters to oppose them are desperately needed. There seems to be a general air of pessimism.

A large French troop ship, the 'Ville d'Alger' waits in the fiord; it's too large to moor against the quay apparently. It landed French troops here a few days ago, arriving under the escort of two French destroyers which are still in the fiord; someone tells me that they are all waiting to take the troops off again and back to Mother France where things are going very badly for the French and British armies.

I turn in late.

26 April

Woken at 05:30 hours by heavy AA fire from the direction of the fiord. Ships are having a go at a lone Henkel-III which apparently turns up early every morning for a quick look-see.

It flies away undamaged.

The interpreter, Harborg, turns up with three sets of skis. He is a local Norwegian conscript about my age and speaks good English. We spend all day looking for likely airfield sites but find it impossible to make a judgment given that all meadows are covered by about five feet of snow and we have no idea of what lies underneath it. This is my first time on skis and I don't do well.

An exhausting day, fortunately without any aggressive action by the Luftwaffe. Back in bed after finding some hot food at about midnight.

27 April

What a day!

Woken at about 06:00 by the windows of the hut shattering inwards and the sound of bombs bursting nearby. Sexton and I step outside to see the fireworks display. All the warships are banging away at bombers flying high over the fiord; we see the shells bursting at about 10,000 feet above our heads. heads which are protected, probably completely futilely, by our tin helmets. I hear a loud rushing sound and witness seven bombs from one aircraft descending on the quay-side about a mile away. A wag nearby says, "There goes the railway train."

The stick of bombs hits the main British ammunition store and the whole horizon dissolves into explosions, flame and indescribable noise. Ships all along the quay cast off and move into the centre of the fiord where they can attempt to manoeuvre away from falling bombs. Ordnance from the destroyed store continues to explode and burn for the whole morning. I'm told that there have been several casualties with the bodies of the two storekeepers completely disappeared.

I find the abandoned Skua nestling between rocks and, as Sexton has decided not to attempt an airfield recce today, I look to see if anything is salvageable. I remove three compasses easily but will need tools if I'm to get the machine guns out of the wings.

Later in the afternoon the Luftwaffe revisit the scene and

bomb some more. Calcutta is stuck by splinters from a near miss and registers eight wounded. The Admiral visits GHQ while I am there and I hear him say that it was lunacy to have such a big ship as Calcutta sitting in the fiord as a target for Jerry.

Just before I turn in a Heinkel-III flies low along the road leading out of Namsos and lets loose its machine guns. I wake up later hearing noises coming from the quay-side. I look outside and see a big merchant ship unloading a battalion of French troops and about a dozen mobile Bofors Anti-Aircraft guns, weapons that are supposed to be very effective against aircraft.

28 April

Usual early morning recce by the Heinkel.

Harborg has obtained a very dilapidated Model T-Ford for use in our airfield search expeditions although he is not available to join us today. I've christened it 'Willie'. I borrow tools and drive out to the Skua where I manage to remove its four Browning machine guns by 09:30, just as six Junkers-87 Stukas fly over me and then start their screaming dives towards the military encampment on the quay side. I take cover between two rocks on the roadway near the Skua; it's a pretty good shelter and I still get a view of the fireworks. Three of the bombs hit the already scarred and burning quay seemingly without causing any more damage while the other three fall harmlessly into the water. The pilots were probably put off by the intense fire coming from not only the warships but also the Bofors guns that were landed just yesterday. The aircraft fly away; one appears to have been hit as it is manoeuvring erratically.

I return to the Skua but just 30 minutes later two Heinkel-III turn up. I squat between my two rocks again while they attack some target further down the fiord.

I take the Skua's machine guns to the FAA armoury on the quay.

Everything quietens down until early evening when a lone

Heinkel-III, assumed to be on a Recce patrol again, drops its bombs onto and around a trawler causing damage to it. I hear later that this was the 'Arab' and had been requisitioned for anti-submarine purposes at the beginning of the war. Apparently its Captain, a Lieutenant Commander Stannard, is known for his coolness and did an excellent job in manoeuvring his charge away from the worst effects of the bombing and thereby saving all his crew.

In bed fully clothed (again) and writing up this diary and determined to get on with the job of finding a landing field tomorrow.

29 April

It's been a long day and I can hardly keep my eyes open as I write up the events I witnessed in this little diary.

Usual morning recce by the Heinkel, who, after last evening's performance got a pretty hot reception and veered off.

At about 07:00 Sexton, I and Harborg get into Willie and are about to sortie out to some likely looking sites, at least according to the very poor map we have, when six Stukas suddenly appear overhead and start diving at a small warship emitting the unnerving scream of their sirens. I see that it is HMS Bittern that is under attack. I have met her captain, Lieutenant Commander Mills, who told me that she is what is called a 'Sloop' and weighs about a thousand tons. She twists and turns in her efforts to avoid the diving aircraft and their falling bombs, but the fiord is narrow and she has little room for these manoeuvres although I sense that Mills is doing his very best to save his ship and crew. Other ships are firing at the Stukas and I see one burst into flames and scuttle off down the fiord at two hundred feet; I am sure that it has crash landed somewhere. Only two of the six bombs explode; they miss Bittern but cover her with spray.

We head off in Willie and find our destination about 30 miles away from Namsos which we can still see as we have climbed quite high, Willy puffing and wheezing all the way and having to be continually replenished with water. We see that more aircraft are attacking Bittern; we see her struck and a plume of smoke rising from her; it looks serious. There are five more raids on her, on other ships and Namsos itself during the day. We stay away until it seems to be all over, and we have still not found a possible landing ground.

Back at GHQ that evening I'm told that Bittern has been hit by a large bomb that set off the depth charges stored on its stern, destroying the back end of the ship. Twenty-nine sailors have been killed and a further seventeen seriously injured; survivors were taken off by other ships moving alongside. Bittern was not sunk by that bomb, but clearly beyond further use to X-force she was sent to the bottom of the fiord by a torpedo from the destroyer, HMS Janus. A trawler was also sunk by German bombs and another damaged but it is believed that at least three German aircraft were shot down.

And so to bed, it's past 02:00. I think I may be walking home if this loss of ships continues.

30 April

Heinkel recce a bit later this morning; just one quick pass then off, but back five minutes later and loosing bombs on to the quay.

Most of the warships move away from Namsos towards the mouth of the fiord which being wider and not hemmed in by high hills gives them more room to manoeuvre when under attack; but while they make their moves so does Jerry in the form of five bombers, Dorniers I think, but their aim is poor and their bombs fall harmlessly into clear water.

Then a single Stuka flies over and machine guns the GHQ just as I arrive there, but causes no casualties. As it departs it deposits a big bomb onto the road leading away from the town. Again, no significant damage done.

Lots of rumours and counter rumours at GHQ, and throughout the whole base. It looks as if Namsos is going to be evacuated. It's obviously untenable as a base from which to counter attack the German Army in the Norwegian hinterland without air cover, so best remove the troops to fight another day at another place and salvage as much equipment as possible.

In any case Harborg, who is now totally pessimistic about the future of Norway in particular and the French and British cause in general, believes that, even if Namsos is held, building a landing strip for British aircraft is totally impossible. The lack of large scale maps makes identification of potential sites difficult, and on the ground evaluation is impossible due to the snow. All suitable equipment to clear snow, or compact it, is held in Oslo and Oslo has been held by the Germans for nearly three weeks. Some Norwegian turncoat by the name of 'Quisling' appears to be trying to take charge and collaborate with the Nazis. Harborg adds that much of the local population is resigned to occupation by the Germans and does not wish to seek retaliation by overtly helping to build the airfield.

1 May

I wake up convinced that we will evacuate Namsos, and soon, so I return to the Skua to remove as much equipment as I can and hand it in to the FAA stores near the quayside. As I do, a few German bombers make a short attack on Namsos town. Only one 'railway train' bomb stick is dropped before the aircraft are driven off by our AA guns. I believe one attacker is damaged. I decide to take the opportunity to walk through the town. I know that it is a legitimate military target with its large concentration of British, French and Norwegian forces but I still feel a huge rage against the destruction that surrounds me. There appear to be no houses at all left standing in the main street. Everything is levelled, razed. All that remains of the church are two damaged walls. I recall Harborg telling me that nearly 4,000 residents are now homeless although, against all odds, only twenty or so of them have perished in the German air attacks.

I write up this dairy as I await developments.

2 May

I hang around GHQ. Orders seem to be being transmitted to troops in the field to return to their Namsos bases.

In the afternoon another air raid on the town, short and not very serious. Namsos is already so badly damaged that I doubt that this attack achieved anything for Jerry.

It's now early evening and the order to evacuate has just been given. It seems that all military equipment is to go on HMS Carlisle, an anti-aircraft cruiser and sister ship to the Calcutta, while personnel are to go aboard the destroyer HMS Alfridi by 21:00 hours and then be ferried to warships and troop carriers waiting nearer the mouth of the fiord.

I stroll a little out of town and watch the troops coming in. The French Chasseurs Alpins are particularly impressive, although obviously exhausted, their discipline seems still superb and they appear to have all of their kit, including their skis strapped across their backs. They await loading onto Alfridi as do The Royal Lincolnshires and other troops that I can't identify.

I and the other members of the Sexton party take our kit onto Carlisle and are told to stay on board while Alfridi and other ships start ferrying troops out of the port under cover of the advancing darkness. I find my way to the wardroom where I am offered a drink and make conversion with Carlisle's officers as they come in and out to grab a bite to eat between attending to their duties on deck. I continue to be offered and accept naval gins. By midnight I'm curled up in an armchair and falling asleep.

3 May

I wake up to a running breakfast being served, and join in. We are running to get clear of the fiord.

A klaxon sounds four times and the Carlisle officers dash away from their breakfasts. The vessel's 4-inch AA guns fire for a few minutes then all is quiet and the officers return to their breakfasts. They appear calm and laugh a lot, but the strain of the past weeks shows in their faces.

Action stations sound again and I go up on deck with Mills, the Captain of the sunk Bittern. We come to a 4-inch gun which immediately fires. I dive for shelter thinking we are under attack and land on my bum, much to the amusement of Mills. There are German aircraft attacking ships all over the fiord. I see two shot down. I also see the French destroyer 'Bison' hit by bombs and start to sink after a huge explosion in her magazine. Alfridi and two other warships rush to her aid and take off survivors.

Alfridi finishes off Bison with her guns; she sinks.

The air versus sea battle goes on for hours. Suddenly a group of Stukas targets Alfridi. She is hit by their bombs and catches fire and I see a large hole in her side. Her captain puts her into a tight turn so that the heeling of the ship keeps the hole above water while the crew assemble on deck. Then two destroyers race up to her, she slows and starts to settle by the bow as the destroyers take off the survivors. These destroyers then come under attack themselves. I'm standing next to the Admiral and express my disgust at Jerry's actions but he calms me by saying that, rescuing survivors or not, the destroyers remained legitimate targets.

We reach the mouth of the fiord and turn towards the south and Scotland. Jerry continues to harry the convoy. I ask how the land-based German aircraft continue to find our ships so easily and am told to look at an aircraft shadowing the convoy well out of the range of any of the AA guns. The Navy call it 'Shad', but it's actually a Heinkel-115 and it radios the convoy's position to the Luftwaffe and any Jerry submarines in the area.

I return to the wardroom in the evening to reserve my sleeping chair for the coming night.

A young officer asks me, "Weren't you supposed to be on the Alfridi?"

I suddenly realise that if it hadn't been for the Carlisle's wardroom hospitality of the previous evening I would have been on the sinking ship. I nod my head.

"Fifty-three of the crew dead," he tells me. "Plus about a

dozen of our soldiers and half of the Frenchmen plucked from the Bison."

I realise that I have now witnessed death at first hand and contrast it with my cosy little life flying a Lysander from Southern England not much more than a week ago.

4 May

We now have RAF aircraft keeping guard over us and Jerry has ceased his attacks. I'm told that, apart from those in Alfridi, all 12,000 French and British troops were successfully evacuated from Namsos. I wonder if I will ever see that town again. I suppose not.

We steam on.

5 May

Arrived Scapa Flow at 04:00 and transfer to the troop ship 'Duchess of Athol.' A seven ship convoy forms around us this evening and Sexton, who turns up from God knows where, tells me that we may be going back to Norway. In the meantime I find a shore billet at a large house in the nearby town of Leith.

I've lost contact with Flying Officer Ball and his airmen.

Chapter 4

Bodø

<u>**10 May 1940**</u>

I leave my billet in Leith by the side of Scapa Flow and re-join the 'Duchess' where I'm allocated a bunk. We move out of Scapa as one of a convoy of troopships escorted by an assortment of warships. We are going to Bodø which is further up the Norwegian coast than Namsos, to try and build an airfield there for RAF and FAA fighter aircraft that are currently based at Bardufoss. They are to provide air cover for the troops that we are taking to Bodø and others that are already there. We have been joined by more RAF personnel to provide logistic and technical support for the expected aircraft.

Hear that Germany has attacked the Low Countries and France. Phony war has really ended now.

RAF Sunderlands take turns in escorting us, and we see no sign of Jerry.

<u>**11 May**</u>

Heading almost directly due North. Sunderlands still keeping Jerry away.

12 May
Weather deteriorating, no sign of Sunderlands or Jerry.

13 May
Still no air cover as we approach Norway.

Heinkel 115 appears in the evening as we moor at Bodø. Seems smaller than Namsos and not so damaged.

Unloading of troops, British, French and Norwegian, going well. They seem in good spirits.

Staying on Duchess for the time being.

14 May
Sexton and I get off the ship and start to look for possible sites. We don't have to look far as there is a suitable area right by the town and facing into the sea. Although it is criss-crossed by power cables and very soggy.

We negotiate successfully with local officials for housing for the RAF contingent.

We are introduced to Mr Wick, a local who works for the Norwegian Roads Department. He agrees to act as our project's civil engineer and will engage the local labour that will be needed. He speaks good English. In addition to the airstrip itself we will have to build air raid shelters and crew rooms for the pilots when they arrive. This time we have got to get it right so that Bodø can be defended from the sort of aerial destruction I saw wrought on Namsos.

15 May
We have started! And so has Jerry. Sinking a troop transporter in the water near Bodø.

We have hired 120 men at one kroner per hour and have divided them into day and night shifts, although a lot of the night shift is spent in the lingering sun. The long daylight hours of this northerly location which is just above the Arctic Circle will help us, but it also helps Jerry. We have installed an air raid warning system linked to the town.

Air raid sirens all night, mainly false alarms.

16 May

Moved off the Duchess and into a chalet complete with a bath, what luxury. Excellent weather, am spending all my time at the strip which is now marked out and has some drainage installed.

Wick estimates that we will need 15,000 cubic feet of soil as filler. We don't have any trucks so we have hired 25 horses and carts to move this earth.

17 May

The ground is too boggy to use as is, so a surface has to be laid comprising thousands of turf sods. Manpower is pouring in, it seems the whole town is volunteering to help in a multitude of different ways. All seem keen and enthusiastic to help keep Jerry at bay. But we will need more labour so have engaged a further hundred men.

We have started to excavate air raid shelters by the airstrip because our efforts are soon sure to draw the attentions of Jerry. Sexton thinks we will be finished in two weeks. I think three is more likely.

The heavy cruiser HMS Effingham was travelling at full steam bringing in more troops when it hits a rock fairly near to us and is wrecked. Luckily without casualties.

18 May

Everything going well. Sexton may be right about the timescale. He is leaving me to oversee the construction of the airfield while he deals with the logistics, manpower and administration tasks for the arrival of the aircraft and aircrew. He has also arranged for all the overhead cables and pylons to be removed from the vicinity of the airstrip.

Nine Ju-87 overflew us but were probably looking for targets in the vicinity of ground forces clashing somewhere in the interior. I realise that we have to have sufficient shelters on the airfield to provide protection for the 200 or so men labouring to build it, so I make the excavation of more dugouts a priority.

19 May

Wick calculated that we will need about 175,000 sods for the surfacing of the airfield. I have calculated that we will need about twenty shelters. Work continues on both requirements.

20 May

50,000 sods cut by midday from a field about two miles away from the airstrip area. I tell Sexton that I am now predicting strip and shelters will be ready on Saturday 25 May. He says that he will advise the RAF base at Bardufoss that aircraft coming from there can arrive on 26th.

Mid-afternoon six Ju-87 bomb Bodø. Three houses set on fire. Work on the airfield slowed as men took shelter or rushed away to inspect damage, but back up to speed in early evening and continued all through the night.

21 May

Misty morning is keeping Jerry away. Just one Heinkel-III overhead drops one bomb through the mist, no damage.

Levelling of the airstrip in preparation for the laying of the sods has started and is going well, as is the digging of the dugouts which will have bomb-splinter-proof roofs (I hope). But we only have 50 men for the sod cutting, so have asked the local Chief of Police Mayor to get us more. He scours Bodø and a couple of nearby villages and more help arrives pretty quickly. So much in fact that we start to build Officers' quarters in the form of a reinforced above-ground hut with accommodation for fifteen and a basement to serve as the flight operations centre.

Underground power and telephone cables are being laid.

22 May

We are making great progress with hundreds of men now on site. I have 200 on day shift, another 200 on night shift and 75 horses and carts which are bringing the turf sods to the airstrip.

Late afternoon a Heinkel-III comes over and drops 6 bombs near to the airfield killing three soldiers and wounding twelve more. Work interrupted for five hours but resumes later in the night.

23 May

Levelling of the airstrip continues and by day's end half its length has been turfed to a width of 50 yards. However, I am not happy with the firmness of the surface which I do not believe will take the weight of an aircraft. I consult with Wick and we decide that the sods are to be covered by wire mesh.

At 20:00 hours shots are heard from the direction of the Quay and news comes through that the Germans are attempting a landing from the sea. Many of the labourers disappear until it transpires, and they are convinced, that it was all just a false alarm.

24 May

Splinter-proof shelters now all completed and the bomb-proof aircrew cellar nearly so. Nine Ju-87 drop bombs into the harbour area without causing any serious damage, but then machine gun the airfield workers. We are lucky to have no casualties but for the first time I feel frightened.

25 May

Mid-day and the strip is now complete. It is 50 yards wide by 700 yards long. Just big enough we think. We have used over 160,000 turf sods in its construction. We will keep 100 men on standby at all times to fill in bomb holes as Jerry makes them, which we feel is inevitable. RAF ground staff have arrived from Harstad along with tools, fuel pumps and fuel in drums that they site at three dispersal points for servicing the aircraft which are expected to arrive tomorrow. These aircraft are needed to provide air cover for the withdrawal of British and Norwegian troops from the Bodø area. We are going to scoot off again!

A Norwegian girl, Ingrid, visits my billet after I've had supper. She says that she has some vital war material that has to be taken to England to be kept out of German hands. I ask what it is, maps perhaps, I was thinking. She tells me that its whale oil, in a large metal drum. I know that the Norwegians are big whale hunters but so are many nations. I ask the importance of this particular oil. She tells me that it is from the Sperm whale and is very special because it doesn't go thick at low temperatures and therefore it's used for aircraft instruments. As she tells me I remember from somewhere, that it lubricates gyros, automatic pilots and so forth. I tell her that I have no real means of getting it to England but if she can get it to the airfield, I would help if I can. She tells me that she and the barrel arrived with the ground party from Harstad, and the barrel is now already safely stored in one of the air raid shelter pits nearby.

26 May

Jerry aircraft all around in the early hours of the morning but cleared off later.

Three Gladiators of 263 Squadron arrive from Bardufoss at 14:00 hours and all immediately bog down on our carefully prepared landing strip. The biplanes stream-lined wheel fairings clog up with mud. They are extricated by the ground crew and moved to an area of the strip about 50 by 300 yards long which is less boggy than the remainder. It's not really big enough for safe operations, nevertheless, Lieutenant Lydekker who is actually FAA, manages to take off to keep Jerry away as the other two aircraft are refuelled.

I have my doubts about the effectiveness of these obsolescent biplanes against the seemingly much more modern German aircraft they will face.

Two Heinkel-III appear and Flight Lieutenant Hull and Pilot Officer Falkson attempt to get airborne. Hull succeeds but Falkson crashes because of the poor airfield surface. The Gladiator is so much scrap although Falkson himself appears unhurt but obviously shaken.

Lydekker sees off the two Heinkels and is then recalled to stay on the ground while Hull heads off to provide air cover for troops under attack at nearby Saltden. By the time he returns out of ammunition he has shot down or damaged three JU-52 and two Heinkel-III. So much for my doubts about the Gladiator!

For the remainder of the day the three pilots take turns to provide continuous air patrols with the two serviceable aircraft. No more Jerry aircraft try their luck over Bodø and the troops to be evacuated (about 2,000 I'm told) arrive without further molestation from the air.

Wick comes up with a solution for the poor surface of the wire covered sods. We will lay snow boards over the surface of the airstrip. By midnight we had laid 300 yards of them. Just enough we and the pilots think.

I write up this dairy then get to bed at 04:00. This day the strip has done its job.

27 May

Wake at 07:45 to sound of heavy bombing. Dash out of hut and see twelve Ju-87 accompanied by four Me-110 fighters. Lydekker manages to take off while Hull struggles to start his engine. Eventually he too gets airborne. I see Hull damage a Ju-87 then both Gladiators are chased away from the airfield vicinity by the Me-110s, for which they are no match. The airfield is bombed but no damage to the airstrip at this time although some of the other facilities are damaged. Repairs started immediately. I peak into one of the dugouts where I find the metal drum bearing the legend 'Sperm Whale Oil' in rather amateurish lettering.

I hear that Hull has been shot down and crash landed at some place called Skagodden. He is badly wounded apparently with bullet wounds to the head, knee and hand and has been taken to the nearest hospital. Not knowing about this and thinking that Hull has returned to Bodø, Lydekker flies on to Bardufoss, under continual attack by the German planes he lands there wounded in the neck and shoulder, and is also taken to hospital. We have no air cover.

18:00 hours the Ju-87s and Me-110s return, attacking the airfield firstly with bombs which completely destroy the airstrip, then machine gunning everywhere. In a lull I dash out of my shelter and search for the rest of the RAF men. They are all okay, but badly shaken.

Ten minutes later I hear enemy aircraft returning. I'm in the open and my nearest shelter is a water filled ditch into which I scramble. Bombing starts immediately and I feel the ground shake as the bombs hit the airfield, then Jerry's efforts are redirected to the town and I witness the systematic destruction of Bodø. The hospital is the first building to be hit and goes up in flames, then the rest of the town is razed before my eyes and everywhere is machine gunned. I'm wet through with the icy ditch water and praying amid the noise and mayhem as I've never prayed before.

The firing eases, I venture forth from my ditch and find Wick with a young airman. The machine gun strafing starts again so we all three dive back into the icy water filled ditch. The fury abates and we dash across about 200 yards of open ground to reach the splinter-proofed RAF Headquarters. We are exhausted and as pale as sheets.

We revive ourselves with a beer each. Then the sick and wounded from the destroyed hospital begin to pour in. Falkson is driving an ambulance and the place is turned into a casualty clearing station. Nurses come in along with doctors and the RAF Doctor, Scott. Two pregnant local girls arrive, then the Flight Sergeant and the rest of the RAF contingent. No casualties.

Sexton comes and asks if I think it's possible to repair the airstrip. I truthfully answer, no. He disappears. I think he is helping to plan an evacuation or even a forced march of 120 miles across mountains to the relative safety of the main RAF base at Harstad. We try to rest against that possibility.

We scrounge food from wherever we find it. Sleep hard to come by as we shelter in the RAF HQ.

28 May

We decide to get away from the airfield as it's likely to remain a key target for the Luftwaffe. We form up all the RAF crew, scrounge as much kit and food as we can and move into the hills. There we make our own individual funk holes. I find a good site under a huge rock. In the evening we send out a party to scrounge more food.

Jerry raids Bodø again but everyone round me seems to be asleep by 22:00 hours.

29 May

Woken up by the sound of aircraft and machine guns, snuggle further into my funk hole. During the day we stay in the safety of the hills, I find two of the men have local girls in their funk holes. I ignore them, silently wishing them well. Later I make my way to the Navy HQ and cadge a couple of tots of rum.

30 May

Again woken by machine gun fire which continues on and off all day. Sexton turns up in a car and we drive to the airfield where he takes lots of photos. He insists that the airstrip is repairable. I argue that we now have neither labour nor transport, he counters that the RAF ground crew will have to fill the craters by hand. The thought of being in the open filling craters while being machine gunned by Stukas terrifies me and it's an order that I don't want to have to pass on to the men. Then we hear that two destroyers are coming in tonight to take us off. Very glad tidings.

22:00 hours we move out of the sheltering hills in small parties and make our way through the remains of the town to the supposed rendezvous point for embarking on the ships. Not a thing stands in Bodø. The church, hospital, hotel, everything is gone and there is a stench of burning flesh. Just a few chimneys stand sentinel as monuments to the madness of the Nazis.

We reach the docks and wait nervously while we are allocated billets. It seems that we are not leaving tonight after all. The first offering is a wooden shed which I vigorously refuse for myself and on behalf of the men. Eventually we move into the stone built Custom House having smashed down its door. The army units, British French and Norwegian, are being evacuated ahead of us. I suppose they are needed to fight in France or elsewhere.

31 May 'til 6 June
We wait anxiously in what is fast becoming a stinking hole. Our clothes and our bodies are filthy. Rumour and counter-rumour swirl around all day, every day. Our ground troops seem to have all been successfully evacuated.

We hear that the Germans are driving us out of Norway just as they have driven our army out of France. There is a major evacuation taking place at Dunkirk apparently. This war is not going well for us. The men and I, are getting very nervous. Will we get out before the Germans arrive? Will we spend years in prison camps? I have no answer for them or myself.

Amazingly I am told that only about a dozen civilians were killed in the bombing of Bodø, although many more were wounded.

On top of all this the weather has turned very hot adding to our discomfort.

7 June
Still no real news. Went exploring and had a bath in a horse trough so feeling a bit better. In the early evening the RAF contingent finally boarded a destroyer and departed broken Bodø.

8 June
Heading home.

Eugene's Story

Chapter 5

And that was it. The final words, 'Heading home' and nothing more. I flicked through the remaining pages of the note book but all were virgin blank.

His narrative did give rise to questions in my mind. What had happened to Flying Office Ball and the radio operators? Did they too take the journey from Namsos to Bodø? And how did Colin get 'Home'? If, as his diary said, the RAF contingent set sail on 7 June why is his last entry 'Heading Home' made a day later? And what happened to the sperm whale oil? He made no further mention of it so presumably it was left behind in that dugout on the airfield to be found by the Germans perhaps?

But this was all trivia compared to what the diary had revealed. I now knew what had happened to Colin over just six weeks of his life when he was twenty-six years old. I knew virtually nothing else about him except that he would be dead by thirty. Yet these forty or so pages written in pencil with a beautiful hand had opened a window to my father through which, in a way, we could look at each other and shake hands. The diary showed how he behaved in very trying and totally unexpected circumstances and from it I saw him as brave, but not ashamed to admit to fear. Obstinate perhaps, resourceful certainly, compassionate and lucky, in Norway at least. I at last knew some intimate things about him, and I was proud to be his son.

I passed these new feelings of mine onto Ian, and he said that the diary had had exactly the same effect on him.

"I mean," I said, "I had no idea that we had invaded Norway during the war. Or tried to at least. That period, summer 1940, has always been overshadowed by the so-called miracle of Dunkirk and the Battle of Britain. And then there is the horror of the bombing of both Bodø and Namsos. He saw it all."

"Well, you can read about it. There are several good books covering what was in all intents and purposes a complete fiasco," Ian replied. "And something else you probably don't know, he got an award shortly afterwards. The OBE."

"The Order of the British Empire? Is that one of the medals in the photo in Mary's room?"

"Yes, I've checked. It's the first on the ribbon row and here it is straight from his tin box."

He opened a leather covered hinged box not much bigger than a glasses case. Inside were six medals suspended by coloured ribbons from a long clasp. The left most one was in the form of a silver cross topped by a crown and at its centre was an engraved portrait of King George VI and his Queen Elizabeth. The ribbon, a little faded, was red, almost maroon, with three thin silverish stripes. It was a handsome thing and I caressed it gently with my figure tips.

"But they don't give OBE's to soldiers or airmen in the middle of a war, do they?" I asked. "I thought it was the type of thing you get as a reward for years of dedicated service. The sort of honour that you might get, would have got."

Ian smiled. "Yes, I'd have probably got it just before my scheduled retirement."

"And what is this other medal next to the OBE?"

"That is a Distinguished Flying Cross, otherwise known as a DFC. RAF pilots and other aircrew got them, commissioned officers that is. The non-commissioned had to settle for a Distinguished Flying Medal, the DFM, I believe"

"Are you sure it wasn't the DFC that he got for building that airfield?"

"No, that has to be for flying. He would had to have shot aircraft down I think and more than one. One of those three Gladiator pilots, Hull was it, ought to have got a DFC, probably did I expect. I guess it would be possible to find out about the OBE, but as Mary has never mentioned it, along with so many things about our father, including the DFC, perhaps it is something to tackle her with right now."

I nodded. I wanted to know as much as possible about Colin, my newly discovered father.

"Would you like to know more about the Norway campaign?" Ian asked. "There is a fellow I used to work with, although much older than me, Eugene Russel. He's a font of knowledge about the Second World War and has the OBE himself, so might be able to shed some light on Colin's award."

"Maybe. Yes. I'll think about it." I replied.

"While you are in your 'getting to know your father'

mood, have a look at his flying log book," Ian said, handing me a handsome, green leather-bound book with the name 'Colin Mitchel RAF' embossed in gold letters on its cover.

"It's got his whole flying career in it starting from his first training flight in Lincolnshire, then his time in India when he was 21 years old, then right through the war and into peace time, just. He flew lots of different types, even Spitfires. He shot down five enemy aircraft, that's where the DFC came from I expect. It's got all the places he served in, India as I've said, England and Norway we know from the diary, but also Malta, Egypt, Kenya and Burma."

I took the log book and read through it during the remainder of the days that I stayed at Westgate during that visit. The terse entries in the log contrasted with the emotions shown by Colin in his Norway diary so I learned little more about his character from it, but as he flew almost continually throughout the war, even when being rested from offensive operations, I gained an understanding of what his life had been like. I was right, he had been lucky. Right up until that fatal trip over Germany in September 1945.

Back in Aberdeen I told Fiona about the diary and showed her Colin's log book. She was immediately interested and urged me to follow up Ian's suggestion to talk to his friend.

"You know what he was doing in Norway but you don't know why he was chosen to go there. Why did this man, Noakes was it, seek him out?" she urged. "And you may uncover something about that mysterious OBE."

I phoned Ian to ask if he could put me in touch with his friend Eugene.

Six weeks later I travelled down to Westgate by air and train as usual to stay with Ian and Mary and to give me the opportunity to go from there up to London to meet Eugene Russel. Pressure of work prevented Fiona from coming with me.

I had first spoken to Eugene on the phone from Aberdeen. His voice was rich, full and fruity, like a Shakespearean stage actor's, and he seemed enthusiastic to meet me. I guessed that Ian had already spoken with him.

"Tuesday would be good. Meet me at the RAF Club, my boy, near the corner of Piccadilly and Hyde Park. Bring up a copy of your Pa's diary if you can. There's parking nearby."

I said I would be coming up by train and I'd get a cab from Waterloo.

"Excellent. Meet me in the lobby at twelve. There's quite a lot of security at the entrance, hang over from the IRA days, just ask for me and they will dig me out of the downstairs bar."

Two days later, with a copy of Colin's diary in a small briefcase, I passed through the RAF Club's security turnstile at exactly mid-day. A lady behind the desk phoned down to the bar and asked for Mr Russel to meet Mr Mitchel in the lobby. Eugene came rather ponderously up the nearby stairs and clasped my right hand with both of his. Incongruously, they were rather small and soft, but he was big, very big. Well over six foot and of enormous girth. Earlier in his sixty plus years (as I reckoned) he had probably been quite handsome, but a large nose mottled purple by a love of alcohol had long left Adonis behind. I was reminded somewhat of a male elephant seal, something seen in a David Attenborough documentary perhaps. But his smile was full and genuine and his eyes sparkled with intelligence, shrewdness even.

"Delighted to meet you," he greeted me as he pumped my arm before releasing my hand. "No problem knowing who you are. You look very like your brother." He dropped that subject immediately. "I chose this place, I'm a long time member, rather than my normal Whitehall club because we are less likely to be disturbed by some old crony of mine."

He guided me along a corridor hung with a multitude of aviation pictures, some autographed, and into a spacious formal dining room hung with portraits of distinguished looking airmen, none of whom I was able to identify.

"They rather overdo the pictures here I think," Eugene said as a waiter guided us to a corner table. "They do plain'ish but good food here, nothing over the top. Fish is always excellent. A Dover sole is usually on offer, otherwise the steaks and Guinness beef pie are always good bets."

We both ordered a steak and he chose a good looking bottle of Macon to compliment the meat. We each had a gin and tonic to wet our appetites, then we ate and we talked, with Eugene doing most of the talking.

"Your brother Ian. Now he is a clever chap. Would have probably made undersecretary but for that wretched disease. Said that you would like to know something about the Norwegian foray and your Pa's part in it. How is Ian doing by the way?"

"He gets by, very brave, doesn't complain but hates being confined to a wheel chair."

"Confined? Poor chap."

"Well, not really confined as such. He uses it to go out. He can just propel it by himself, or sit in the garden, but in the house he uses an arm chair, or a dining chair for meals. He can still stand and walk a little, lives on the ground floor so no stairs, can get in and out of bed by himself but needs help for showers in case he slips. He can't manage a bath now. He asked me to pass on his regards to you."

"Which I reciprocate. How sad. No sign of a cure on the horizon?"

"None that I know of."

"I believe it, Muscular Dystrophy, is hereditary?"

"Generally, but not necessarily I understand it depends what sort it is."

"But you haven't been touched by it?"

'No, not at all, and I'm well past the danger years. Statistically at least."

"Splendid, splendid," Eugene commented. But I'm not sure if that was directed at me or the large steak that had just appeared in front of him. Mine was distinctly smaller as was my portion of chips, for which I was glad. It seemed the RAF Club's catering staff surely knew their customer. The wine was a good choice. I wondered how much that was going to hit my pocket as I supposed that I would be treating Eugene.

A few mouthfuls later, Eugene began to earn his meal.

"It was really all down to Churchill, almost a repeat of his debacle of forcing the Dardanelles and the Gallipoli campaign of the first Word War. It had some very unexpected consequences. Some of which were good and meant that the Norway episode was not quite the defeat for us that some made out. One consequence was the final impetus for the resignation of Chamberlain, who was not nearly such a spineless incompetent as has often been suggested, by the way. But, it catapulted

Churchill into his wartime leadership role, thank God. But we don't have the time, and I don't have the inclination to relate a blow by blow of what happened, although I could. I will just give you an outline of what transpired."

He then produced a masterful summary of the failed campaign to deny Norway to the Nazis. I supposed that this talent had been honed in his career as a civil servant. The skill of providing essential briefs to politicians so as to make it appear that they understood some knotty problem about which they actually had not a clue. I was impressed and the nearly two hours we spent over lunch, the bottle of Macon and finishing with stilton, port and coffee, flew past.

--///

In the beginning of 1940, the Germans had pacified Poland and Czechoslovakia, successfully 'Anschlussed' Austria and had a non-aggression pact with the Russians. Over in the West all was quiet with France, the Low Countries and England, the period known as the 'Phony War'. But Britain, and France in particular, had a horror of a re-enactment of the trench warfare of the previous conflict with Germany. They thus hoped to avoid this by opening a second front away from the traditional Germany-France battlefields. Churchill was an avid supporter of this while Chamberlain, then still British Prime Minister was, at the best, ambivalent.

But Hitler knew that he would soon be marching on Moscow and would inevitably have to face-off with France and Britain. He wasn't unhappy with Germany's balance of land and air power against these foes but despite a frantic building programme, he knew that the German surface fleet was no match for the Royal Navy.

He and his staff reasoned that if the eminently defensible ports and fiords of the rugged Norwegian coastline became home to British naval units then the whole of the North Sea could be closed against the movement of German shipping both military and merchant. Furthermore, a long conflict would necessitate a secure source of iron ore for German industry and this material had to come from Sweden, preferably through the Norwegian specialist ore terminal at Narvik. Now, Norway is effectively a long, tapering strip of land running North-South and attached to Sweden along the whole of its Eastern border. Narvik is a good three quarters of the way up this strip and only about 40 miles from the Swedish border as the crow flies. Hitler also had a detailed plan for the invasion of France via the Low Countries which was supposed to kick off in May 1940. So, if he was going to keep Norway from Britain, he reasoned that it had to be invaded during the early spring of 1940.

The German military staff knew that to simply try to march up the length of Norway to reach Narvik, having first swept through Denmark, was impracticable. Much of the terrain was unsuitable for the type off Blitzkrieg tactics that the German Air Force and Army had become adept and successful at, so a plan was developed involving the simultaneous landing of ground forces at six locations up the whole length of Norway, starting with Oslo at its southernmost tip. These forces, comprising six 'Groups", would have to be convoyed by sea and protected by warships of the Kriegsmarine, the German navy. And the six flotillas of warships accompanying each Group had to be powerful enough to withstand attack by the British Home Fleet which lay just across the sea gathered at the Northern tip of Scotland. Hitler was taking a huge gamble with his limited surface fleet. He was not only committing twenty-one major warships plus numerous support vessels to landing the six Groups, he was also throwing in two of his new battleships, the Scharnhorst and the Gneisenau. The predicted prizes for these German forces included not only the securing of the vital iron ore supplies but also access to the fortress-like anchorages that the Norwegian fiords would provide to German warships destined to raid British North Sea shipping. Furthermore, airfields would also be available for German bombers to attack not only allied shipping convoys but also to raid airfields in Scotland and the North of England. All in all, the Germans were committing over 100,000 troops and 1,000 aircraft for the subjugation of Norway.

At the same time that this meticulous German planning was being finalised, the British defence chiefs, goaded by Churchill, were planning a sort of pre-emptive strike into Norway to protect Narvik. Britain also needed access to the huge Norwegian fleet of merchant shipping that would be needed to sustain the British Isles if, as surely would be the case, the German submarine fleet succeeded in decimating logistics convoys as it had done to a certain extent in the First World War. And all this would have to be arranged and performed while, outwardly, seeming to respect Norwegian neutrality. The planning was far from meticulous and parts of it defied logic. There was also a preponderance of very senior admirals and generals involved in conducting the operations carrying fancy titles which might not have reflected their actual abilities. In addition to the British Army the ground forces were also to include Polish and

French troops. In all about 38,000 soldiers were to be committed to what was to be known as the Allied Expeditionary Force, 'Force X', which, it was hoped, would join up with a fully mobilised Norwegian Army estimated at about 55,000. In stark contrast to the German plan, the need for strong air cover was hardly considered.

The German invasion of Norway started on the 3rd of April 1940 when the six invasion Groups moved from Germany up the Norwegian coast. They were spotted by Allied ships and aircraft although their intentions were not known. However, there was a degree of muddle and miscommunication among the Allied warships and between the leaders of the Navy and the RAF, this was exacerbated by a period of poor weather which delayed not only the deployment of Allied forces but also the progress of the German groups. Nevertheless, skirmishes did occur between the opposing warships with casualties on both sides. The British battleship Renown found the Scharnhorst and the Gneisenau, damaged them both and forced them to flee north. The German ships were faster than the Renown and made good their escape.

The German Heavy Cruiser, Blutcher, was sunk by Norwegian shore guns and torpedoes as it accompanied 5-Group entering the fiord leading to Oslo, while another cruiser was also damaged. These setbacks delayed the sea-borne invasion forces but, by the time troops were eventually disembarked on the 8th of April, Oslo was already in German hands, having been taken by airborne forces landed at a nearby airfield. The Norwegian government had already partly mobilised its armed forces but little resistance was offered at Oslo although the Royal Family managed to escape to the north. Orders were given for the Norwegian merchant fleet to sail to either Allied or neutral ports, which in the main it did.

At the opposite end of the country, ten German destroyers of 1-Group approached Narvik and sunk two old Norwegian coastal defence vessels after which the town was surrendered without a fight.

The other four Groups landed troops as planned at four different locations, generally meeting little or no resistance. Much of the coast of Norway, and its capital, was therefore in German hands by the 9th of April, the same day that Germany chose to successfully invade Denmark by land and air. Thus the German objectives had seemingly all been achieved, but retaliation would be coming once the British and their allies could get their act together.

Early on the 10th of April powerful elements of the British Home Fleet stole into Narvik harbour and created havoc among the German warships and supply vessels that they found there. They sunk eight while receiving very little damage to themselves. Further south, however, two British ships were found by German destroyers and put out of action. Between then and the 13th of April, the British chased the remains of the German fleet causing more casualties including a cruiser sunk by naval aircraft.

On the morning of the 13th of April British ships again entered the fiord leading to Narvik and cleared out the remaining German warships.

Churchill insisted that Narvik be reclaimed while Army chiefs preferred to land at Trondheim on the central Norwegian coast. The German land campaign, however, was going well and had the immediate objective of linking up their two forces based around Oslo and

Trondheim, The Norwegians had by now got their act together and resisted fiercely to begin with, but soon large numbers of their troops were seeking refuge in Sweden and by about the 15th of April the whole of Southern Norway was effectively in German hands. An Allied landing at Trondheim became out of the question. On the 12th of April however, some troops had managed to get ashore at Andalsnes on the West coast about midway between Oslo and Trondheim. They moved eastwards to support those Norwegian troops that were still fighting. They were supported by RAF aircraft, albeit obsolete biplanes called Gladiators of Number 263 Squadron, that had made a base on a frozen lake in much the same area. Most of these aircraft were soon destroyed by German bombers.

Another major landing of British troops was made at Namsos on the 14th of April about 80 miles north of Trondheim. Again no air cover was provided. These troops moved inland a couple of days later intending to head off Germans coming up from their strongholds further south. French troops landed on the 19th of April and moved to join the British. On the 20th of April the German bombers destroyed much of Namsos leaving the Allies without a base there. Most of the Allied force moved inland up to 80 miles to engage the Germans, but without air cover they had little chance of success and were soon in retreat towards the coast. The order to withdraw was given and evacuation of the Allied troops was completed with some human and warship casualties in the first week of May. At much the same time, the Norwegian Royals arrived in Tromso in the very North of the country which then became the seat of the legitimate Norwegian Government, such as it was. This failure of the Allied campaign in southern and central portions of Norway set the spark that led to Chamberlain's replacement by Churchill, whose eyes once more turned to the recapture of Narvik.

But, as previously, there was no unified command structure for the Allied force, now largely British, to be despatched to the North of Norway. Inter-service and even intra-service divisions of opinion caused organisational and operational problems. Nevertheless, on the 14th of May part of this force got ashore at Harstad on an island a few miles to the north of Narvik, while the aircraft carrier Furious conveyed a reconstituted 263 Squadron of Gladiators and No 46 Squadron Hurricanes to the same area where they flew ashore to an airfield at Bardufoss.

The British troops joined up with that part of the Norwegian army that was still fighting and moved on Narvik. And further south, more Allied troops were landed at Bodø. On the 13th of May French troops were landed at Bjerkvic, very close to Narvik.

The German army, backed by very strong Luftwaffe units, was moving relentlessly up from the South to relieve the German garrison at Narvik. Nevertheless, on the 28th of May French and Norwegian troops recaptured Narvik. During this period, of course, other German forces were advancing rapidly into France having already subdued Belgium and the Netherlands. Shoving the British expeditionary forces back towards the Channel where they were eventually evacuated to Britain at the beginning of June by a motley collection of military and civilian vessels. The French wanted their Narvik troops back in France and the British similarly saw no point in having forces in Norway while the very shores of

England seemed to be coming under threat. Thus the order for a general withdrawal from Norway was given and by the 8th of June all had been evacuated, including the Norwegian King and his immediate family who travelled to England, as did many Norwegian soldiers, sailors and airmen.

On the 10th of June, Norway officially capitulated to the Nazis and suffered five years of occupation with a puppet fascist government headed by the despicable and despised turncoat, Vidkun Quisling.

--///

Eugene had spoken for a good fifteen minutes without pause. As I thanked him the waiter came over with a large brandy for him, Had Eugene made some secret sign I wondered. He asked if I would like a digestif of some sort. I settled for a coffee.

With half of his brandy gone and the coffee set in front of me, Eugene spoke again. "Did you bring a copy of your Pa's dairy?"

"Yes," I replied, opening my briefcase and handing him the brown envelope which contained the copy of Colin's diary that Fiona had made in her office. He lay it on the table, unopened, by his left hand.

"He was at both Namsos and Bodø trying to build airfields so that the towns could be protected against the Luftwaffe. The Namsos field never got going, but the one at Bodø did operate for a day or two defended by three pilots flying those Gladiator aircraft you mentioned, but despite their efforts the town was virtually obliterated by bombing. So I suppose he didn't really achieve anything."

"Well let me read it and I'll tell you what I think. Somebody obviously thought he'd done a good job because Ian told me that he was awarded an OBE."

"He did get an OBE, that's true, but if it was for his Norway saga neither Ian nor I are sure. We are hoping that you may be able to shed some light. You've got one haven't you?"

"Other Buggers Efforts! Yes, I've one. It would be unusual if I hadn't got one after forty years of devoted service, attending meetings, drinking appalling tea and tasteless biscuits, and briefing temporary Lords and Masters who have very little idea of what the real world is about. I deserved it. Well that's my opinion any way."

I murmured something about my being sure that the award was well deserved, but he continued speaking over my words.

"Anyway, the Luftwaffe certainly appreciated your Pa's efforts because they turned Bodø airfield into a major airfield for their operations and now it's an important Norwegian and NATO air force base and a small airport in its own right. You should go there sometime. I've been, a few years ago, the town's all rebuilt now of course and quite pretty."

I wondered what had taken him there.

"So quite ironic about its Luftwaffe history but there is a lot of irony in the consequences of the abortive Norway Campaign. Are you interested in hearing some of them? It'll be a bit of a lesson in the law of unintended consequences."

I nodded.

"Well, firstly, the Germans successfully invaded Norway. The Norwegians held out for a total of 62 days which is longer than any other country they invaded, other than Russia of course, but the Nazis still took it. Thus they gained their desired access to Swedish iron together with bases from which to attack Allied shipping in the North Sea and later, in particular, the convoys carrying armaments to Russia. So their plan worked at the cost of about 1,300 German deaths on Norwegian soil. The British had nearly 2,000 deaths in the land battles alongside about 500 French and Polish. The Norwegians had about 900 military deaths on land and about half that number of civilians. But the German troops holding down Norway for the duration of the war could probably have been put to much better use defending the Fatherland once the Allies started to push back on land." He paused and swirled his brandy before continuing.

"You may have noticed how I have been, until now, expounding on land casualties. However, the losses at sea of both men and material were much heavier for both sides, but Britain was better able to withstand these losses because of its much larger fleet. The Germans lost about 2,400 dead at sea of which up to 1,000 occurred when the heavy cruiser *Blutcher* was sunk while attacking the defences of the port of Oslo."

"One thousand, from the sinking of one ship?" I exclaimed.

"Well, there has been some argy-bargy about the figure: some put it as low as 250, but that would have been sailors only. There were almost certainly a lot of troops on board and it is generally accepted that they made up the bulk of casualties. The Germans also lost two more cruisers, ten destroyers, six submarines and some twenty other smaller ships. Oh, and when the *Scharnhorst* eventually was sunk in 1943 by a British battleship, nearly 2,000 German sailors lost their lives in that one incident.

Britain lost two cruisers, seven destroyers, one submarine and the aircraft carrier *Glorious* which was sunk by the *Gneisenau* and *Scharnhorst* pair after departing Narvik carrying evacuated soldiers along with the airmen and aircraft from Bardufoss. Some 1,500 souls perished with *Glorious*, over half of all those lost by us at sea during the campaign. So some sort of pay back for the loss of the *Blutcher,* I suppose.

The Poles, French and Norwegians all lost two or three warships. Of course there were also large numbers of merchant ships also sunk.

And talking of casualties, those three Gladiator pilots, Falkson, Lydekker and Hull, all died eventually and all so very young.

Falkson was on the Glorious when it was sunk.

Lydekker returned to flying for the Fleet Air Arm. He was lost in 1942 when his aircraft carrier was sunk by a German submarine off the coast of Africa. There were only twelve survivors out of that ship's compliment of over 500.

Hull was shot down and killed in September 1940 during the Battle of Britain.

I believe there is now a monument to them all at Bodø.

But returning to the Norwegian campaign, effectively Britain lost the land battle but won the sea battle. Britain also learned that it had to greatly improve the ability of its fleets to combat hostile aircraft and so started an ambitious programme of aircraft carrier building.

The Germans discovered that the idea of the Norwegian fiords providing safe berths for its capital ships was something of a mirage. Although they did manage to emerge from their hiding places to harass and sink North Sea shipping, they were repeatedly attacked, with success, by the RAF bombers and the Royal Navy in the form of midget submarines. Thus, it can be argued, that Norway became somewhat of a liability to Germany. Similarly, it can also be argued that the depletion of the German surface fleet had the consequence of the Nazi's deciding to put most of Germany's warship building resources into its submarine fleet, with near calamitous consequences for Britain."

Eugene placed his napkin on the table and picked up the envelope.

"Well, I must be off," he said, indicating to a passing waiter for the bill which came almost immediately.

"I would like to pay," I said.

"Oh, no, you can't because you are not a member. My treat, I'll just sign it." Which he did. "And next time we will meet up somewhere where you can pay. Look, I'll read the diary and do a little investigation about the OBE. Give me three or four weeks then phone. Ian, presumably, gave you my number."

I confirmed that yes, Ian had passed on his number and we left the RAF Club together. I thanked him for the lunch and his impressive exposition which he dismissed with a slight wave of his hand He hailed a cab right outside of the club while I walked to Green Park underground, and thence to Waterloo station and my train back to Westgate.

I told Ian about my time with Eugene. I said that I now had a good understanding of the environment surrounding Colin's time in Norway, and that I was appalled by the number of lives sacrificed for no apparent advantage.

"And, because of the publicity and self-congratulation surrounding the so-called Miracle of Dunkirk, the

Norwegian Campaign seems to have been swept under the carpet. I certainly had no knowledge of it."

"Neither did I," replied Ian. "Until I read a book called 'Narvik' about a month ago. It's a bit dense in places. I've left it by your bedside. But Eugene seems to have covered all the important points."

Chapter 6

I returned to Aberdeen, Fiona and my work, to wait out the five weeks before my contract would allow me more free time to see Ian and Mary again. I gave Fiona a comprehensive account of my lunch at the RAF Club.

"But what about Mary?" she asked.

Fiona and Mary had developed a real affection and respect for one other and I knew that Mary would have liked us to get married and produce a grandchild. Now 38 years old I was, according to Dr MacGregor at least, well out of the danger zone for contracting Becker's MD, which he confirmed was now proven to be wholly hereditary and passed down by mothers exclusively. He urged that there was really no risk of a son of mine contracting the disease unless, of course, Fiona was a carrier, or her mother, which seemed highly unlikely as she had had five healthy children, now all adults of course. Ian's advice had also been unequivocal, "Go to it, I'd like a redheaded niece or nephew."

I explained my feelings to Fiona about discussing Colin's war with Mary, adding that Ian was of the same mind. "Just as I have never felt the lack of a father so, I believe, Mary has not felt the need for a husband, at least not since a year or two after his death. And as I've told you, I think she prefers the company of women."

"She might be at home with relationships with either sex. I and several of my girlfriends have had lesbian dalliances of varying intensities, particularly in our late teens and early twenties. We regarded it as quite normal, then we all followed the straight path, except for Meredith that is."

"Meredith?" I queried. "Really?"

Meredith was the one woman among our circle of friends that was Fiona's equal in beauty and intelligence. "But she is always surrounded by admiring men, and she has had long term relations with at least two that I know of."

"It's a convenient ploy. She does have a long-term relationship but with an older woman, her professor at Edinburgh University. They meet most weekends down there. She shields the relationship because the prof' doesn't want to come out, although Meredith would willingly admit to being gay if you were to ask her. She doesn't want to be pestered by other lesbians, most of which would be able to detect that she's gay, while working here in Aberdeen so she seeks out the company of men. Or rather they seek her out and the two male partners, that you believe you have perceived, are both gay themselves."

"Okay, that's a nice little lesson on a subject I knew little about."

"Really? Did you never experiment with other boys in your early teens? Or whenever puberty hit you? Surely a little bit of fondling at least, at some time?"

"You were asking about Mary," I countered, trying to steer the conversation away from the direction she had just chosen. Not because I would have been particularly uncomfortable about discussing my boyhood experiments with her but rather because she had that look on her face. Cat like, she would stare at me in a challenging way, the corners of her lips slightly upturned as if about to smile and the tip of her tongue just visible. I called it, to myself only, her 'I want it, and I want it now' look. She had seemed to me to have become rather more sexually driven than at the beginning of our relationship. She could be a lot of fun and very demanding. But I really did want to get the topic of Mary and the diary put to bed, so to speak, if only to clarify my own mind. She affected a pout, but then settled down to listen to me.

"I did suggest to Ian that we talk about the contents of the diary with Mary, but he was dead set against it. He argued that, because he spent far more time with her than I did, his opinion should take precedent over mine. I could only agree. His main point was that Mary seemed to no more consider Colin to have been a husband to her than I considered him to have been a father to me. I said to Ian that I had learned a lot about Colin from his diary and from Eugene's description of the historical environment in which it had been written, and I felt that I did have a son-like attachment to him. 'Maybe Mary would benefit in a similar way,' I had suggested. But Ian countered quite forcefully that we could not take a risk on that. He said, 'Maybe she didn't even really like the guy! We just don't know. It was a wartime marriage, and he was away much of the time as you can see from his logbook. Just how close could they have been?' In the end, I accepted Ian's opinion."

Fiona nodded and I continued, "Mary would surely have opened the trunk after Colin's death, almost certainly read the diary, but she hadn't brought the subject up after giving the trunk to Ian, so to his mind it was clear that she did not want to discuss Colin's war record. I now think Ian is right."

"Okay, that seems clear. So what are you, or Ian, going to do next?"

"Well, I think you should read the diary again. More thoroughly, like a lawyer and let me know if you think the award of the OBE is connected. I'll wait three or four weeks then give Eugene a call to see what he has discovered. We could both go down to Westgate in five weeks' time and maybe meet up with him."

"Yes, I can get time off then, but I think it might be better for you to see this guy Eugene alone, he might have some State Secret to impart. I want to spend time with Mary and Ian again anyway. How did you find him health wise?"

"Much the same. He has his good and bad days. It's been established beyond any doubt that what he's got comes down the mother's line and only affects their sons, and then not always. It's a statistical lottery apparently. It's as good as certain I'm not going to be affected and I can't pass it on to a daughter so you and I should be okay to have kids; if that's what you want."

"I'm not quite ready yet. Not because I in anyway doubt our relationship, but I do have a really good job that would be very hard for me to give up."

"It's the Eighties for goodness sake, surely your company will keep your job open?"

"Oh yes, certainly, in fact they have told me so. But I want to see the resolution of the Atlanta oil rig sinking case. There is going to be a lot of law suits against the builders and operators, and we are handling most of them. It could all last another eighteen months or more, so I think we are on track for your fortieth to make an honest woman of me. But I don't mind being the pregnant blushing bride."

"Fine, but Meredith is now taboo."

--///

When I telephoned Eugene he sounded quite excited.

"Splendid, young man, simply splendid that you've called. Very, very interesting stuff has come out from my reading of your Pa's narrative. He was a brave chap too, what a pity he didn't make it back to civilian life. But, then, if he had who knows where his Norwegian story may have led him."

"But what about the OBE, is that what he got it for, Namsos and Bodø?"

"Well I found the announcement in the London Gazette for 1st January 1941. The entry gives no more than his name and rank, Flight Lieutenant still, in a list of some forty-five other RAF recipients. What is most interesting about this award is that as a Flight Lieutenant he was the most junior officer on the list. All other officers ranged from Squadron Leader up to a bevy of Air Commodores, so he was in distinguished company. But I'm with your brother on this and, after taking advice, I am sure that the OBE is not awarded for gallantry. It's normally for prolonged good service, not a single act and it was a very unusual award for a twenty-six-year-old Flight Lieutenant. So I've dug a bit deeper and it's all to do with whales."

"Whales?"

He let out a great snort of a laugh. I could sense that the whole of his large amorphous body was shaking.

"Sperm whale oil, actually. Remember the bit in his dairy when some Norwegian woman turned up at the Bodø airfield with a barrel of sperm whale oil that she needed safeguarding?"

"Yes, but there was only the one entry, neither she nor the barrels were ever mentioned again."

"Nevertheless, that barrel and the woman, I'm just flicking through the pages you copied, yes 'Ingrid', is the key to the OBE. Sounds like something out of Gilbert and Sullivan doesn't it? 'The Key to the OBE'."

I suspected he was still being affected by a long and rather liquid lunch.

"Well, sorry about that rather poor joke. It's actually a very serious story. I don't know all the facts but I have a friend who does, Clive Somerfield. He is pretty ancient now and doesn't travel much, so if you want to know the whole story you will have to visit him at his home near Aldermaston."

"Aldermaston? Isn't that where the Atomic weapons place is?"

"That's right, the Atomic Weapons Research Establishment, AWRE. He used to work there, well after the war that is. Before that he was a Cambridge Don. I'll fix up a visit if you like, I'll come if I can. You could drive there from your place in Kent, cross country, not too far really."

"Yes, yes please, contact him. My partner Fiona is very interested in my father's story. Do you think she could come with me?"

There was silence for a few seconds, then, "You might be required to sign the Official Secrets Act before Clive reveals what your Pa and Ingrid did. I'll check with him to see what he thinks. He may not want to tell the story to two people. Although I suspect that may well be silly, you would only tell Fiona anyway."

"Official Secrets Act! For goodness sake, it all happened forty years ago!"

'Yes, yes silly of me. Comes from having been in the defence business for so long, you get used to keeping your mouth shut. Look, I'll get back to Clive. When will you next be down here?"

"I've got a week off starting the weekend after next, so any time then."

"Good, you wrote a phone number on the top of the envelope you gave me, is that your Scottish number?"

"Yes, that's where I'm phoning from now."

Eugene phoned back three days later.

"How about the Monday after next, midmorning for coffee?" he asked.

"Yes I can make that. Are we meeting at Mr Somerfield's?"

Eugene gave me the address. "I won't be there, I'm sorry, another appointment, but Clive says it's OK to bring what's her name... Fiona?"

"Yes, Fiona. Thank you, she will be pleased."

"OK, my boy! I think that you are both in for an interesting time. Let me know how it goes."

Fiona was delighted to be going to Aldermaston with me. We flew down to London the following weekend, rented a car and drove down to Westgate. Ian asked me not to tell Mary about the impending trip, but insisted that both Fiona and I gave him a full debrief on our return.

We had looked at a road map and discovered that the journey was quite long and possibly tedious if we were to follow a cross-country route. So we departed early and followed motorways as far as possible up towards London then westwards to Reading then turned down towards Aldermaston. Clive Somerfield's address was a little out of the town and to get there we had to pass the large, fortress like compound of the Atomic Weapons Research Establishment, with its several rows of high perimeter fencing and large elevated piping running hither and thither. It was not the sort of place where you would want your car to breakdown.

We turned into the gravelled forecourt of a large, detached Victorian house, three stories high, maybe four if the attic were counted. I parked the car by two others near to a short flight of steps leading to a very large double front door. It was just the sort of home that I would associate with a Cambridge Don, although I wondered how he managed to fill such a large place. The answer was in the bell pushes by the side of the door. There were four, each bearing a different name. I pressed the bell marked 'Somerfield' and a female voice answered 'Hello' through a small loudspeaker.

I identified myself and Fiona, a buzzer sounded and the voice said, "The front door is open, just push it and I'll be waiting inside."

She was waiting at the foot of a rather splendid flight of balustrade-lined wooden stairs leading up to two landings that I could just discern among the heights of the gloomy stairwell. She was tall, smartly dressed and perhaps in her mid-fifties. She greeted Fiona first, which I thought was a nice touch, then shook hands with us both.

"I'm Jane," she began, "I housekeep for Clive and live at the top of these stairs. It keeps me fit running up and down them. The lights come on automatically once you start to climb. There are two other flats up there, both let to couples. Clive owns the whole building. It used to be full of his family but his wife died and the children moved away years ago. He now confines himself to the ground floor flat which is twice the size of any of the others. But I'm prattling on... It's he you want to see, not me. I'll bring in coffee and tea in a few minutes, then I'll leave you alone."

She opened a large door behind her and ushered us in to a

spacious, comfortable sitting room. Clive Somerfield was sitting almost facing the door in a high back chair with his feet resting on a low stool. He looked very old but his eyes were bright and had the piercing, steady look of high intelligence. He stretched out a translucent but steady hand to greet us. He was clearly not about to stand. Fiona and I gently shook the hand in turn.

"Clive Summerfield," he said with a strong voice. "I'm pleased to meet you, and this gentleman," he added indicating a man who had been seated out of our sight behind where we now stood, "is Mr Rupert Noakes. A sort of a minder although he is nearly as old as me."

This was not quite true, I think the second man could have been twenty years his junior although still perhaps seventy. He rose and shook our hands, smiling, but guarded I thought. Tall, slim, very well dressed in a dark suit and looking very fit for his years. He could still have been a working civil servant I surmised, and my immediate inclination was that he was not the sort of person to be addressed by his Christian name on first acquaintance.

"Let's all sit down," Clive suggested.

Fiona and I sat down in high back chairs matching those of Clive and Noakes. There was a small table by the side of each chair. Jane came back into the room pushing a trolley table, offered us tea or coffee and served our choices, with biscuits, onto our individual tables. To my surprise it was Noakes who spoke first.

"I knew your father. Flight Lieutenant Colin Mitchel as was. I was the person that sent him to Norway in 1940. I also met him after his return, and I know how and why he got his OBE."

'Of course,' I thought to myself. Noakes was the name my father had written in his dairy. He was the Squadron Leader that approached him at RAF Ickenham in April 1940. "Yes," I responded. "Yes, he mentioned your name in his dairy. You were a Squadron Leader. So you were RAF too."

"It was an honorary rank, purely for the duration of the

war. Before then I was a sort of policeman, and after it also. But I worked a lot with the RAF so it helped things that I wore the same uniform. It was fairly common practice to put civil servants into uniform, it helped to define pecking orders. But to return to the OBE, your father undoubtedly deserved some sort of recognition for his work, under enemy fire remember at Bodø and Namsos. You have his diary, but I have seen the situation reports he compiled every few days and those of his boss, Wing Commander Sexton, so I know what went on. But the point is that his activities were not restricted to attempting to build airstrips in very difficult circumstances, and my guess is that he did not include these activities in his diary?"

"No," I replied. "Not unless it is something to do with that drum of whale oil that he stored. He only mentioned it once but Eugene Russel, in arranging this meeting, indicated that it had some bearing."

"Indeed it did. But whales, Sperm or any other variety, don't really figure in the story. To understand the importance of what your father did you have to know something about 'Heavy Water'. Perhaps you already do know what it is and its importance to nuclear physics."

"Very little," I admitted.

Noakes turned to Fiona. "And you, Fiona, may I call you Fiona?"

"Yes, of course."

"Do you know about heavy water?"

"I'm afraid not, I'm a lawyer. But I have read Colin's diary and Martin has given me an outline of his meetings with Mr Russel."

Clive spoke. "Then it is time for you to listen to a little lecture on the subject. That's what I do I'm afraid, lecture."

We listened. He spoke fluently with the strong assured voice of a master of his subject.

"I was there at the beginning, the very beginning, studied at Cambridge with Rutherford and Cockcroft. Sir John Cockcroft, who with Walton is credited with splitting the atom, 1928 if I remember rightly. I was much younger than them, they shared the Nobel prize for that. I had a junior role in it all until John left to set up the nuclear stuff in Canada in 1944, then I was promoted pretty quickly. When he returned after the war to set up the Atomic Energy Research Establishment, AERE, in 1946, he asked me to join his team, which I did. Later I was persuaded to get involved in Britain's nuclear weapons development programmes and ended up here at AWRE. It was all to do with nuclear fission anyway, just the outcomes that were different. I even met both Fermi and Szilard before they went off to America and the Manhattan Project. As I said, nuclear fission was what it was all about, but if you have fission you are likely to get a chain reaction unless you can control it in some way. The physicists doing the research before the war, here and in Germany and France, knew that you needed either pure graphite or heavy water to be the moderator of the electrons emitted during radioactive decay. The moderator is the means of control, a sort of sponge for stray electrons. You surround the nuclear reactor, the sort of thing at the heart of a nuclear power station, with the moderator."

Clive paused for a moment. Fiona and I nodded together to indicate that we were following so far. He went on.

"The water molecule, as I'm sure you know, comprises two hydrogen atoms and one oxygen atom, hence H two O. Heavy water is exactly the same except the non-oxygen atoms are an isotope of hydrogen called 'Deuterium'. The nucleus of the normal water hydrogen atom, called 'Protium' comprises just one proton while the Deuterium nucleus has both a neutron and a proton which makes it roughly twice as heavy. Hence heavy water, or more accurately 'Deuterium Oxide'. Heavy water is nearly completely pure Deuterium Oxide, but it usually contains a little ordinary water and a pinch of something that is a sort of hybrid of the two molecules that I've just described. Conversely, our ordinary water, from our taps say, usually contains a few Deuterium Oxide molecules. And the weight of heavy water, or more accurately its specific gravity, is only a very little more than that of ordinary water because it is only the very light Deuterium atom that is heavier. The much denser oxygen atom is common to both and remains unaltered.

This clear liquid, heavy water, is death to neutrons emitted by radiation but generally benign to life. It is a by-product of the electrolysis of ordinary water. In the early 1930s the Norwegians built a huge hydroelectric plant at a rather inaccessible place called Vemork for the purpose of producing an artificial fertiliser based on ammonia. Vemork is in the south of the country about 60 miles west of the capital, Oslo. At maximum capacity, the fertiliser process could produce about 12 tons annually of a water-like liquid with an increased concentration of deuterium oxide molecules, about one molecule in two thousand or so. The Vemork plant produced much more electricity than that needed for the fertiliser plant. The Norwegians realised that this surplus electricity could be used for further electrolysis of the watery by-product to produce heavy water. They installed a complex of cascading electrolysis chambers and by 1934 Vemork was the heavy water producer to the world but with a capacity deliberately limited to 10 kilos per month." He paused again. We nodded again. He continued.

"Vemork is near Telemark. You may have heard of the film 'The Heroes of Telemark' which dramatises the true story of the destruction of Vemork by Norwegian saboteurs during the war. The Germans rebuilt the plant which was then repeatedly attacked by Allied bombers until rebuilding was abandoned. Anyway, the relevance of heavy water to nuclear energy and nuclear weapons became increasingly recognised in the late 30s and early war years by the Germans, British, French, Americans and probably many others. The Germans, in particular, thought heavy water to be a better candidate for the control of nuclear fission than graphite, although the French favoured the latter.

The Vemork hydroelectric plant and its store of heavy water was thus an attractive potential acquisition for the Nazis and may have figured among their reasons for invading

Norway in 1940. But just before that invasion actually started, agents of French military intelligence removed all of the heavy water kept at Vemork. All 185 kilos which was effectively the world supply at that time, with the agreement of the plant's manager to 'lend' it to France. They secretly and with some difficulty, transported it to Oslo, then Perth in Scotland and finally to France. It was hidden by Curie when France was invaded but eventually spirited out of that country, along with several eminent nuclear scientists, to England during the Dunkirk evacuations aboard the steamship 'Broompark'. The ship arrived safely in Falmouth on 21 June and its captain was awarded the OBE."

"And that is my cue," interjected Rupert Noakes. "That OBE, and your father's."

Chapter 7

While Clive's description of heavy water and its Norwegian connection was delivered in the measured, precise and authoritative style of an academic and educator, Rupert Noakes spoke in a chummy manner as if sharing a secret, or trying to persuade one of a point of view. I supposed this might be because he had spent a lifetime influencing people to a particular course of action, or perhaps even interrogating them. He sounded like a sophisticated, urbane policeman which is what I guessed he might be.

He began to speak.

"Eugene contacted both Clive and me about your father's story at more or less the same time which is why we," he indicated Clive, "decided to team up to meet with you both today. I haven't seen your father's dairy but Eugene briefed us on the relevant bits."

"And the relevant bits concern whale oil and a woman called Ingrid," I interjected.

"Yes, Martin, that's about right," replied Noakes with a broad smile. "But I want to go back a bit further than that. I was working in Whitehall in early April 1940 trying to make sense of the implications of an Allied withdrawal from the

Norwegian fracas. We knew we had to get the Norwegian royals out along with key members of government, but there were other things we needed to extract as well as the important personages. These included Norwegian Army, Air Force and Naval personnel which could be used to bolster Allied forces, and of course the huge Norwegian merchant marine. We knew the French were handling the heavy water movement but there was other stuff to get out as well, including the nation's store of gold bullion for example, 50 tons of it, held in Oslo and being transported northwards in an effort to avoid advancing German troops. Other valuables, like crown jewels, artworks, sensitive government papers, maps, plans of munitions factories and dockyards, possibly even captured German code books. We had no real idea of what might turn up at those ports scheduled to be used for extracting our troops, Namsos, Narvik, Bodø, or anywhere else. What we did guess is that the Army Staffs of the British, French, Norwegians, were more likely to be concerned with safely getting their troops out of Norway to live to fight another day than with the transport of Norwegian artefacts. So a decision was made that the RAF should become involved in this potential recovery task. I was asked to select someone to join the contingent being assembled to help defend Namsos from air attack. A task which included the construction there of an airfield.

There was already much doubt about the likely success of the airfield building project given the known terrain and environmental conditions in Norway at that time of the year. Besides, it was thought, any airfield construction would be completed before the Norwegian stuff arrived for movement to England, thus it was decided that somebody from the building team could be spared if required. I looked for a junior but mature officer with a good service record who was underemployed in his present post. Your father filled the bill. He had served in India before the war had started, was known for his initiative, had been an RAF swimming champion, and was restless flying army cooperation exercises in deepest, darkest Hampshire. Wing Commander Sexton, who had already been selected to have overall charge of the Namsos RAF detachment, was briefed on the possible secondary duties that might involve your father but he was, I think, disinterested in anything that was not of immediate benefit to the RAF. In fact, he played virtually no role at all in what was to transpire. He was, quite rightly, totally concentrated on the need to build and supply the air bases required by the RAF while fighting the Luftwaffe over Norway. But he did insist that your father, goodness, let me stop calling him that, Colin, should be allowed to concentrate on his airfield building task and not be told about his possible other responsibilities unless the need arose. We, that is I, agreed. Now, before we get to whale oil, let's talk about Norwegian gold."

I exchanged a glance with Fiona, 'Is that what this is all about, gold? What about all that talk about heavy water from Clive?' these were the questions we silently signalled to each other. Rupert caught the gist of our glances.

"No, gold's not what brought about the OBE but it has a part to play. A little more patience, five more minutes and all will be revealed. Fifty tons of gold bullion was taken out of vaults in Oslo just before the Germans arrived in the first week of April and taken on a very tortuous journey by road, rail and ship. It was split up and then recombined on its route up the length of Norway, dodging Germans on the way, until most of it arrived in Tromso on or about the 8th of May. It was moved to England about a month later. We were obviously tracking its progress and indeed the Navy played a role in its transportation. At one stage, the fifty tons had been split into smaller lots, some of which were in grave danger of capture by the Germans, and some of which we lost track of. While trying to sort all this out from garbled messages being passed into Whitehall, we received a decoded signal from the Norwegians that a special load from the area of Telemark, which had joined the gold shipment on its route north, had had to be abandoned by the main transport convoy as its prime task of getting the gold out of the country was proving harder and harder. A small, separate party was now going to attempt to move this load to the British at Namsos. You go on now, Clive."

Clive stirred himself in his chair. "Well I'd been hanging around Whitehall trying to persuade a sceptical brass that it was vital the heavy water the French had extracted from Vemork did not fall into German hands. Then a very clever young lady cipher clerk saw the message that Rupert has just described. She knew that Telemark was close to Vemork. 'Could this special load be more heavy water?' she asked me. I discussed the possibility with Rupert, and he dashed up to Scapa Flow."

"Where I arrived," Noakes took over, "just as Colin got there after the evacuation of Namsos on the 7th of May if I remember right. I had to go up there in any case to take charge of some interesting German prisoners that had arrived in Colin's convoy from Namsos. Anyway, I found Colin at Leith House on the little Orkney island of Burray near Scapa Flow which was full of ships of all shapes and sizes. He was waiting for his next convoy to Bodø to form up and was in comfortable shore accommodation meanwhile. It was then that I told him for the first time of his potential second task while in Namsos. Much like I have just described to you, getting stuff out of Norway. But I also told him that there was a particular load that had to be brought back to Britain if at all possible. I didn't tell him about heavy water; I couldn't have described its importance as Clive has just done in any case. Just that it was important and that I had no idea by whom or when he might be approached. I added that we would transmit more information as and when we had some."

Noakes looked at his watch, it was approaching mid-day. "My goodness, I promised Jane that we would be finished and you away from here before she comes in to give Clive his lunch in a few minutes time, so I'll finish this up as quickly as possible. It won't take long."

He stood up and passed a hand over his mouth rubbing his lips and chin as he framed his words. "Well, this woman that Colin mentioned in his diary, Ingrid, turned up at Bodø with a 45-gallon drum labelled Sperm Whale Oil. Yes, it was in

English as well as Norwegian. She saw Wing Commander Sexton first who sent her to Colin. This was on the 25th of May and Sexton immediately despatched a signal to Whitehall as he had been instructed. By this time we knew that the barrel contained heavy water and we also knew that Ingrid and her charge had had one hell of a journey. A journey that would prove to get worse."

He turned to fully face me. "I gather the diary doesn't say much about Colin's last week or so at Bodø while he was supposedly awaiting evacuation."

"That's right," I replied. "The whole of his final week, that first week of June, is pretty vague. And what do you mean supposedly?"

"Because of the importance of the barrel it was decided to get it back to Britain via the main evacuation operation from Tromso, rather than use the Bodø convoy which was thought to be rather vulnerable. A signal was sent directly to Colin to that effect. Sexton, I think, had already departed Bodø by then. And Colin did what he was supposed to do, and more. The barrel, Ingrid and Colin all got onto a small inconspicuous ship travelling from Bodø to Tromso, and on their they were all transferred onto the largest warship in the area, HMS Glorious."

He paused for a moment, then, "You know about Glorious of course."

Both Fiona and I nodded, quite unable to speak.

"Colin survived as did Ingrid. Two people out of the thirty or so that were plucked from the sea after the ship sank, but the heavy water was lost. They recuperated in Scotland, and Colin got his OBE for his short-lived success with the Bodø airfield, his part in trying to get the heavy water to Britain, and his success in getting Ingrid to Scotland where she became a pivotal member of the war effort."

--///

Jane swept into the room with a no-nonsense look on her face, removed the tea and coffee things and said that Clive would be having his lunch in just five minutes. Fiona and I got up to leave. There were so many questions we could have asked about Colin and Ingrid's flight from Norway but we realised they would have to be unasked until some other time.

Sensing that Noakes was departing at the same time as us, and maybe had something to add to his story once we had left the house, we stood to say our goodbyes to Clive. He shook our hands as before but wasn't quite finished with speaking to us.

"Of course, heroic though Ingrid was in getting the heavy water to Bodø only to lose it to the North Sea, its safe arrival in Britain would have counted for nothing more than a magnificent gesture. If her oil drum had been full, the contents would have amounted to 180 Kilos, much the same quantity as the French got away with, but it wasn't full. The heavy water would have been in small, individual, sealed glass phials of some sort and these would have been surrounded by a type of soft packaging, straw perhaps. I would think that there might have been only about 30 Kilos of heavy water in all that were lost. And, in fact, the French 180 Kilos was of little real practical use because, as we now know, useful work towards nuclear energy or weapons development requires much greater quantities. The Germans knew this and, in between having to rebuild the Vemork plant after multiple attempts by the Norwegians and British to destroy it, managed to raise its production capacity to 100 Kilos per month. This greatly alarmed the Allies as it indicated that Germany was getting serious about developing a nuclear weapon. Thus in November 1943 the Americans and British pummelled the area with 150 bombers, sadly killing many civilians in the process but forcing the Germans to give up on Vemork and heavy water production."

Fiona told Clive what a great honour and privilege it had been for both of us to have met him, which was true, and we left the house.

On the steps, just as we were thanking Jane, Noakes put his hand on my arm to stop me climbing into the car saying, "There is a bit more to the story that perhaps you might like to hear. There is a nice old pub in the centre of Aldermaston where we could have lunch before you set off home. Do you have the time?"

I looked at Fiona who nodded enthusiastically. Noakes climbed into our car, he had apparently arrived by train from London and then taxi, and we drove the two or three miles to the 'Hind's Head', large but cosy and with great beer which Fiona likes as much as I do.

Over a light lunch and just one drink each, Noakes opened up on what happened to Colin and Ingrid after the sinking of the Glorious.

"I'm not sure about how they were rescued. All I do know is that thanks to a failure in the deciphering of German naval codes at that time and the jamming of the Glorious's radios by the Germans, we didn't know the ship had been attacked and sunk by the Gneisenau and Scharnhorst until many hours after it had happened. Nearly three days passed before a rescue attempt was underway by which time most of those that survived the actual sinking were dead anyway. Somehow Colin and Ingrid were found and landed in the Faroes, then moved to the West Coast of Scotland and ended up at a place called Arisaig, where they recovered from their ordeal."

"And then what?" I asked. "That was still June, wasn't it?"

"Well I can't remember the exact dates. But what I can tell you is that Ingrid, I believe her surname was Johansen, easy to remember, was considered far more valuable than the lost heavy water. She had worked in the Vemork power plant and, as part of the maintenance team, knew every inch of its layout. She lived nearby with her parents in a village which adjoined Vemork, was a keen cross-country skier and thus also very familiar with the surrounding countryside. What better person to help develop a plan to sabotage the plant and help train the saboteurs? The mission to destroy the plant was given in the first instance to the embryonic Special Operations Executive, the 'SOE', which was formed from Section D of the British Secret Intelligence Service otherwise known as MI6, and with which I had connections.

There were several attempts to destroy the plant. The first was not really by SOE at all and was to involve a drop by paratroopers, but both of the planes they were in crashed and all the soldiers were either killed or shot later by the Nazis. Anyway, as I said, Ingrid ended up at a large house in Arisaig, almost opposite the islands of Egg and Rhum. Those two islands were part of the SOE training organisation and there she stayed providing intelligence to SOE operatives. She probably helped in the planning of the ill-fated paratrooper expedition and she was certainly involved in planning the operation called 'Gunnerside', in February 1942 which resulted in the demolition of much of the Vemork electrolysis equipment. It was that raid that provided the inspiration for the Richard Harris film, 'The Heroes of Telemark'. I lost touch with her when she too was parachuted back into Norway towards the end of the war, but I believe she survived."

"That's a totally incredible story. What a brave person she must have been." Fiona reacted

"Yes, she was, but there were so many others who did similar things, men and women, girls and boys often. SOE had nearly 10,000 of them on its books at one time and many died, sometimes in the most terrible circumstances."

There was silence as I and Fiona let Noake's story sink in, then I asked, "And what about Colin, my father? He was back flying fairly soon I think. So he wasn't anything to do with the SOE was he?"

"No, no he wasn't. But I believe that he did stay some time at Arisaig before returning to duties. He was killed, wasn't he?"

"Yes," I replied. "In a flying accident in Germany just a few weeks after the war ended."

"Another tragedy of war, among so many," murmured Noakes.

The meal was finished and after running Noakes to the

railway station, Fiona and I drove back to Westgate with our minds full of Norway, heavy water and the SOE.

"Are you satisfied with what you heard from those two?" She began.

"Yes," I answered. "Yes, but it's an extraordinary story. Nothing like what I expected to hear."

"Well, what did you expect?"

"Something... something a bit more mundane I suppose. After what Eugene had told me I guessed Colin's award was something to do with that barrel of whale oil or whatever, and therefore something to do with the mysterious Ingrid, but to have been one of the few survivors of a sunken British aircraft carrier, that's beyond my wildest imagination."

"Mine too," Fiona agreed. "Then for her to turn into some form of spy or saboteur and to survive that is just as incredible. I wonder if she is still alive, if she married, had children? How would one live a 'normal' life after all that?"

"We don't know how old she was, but say twenty-five in 1940, that would make her about sixty-five now and much the same age as Mary. Yes, of course, she would probably be still fit and healthy now. Even suppose she was forty then, she wouldn't be older than that, I imagine, if she was going to be parachuted into Norway, she could still be alive."

Fiona was starting to nod off, her habit whenever I drove. She murmured, "I think I'd rather like to meet her, and talking of Mary, are you ever going to get over your aversion to making love to me while she is in the next bedroom at Westgate?"

I let that question pass. It wasn't new.

Fiona's Story

Chapter 8

*F*iona stands in front of the full length mirror of the old bathroom in the Westgate house. It used to be the only bathroom. The new bathroom was created out of the downstairs study of the 1930s building and knocked through to the adjacent large and rarely used dining room. It formed a spacious bedroom suite for Ian after he came to live with Mary and his needs as a developing invalid increased with the decrease in his mobility. Everything in the suite is 'wheelchair friendly' and for the present, Ian manages in it quite well by himself.

The old bathroom was completely renovated in the early 1970s and the small coloured tiles to waist height on every wall reflect the English idea of a modern bathroom of that era. The room is quite large and the bath, wash basin and toilet, which are all in the same shade as the tiles, fit in easily. A shower cubicle was added about five years ago and mercifully is in white.

It is the early evening of the day of her visit to Aldermaston. Martin has just taken Ian out in Mary's car, with the special front seat, to the 'Walmer Castle' for a couple of pre-dinner drinks over which he will tell him about the day's *revelations.*

*Fiona is completely naked, her chalk white body con-
trasting awkwardly with the sickly green, called Avocado by
their manufacturers, of the wash basin and the tiles she can
see behind her extending horizontally either side of her body
and in line with her neat belly button. Her red hair, perhaps
strawberry but often looking ginger dependant on the light or
the potions she is using to tame its tendency to resemble the
aftermath of an explosion in a mattress factory, is hanging wet
down to her shoulders. The freckles on her face and torso vie
for visual prominence with the droplets of water from her
shower. She holds one arm across a breast, the other is
hanging down and its hand is resting on her pubis but not
concealing the coiled hairs that her fingers are gently twining.
She can see her bottom reflected in the mirror over the wash
stand, the single dimple on each cheek is visible. A little larger
than when they first emerged at the age of fourteen.*

*'I've still got it,' she murmurs to herself. 'Still got it at
thirty-five. A good looking broad, emerging from a sea of
green. With longer hair Botticelli could have used me as his
Venus.'*

*She contemplates exploring her crotch further, she moves
her second finger towards her vagina but then pulls it quickly
back into her fist. 'Just teasing myself,' she thinks 'but maybe
tomorrow if Martin won't rouse himself tonight. I don't believe
that I'm really that noisy in orgasm as he claims. He says that
in full cry I could waken the dead, let alone his mother. If Mary
heard her son's usual groaning when in gallop she would think
he was a pig in rut. Which is what he is, I suppose.'*

*She slowly moves her hands down her narrow waist and
measures the swell of her hips, satisfied that there is still only
sufficient fat to provide a smooth surface. 'Bones perhaps a
little too prominent in the pelvic area but generally not bad,
not bad at all.'*

*Her first year or two with Martin had been a sexual
epiphany for both of them. Her maidenhood had been given to
a knowledgeable young Highland Infantry Officer in her home*

town of Fort William. He drifted out of her life a few months later after which she remained more or less celibate until going up to the University of St Andrews to study law. She worked hard and shone academically but her looks attracted a stream of male suitors all seemingly after one thing. She granted it to two or three of them during her five years of study, without commitment or enduring enthusiasm on either side. Then she graduated and without much effort landed her first and only job as a corporate lawyer within an Aberdeen company specialising in the then burgeoning North Sea Oil Industry. It took her three years of long days and late nights of clawing over seemingly impossible and artificial barriers to be properly recognised for her abilities among the male dominated environment, but at nearly thirty she could afford to relax and look for more in life. And that more was found in a noisy Aberdeen bar in the form of Martin.

They were both more than emotionally and physically ready for what occurred between them. 'Yes, it was love at first sight. No, lust at first sight.' She thinks to herself. After a very brief 'courtship' lasting no more than a few days they retired to a grand old hotel in the centre of the city for a week, during which time they could hardly bear to be uncoupled. This state of absolute euphoria lasted another six months or so in which time they purchased a house together. Possessions were moved out of their individual apartments and the new home formed the basis of a partnership which to all intents and purposes was a marriage. Their confidence in each other's company spilled over into their working lives where both were rewarded with increased responsibilities, promotions and an expanded circle of loyal friends.

The passion diminished, as it always does, but was re-placed by an abiding love and respect for each other which evidenced into skilled and satisfying sex for both. They had their own spaces, but not too many unshared secrets, and were happy with each other and with themselves. Martin, of course, had the ever growing concern over the health of his brother, but Ian and Fiona instantly took to each other and he came to regard her as the sister he never had. Mary also greatly approved of her and Fiona's parents welcomed their de-facto son-in-law.

Fiona contemplates her body again. Since reaching her mid-thirties she has recognised a growing sexual hunger. Some of her girlfriends of a similar age to her, including Meredith it seems, reveal that they are experiencing or have had similar cravings which have been parleyed into children or affairs. Fiona does not want an affair, dare not tell Martin of the fantasies she is experiencing in case he is either revolted or tries to turn them into reality, so persuades him, easily, to let her have children and perhaps get married. At thirty-six, she resolves, my next birthday, it's out with the pill.

'How will this body look after one or two births?' she wonders. She sticks out her stomach and turns sideways to the mirror. She imagines stretch marks and cellulite. 'He'll just have to accept them, like any other father.'

She examines the profile of her nose, running an index finger along its bridge. 'Will I,' she wonders, 'develop the bump that Mum has?' The bump is not apparent in the photos of her mother as a young woman when, with the same flaming hair and translucent skin, she looked so like Fiona. 'And what about her knobby finger joints? It's not arthritis. I've seen other red heads with them. Will I get them? I've had her elongated big toes since birth? But the good thing is that Mum is in her sixties and still doesn't have a grey hair on her head. She always says that Celtic redheads keep their natural hair colour longer. It makes up for the thin lips that they are also known for, and the unpredictable tempers.' She pouts her lips. 'Nothing wrong with this pair,' she concludes. 'And I've never been much of an incendiary.'

She dries off the moisture on her body, wraps a towel around her hair and a dressing gown around her shoulders, and retreats into the guest bedroom that she and Martin share when visiting Mary and Ian. She dries her hair with her travel blower and lies down on the double bed. The clock on the bedside table tells her that it's half past five. She has an hour before she should go downstairs to help Mary prepare the evening meal. The men have promised to be back by seven and Martin is totally reliable when it comes to punctuality, and most other things she thinks.

She can't recall the spoken words he had used to rouse her interest in that bar, but she was quite tipsy at the time and the words obviously worked. Besides he was rather good looking, tall enough that she had to look up to meet his eyes and exuded an easy confidence. Of course, the muscular stomach has faded a bit now and there is the beginning of a roll that settles on the waist of his underpants. He still that has confident manner but she has realised for a time that in many ways she holds the reins in their relationship. She finds it hard to admit in these days of the feminist movement that she actually likes the way he opens the car door for her, lets her past first through openings and walks beside her on the traffic side of pavements. 'It's just,' she thinks, 'that he is a nice man.'

Her mind begins to drift. Her mildly erotic thoughts make way for lawyer-like analysis of what she has heard today. Something does not quite fit, something in the timelines, in the chronology of events. Her mind sharpens and she concentrates on Colin's story as told by Clive and that rather sinister Rupert Noakes to whom she hadn't taken at all. She suddenly realises the significance of this second government man. He knew Colin, he sent him to Norway, he had a secret agenda for him, and he was with him for some time after his rescue from the ship wreck. With Mary, and not counting the infant Ian, Noakes is only the second person that she and Martin have met that had direct knowledge of Colin. Despite his premature death, she realises that there must be many more who knew him in the War, including the mysterious Ingrid, probably still alive somewhere. She grasps the question, 'How long was Colin in Scotland with her and the SOE? It couldn't have been very long because Ian was born in 1941, June.'

'Presumably,' she thinks, 'Colin and Mary were married when Ian was born, or perhaps not. But easily verified. Either way they must have had congress, she smiled as that word *came to mind, before the end of 1940. 'Yes, m'Lud, we can all count to nine and September is, as this venerable court is aware, the ninth month of the year, the ninth month of 1940 and nine months before June 1941."*

She pulls her mind together. September 1940 is significant in this story. She realises that there may be an answer of sorts in the flying log book of Colin's that Martin talked about. She wants to look at the book and is tempted to sneak into Ian's room right now and fetch it, but refrains. She will talk to Martin first.

She dresses, brushes out her hair and joins Mary in the kitchen over two gin and tonics.

At precisely 7pm Martin pushes Ian in his wheelchair through the front door and into the kitchen. They look happy and a little lubricated.

Chapter 9

Though I love Fiona very much there are times that I need to be without her company, and one such time is when I am planning to have a one-on-one with Ian. I'm sure she has similar needs when she is out with her girlfriends. I do join her sometimes but I find that the frankness with which they discuss their own, and other peoples, sex lives can be quite disconcerting to a mere male. If I complain and, as is usual, I'm the only man present they tell me to be a token female and to 'deal with it'.

So, no complaint from Fiona when Ian and I went off to the pub after the drive back from Aldermaston. She would have realised that I wanted to talk to him about our father in the light of what had been revealed by Clive Somerfield and Rupert Noakes. She also knew that I was becoming increasingly concerned about his physical condition. I had helped him into the shower the previous evening, something that I had not had to do before, at Mary's suggestion in case he slipped over. I was astonished by how thin he had become. There was little muscle on his calves or thighs and his ribs were clearly visible. His wrists so thin that I could have circled them easily with my thumb and little finger. Yet curiously, his calves were quite plump, swollen even.

He caught my gaze. "It's what's known as 'Pseudohyper-trophy'. They have been getting fatter as the rest of me wastes away. It's like my calf muscles have turned to fat. They don't do anything much these days, I can barely walk now. The arms are better because I use them to propel the wheelchair and to help get myself in and out of it, although that's becoming increasingly difficult."

And then, "But I'm not about to peg out, my doctor says that my heart and lungs are still doing okay."

I again noticed how light he was when I lifted him from the wheelchair into the swivel seat installed in the front of Mary's station wagon as we set out for the 'Walmer Castle'. The wheel chair I folded and put into the vehicle's cargo space, reversing the process once we reached our destination. He insisted in getting the first drinks, rolling up to the bar to place the order then back to the small corner table I had found for us. The barman brought the two beers straight to our table. While he was engaged at the bar I compared how we had been. Two husky youths alike as peas in a pod, to how we were now. One fat, one thin. No one now would take us for twins. Fate had dealt him a cruel blow while endowing me with good health and, of course, Fiona. Then there was Colin; survivor of the Glorious sinking but victim of a flying accident, but with Ingrid surviving the same ordeal and possibly still alive. And then Mary; a widow all this time and bearing the knowledge, I assumed, that Ian's condition came from her womb.

"What are you thinking?" he asked as he rolled back to me. "That's a brown study if ever I saw one."

"Oh, just going over the events of the day. I'll tell you all about it once the drinks arrive."

And I did. I've a good memory and probably managed to recall what Noakes had related near word-for-word, although I did paraphrase a lot of what Clive had expounded about the physics and chemistry of heavy water. In any case, Ian seemed to know about heavy water, probably from his time working on government defence projects.

Ian asked few questions and made few comments until I was done, then said, "So that's' it. That's the story of the OBE. The captain of the ship bringing the stuff to England that the French had sneaked out got one, and Colin sneaked the same stuff out, or tried to, but you did say that it was lost at sea?"

I nodded.

"So he got one also. I assume that the building of the Bodø airfield also contributed to his award. Perhaps these two achievements of his didn't fall into the usual wartime categories of gongs for bravery or similar, so an OBE was recommended instead."

During this time a wave of Ian's hand had attracted the attention of the barman and two more beers had appeared.

"What about Mary?" I asked. "The last time we spoke about bringing her into what we've been researching you were dead against telling her anything and I accepted your decision although I didn't really agree with it. But now I think we have got to spill the beans. Fiona will certainly say something if she has a mind to. She sets her own agenda for a lot of things, and with her neat legal brain she can run rings around me in an argument."

"You have arguments? You two are the most seemingly contented and suited couple I've ever known."

"Yes, we are very happy and compatible and arguments are few because I've long ago learned to avoid them as I tend always to lose. So, what do we tell Mary?"

Ian pondered for a while as we savoured our beers. "I think," he began, "that you should tell her a simplified version of what you have been told today. Just say that we were curious about the OBE, say that we've been told that he got it for a combination of building the airfield at Bodø, helping to get a valuable artefact out of Norway and rescuing a spy from a shipwreck. No, perhaps you should go easy on the spy bit. Call her a Norwegian civil servant or something. But stick to the facts as you know them, Mary may know more about what happened than we are assuming."

"And when?"

"Oh! Tonight of course. Get it out of the way before Fiona lets anything slip. And by the way, I've never understood why she should fall for a lout like you. I would have expected her taste to have been better."

He giggles slightly into his glass, but this touch of school-boy banter, completely redolent of our childhood relationship, reminded me that his mind was in no way following the atrophy of his poor body.

After I had settled up for my round of the drinks with the barman, we left for The Courts, arriving there exactly as we had promised, at 7pm. Fiona and Mary were in the large, farmhouse style kitchen and well into their second gins. A bottle of good Rioja was breathing on the table set for the four of us. A kiss on the forehead for me from Fiona and a whispered 'Good Boy' as I sat down, and Mary served us with one of her secret pasta dishes. I poured the wine, and grasped the moment.

"Mary," I began, "would you like to hear what Fiona and I, with help from Ian, have been up to today?"

"Well," she replied, "I suppose that it's something to do with that trunk of stuff of your father's that I gave to Ian a while ago. I've noticed a bit of secretiveness going on." She spoke with a certain wariness, I thought, but still very much in charge of her near forty-year-old sons, still the mother, still her house, still in control. I began to feel a little like a naughty schoolboy.

"We didn't want to tell you anything until we were sure of our facts," I replied rather lamely. "It's all to do with his award of the OBE. Ian, that is we, thought that it was an unusual award for a young RAF officer in the middle of a war, so we tried to find out why he got it. We already knew about his time in Norway, building the airfield in Bodø in 1940. I suppose you knew about that because it's all in his diary, that notebook in the tin trunk."

"Yes, I read it ages ago. Right after his death I think, but he had told me about his time in Norway after his return to England. And I knew of course that he was given an OBE in early 1941 as a result of his activities in Norway, but it never crossed my mind that it was in anyway unusual. If you look in the New Year and Queen's Birthday honours list published each year you will see that many are awarded."

Ian broke in, "Yes, but OBEs are normally given to MPs, magistrates, senior civil servants and the like, together with military people that have been in the Forces for a long time, thirty years or so. Not twenty-six year olds."

"I never really thought of it in that way," Mary responded. "I was very young you know and thoughts of who or who should not get OBEs never occurred to me. I knew Colin as a brave young man, whatever he had done I was sure he deserved the medal just as he deserved his DFC."

She said the words in a manner that seemed to suggest that she wanted the subject to be closed. I was wondering whether to continue or not when Fiona, I should have expected it, broke in. "But did you know that he had survived the sinking of the warship bringing him home and that he had to recover from his ordeal in Scotland?"

Much to my surprise, and to the two others I imagine, Mary snapped back. "Yes of course I knew that. What the hell! Do you think that we could have got married if we hadn't discussed things like that?"

I think we were all slightly shocked at the words and their delivery. She was always such a cool person. I had hardly ever seen her show the slightest touch of real anger. But she was shocked as well. "I'm so sorry, Fiona, that response of mine was totally unjustified... please forgive me." She rose from her chair and put her arm around Fiona, then addressed us all. "You, quite unknowingly, touched a raw nerve and have broken open a forty-year-old scab. To understand you have to consider that I was just twenty-two years old in 1940. I knew nothing of life. Until then I had had no real boyfriends, had survived art school without getting laid, if that's the correct expression, but then had fallen head over heels for a young pilot whom I barely knew, and whom, if I'm truthful, never really knew. I don't suppose that we spent more than a hundred days together between our first meeting and his death five years later. It was like that in the war, and particularly at that time."

She sat down again and recharged her wine glass. "He phoned me from Hendon the morning before he flew off to Scotland to say that he would be abroad for a while and did not know when he would be back. He told me he loved me. I said the same thing. He could not tell me where he was going or what he was going to do. I understood and accepted that. It was war time and these things happened. That was April the 24th 1940, and I didn't know if he were dead or alive until sometime in June when he phoned me from Scotland with only the sketchiest of descriptions of what had happened to him, and to say that I might not hear from him again for a while yet. Britain was not doing well in the war at that time. The army had been evacuated from Dunkirk and it appeared that all of Europe belonged to the Germans. We were the only ones left fighting Hitler it seemed, and we really thought invasion was likely at any time. Then the Battle of Britain started and I thought he might have been mixed up with that. So I waited and waited, and scanned the casualty lists for his name, and I determined that I would make this man happy if I could, when and if we were next together. But then, a week or so before Christmas, he sent a telegram to say he was on leave and coming down to London to stay with his parents and was looking forward to seeing me then. That's how we met you know. Byron and Colin's fathers were in the same local masonic lodge and I went to a party given by Colin's parents at the end of 1939 to celebrate his return from three years in India. We got engaged on New Year's Eve and married just three weeks later."

I wondered why a slight smile puckered Fiona's lips.

"That's what a girl did in those days," Mary concluded. "You grasped your opportunity and to hell with planning for the future. We knew all about the appalling slaughter of the First World War where a whole generation of men, nearly two generations in fact, almost disappeared and thought it all might well happen again. Same enemy, same battlegrounds. If there was a chance of happiness with your man of the moment then you took it. You took him and would live with the consequences. Consequences which for me did not involve a peacetime life with Colin. That's an end to it, I don't want to talk about him or the war anymore."

She was choking up, and we three others at the table sat in shock for a while. We had never heard her talk like this before, never even heard her say that she loved Colin. This man who for so long had been no more than a faint shadow in my life was gaining presence and flesh in my mind.

But as we all expected, this tough lady, my mother, quickly regained her composure. The remainder of the meal, and of the evening, passed pleasantly enough.

In bed together, after watching the 10pm news on the downstairs, and only, television, Fiona put her arms around me saying "Don't worry, it's not sex, just a cuddle. I know the rules unless you want to break them tonight?"

I kissed an exposed nipple, and said, "We will be home tomorrow night, can you wait until then?"

"Mmm, well I don't really know," she teased. So I turned my kiss into a little nip.

"Okay, okay," she feigned shock and pain. "But let's talk instead."

"Yes," I replied. "But let's start with that smile of yours when Mary getting married a month after getting engaged. What was that all about?"

"Oh, men! Why is it you can't remember birthdays and other important personal stuff?"

I had no idea what she was talking about, and she sensed it.

"For goodness sake. When is Ian's birthday? When was he born?"

"Beginning of June, 19–"

"1941, of course." Exasperation in her voice. "And you don't even know the day! Now, think of the September before that."

The penny dropped. "Oh my God," I exclaimed. Mary and Colin were at it as soon as they got engaged."

"Before, of course." Fiona shot back. "September '40, or October at the latest, unless Ian was very premature and that's what all that talk of hers was about. Taking one's chances and damning the consequences. They must have got together after that so-called phone from Colin in June and well before their engagement. She skirted around that, didn't she? Good for them!"

"Yes, good for them," I agreed. So my parents were quite human after all and not the paragons of virtue that I had assumed as a child, and had continued to assume as an adult because I had never had a father in my life to judge. "Is that what you wanted to talk about?"

"Well, sort of, connected anyway. While you were out I was running over what that guy Rupert Noakes, I didn't take to him, too smooth by half, had told us. And you'll say 'typical, lawyer's mind', but something doesn't quite fit in the chronology of what happened. Did Colin stay up in Scotland all that time? The whole last half of 1940? Mary told us that she didn't see him from April until Christmas but we know she must have. Was he mixed up in that dodgy SOE outfit? Just what was going on that kept him from coming down south to see the girl that loved him, or did he get her to travel up to Scotland secretly to meet him in some Glasgow hotel? It doesn't quite all add up."

"Well," I replied beginning to feel sleepy and not really following Fiona's logic. "I can't remember everything that was in his flying log book, but I do think that there were entries included sometime in the last bit of 1940."

"Let's check tomorrow, ask Ian to let us see the log book again."

"Ok." I murmured. "Good night, Darling."

--///

Fiona took a phone call from her office early the following morning just as we were all sitting down to breakfast.

"Hold on," she said into the phone, then addressing the three of us at the table. "Apparently I have to be back at the office tomorrow to sign off some statements that are due to be submitted in court the day after. I'm very sorry Mary, I know I said we would stay a week this time but I really have to get back. I can get a plane from Gatwick this afternoon and Martin could stay here of course for a few more days."

"That's alright Fiona," Mary replied. "It's a pity that you have to go but I know how these things are."

"I'll come back with you, Fiona," I interjected. "And come back down again as soon as I can."

"OK by me," Ian added, and Fiona nodded her agreement.

Fiona returned her attention to the phone. "Please book seats for me and Martin from Gatwick to Aberdeen for some time after lunch today. I'll sort out paying for them once I get back." Then rang off.

Ten minutes later her office rang again to confirm that two tickets had been purchased for the mid-afternoon flight. Mary went outside to talk to the man who had just arrived to clip the garden hedges and I took the opportunity to ask Ian if I could take away Colin's log book again."

"By all means, it's yours as much as mine. There is other stuff in the box so why don't you move it from out of my room into yours then sort through for anything else you might find of interest."

Fiona helped me move the trunk. The green hide, gold embossed log book was still inside, lying on top next to the medal case and Norway diary. They were resting on an RAF flying suit complete with the blue and silver epaulet rings, two thick, one thin, denoting Squadron Leader rank. "So he wasn't buried in his flying suit," I remarked to Fiona.

"I remember you telling me that he was a passenger in the aircraft that crashed, so perhaps he was wearing his uniform rather than a flying suit. Anyway, you don't know how badly the body was mangled in the accident. Who knows what he was buried in, and I don't think it's the sort of question we should put to Mary."

"No, of course not." I pulled out the suit and underneath it was a uniform hat, a forage cap and a pair of flying gloves and another soft backed book. This book was wrapped with a kind of parchment cover with a hand drawn cartoon of a pilot sitting in a chair with his feet on a desk with a pint glass of beer in one hand and a smoking pipe in the other. The cover was labelled Colin Mitchel, again by hand, with 'PO' for Pilot Officer, scratched out. Similarly scratched out 'FO' for Flying Officer and 'Flt Lt' for Flight Lieutenant. The 'S/L' for Squadron Leader remained untouched. I opened the book and found that it was another recording of Colin's flying career. The cover was taped on and I gently pealed part of it off to see that is was an official RAF publication to be used by aircrew to record all their flying. Each page contained headed columns into which various flying data were recorded. Flipping through this log I realised that this was his working copy. Entries were made with a variety of pens and pencils, and every now and then there was a sort of official certificate summarising the preceding entries and signed off by a flight or squadron commander. At some time, Colin had transposed all of these entries into the green book: perhaps at war's end just before he died?

Fiona, too, was looking at this book as I made my examination, and reached out to take it from me.

"No, not yet. If you have it now you'll dive right in and I think we should be sociable and spend the next couple of hours with Mary and Ian before we head off. I'll pass it and the other one to you once your day in court is over, and I promise I won't look at them any more until you've had a go."

That night, back in Aberdeen, as she slipped under the sheets beside me Fiona said, "That's it Martin, I'm pulling the plug, abandoning the pill. Get me pregnant, strictly the missionary position for a while. And blow jobs are out."

Chapter 10

*I*t is Friday, two days after the flight back to Aberdeen with Martin. Fiona is by herself in the house. She has already lost two days of the week's holiday she had planned so is definitely not going into the office today. Yesterday in Court was very tedious with her opposition arguing every clause of the compensation offer to their client, but a settlement of sorts now seems possible. She is happy within herself. Martin is being very supportive about her wish to become pregnant, both mentally and physically. If it doesn't all click in six months or so he has agreed to go with her to her doctor for guidance.

She walks around the house imagining how it might suit a family of three, or more. The single bathroom, nicely modernised, off the landing has to serve the four bedrooms that surround it. But she has already had a go at persuading Martin to have a modern en-suite built in the corner of the very large bedroom that they share. 'A baby should be the clincher for that', she thinks. 'And one of the spare bedrooms will make a splendid nursery: the one right next to the bathroom, perhaps a door could be knocked through.'

She realises that she is already nesting, so clears her mind of gurgling babies and soiled nappies.

She has deliberately refrained from looking at Colin's two flying log books until this morning. Martin won't be back until about 6pm after which they plan to have dinner together at a good Indian restaurant within walking distance. She enters the large downstairs room that she and Martin now use as a study. They have a desk each. She opens the top drawer of her desk, pulls out the books and places them on the desk top.

She opens the green log book and examines the records for 1940. The entries for the year up until the 22nd April are all quite similar. Three or four flights in a Lysander every week from RAF Ickenham, each lasting anything from twenty minutes to over two hours. A crewman is carried on most flights and identified by name. Almost all of these flights involve either some form of training with the Army or patrols along the Sussex coast. The hand and pen, which Fiona now recognises as Colin's, are identical for all of the entries. Those dated for the 24th of April 1940 record his flights in a Flamingo from Hendon to Evanton and then in a Sunderland from there to Namsos.

Entries in the green book cease for the period that Colin was in Norway then restart on the 1st of July. Fiona notes that although these later entries seem very similar to those earlier in the year involving Lysanders out of Ickenham, the flights are generally of shorter duration and very much less frequent. Then, on the 15th of September 1940, flights in Hawker Hurricanes from a place called RAF Speke start to be recorded. Fiona takes the copy of the RAC Road Atlas of Britain from one of the study's book shelves and finds that Speke is now Liverpool airport. So Colin has moved from the south of London to many miles north on the west coast of England. 'Now Mary,' Fiona considers, 'you ought to have been able to get a train from London to Liverpool even in wartime. So why did you say that you didn't see him until that Christmas?'

With the green book turning up nothing else sounding particularly unusual, Fiona turns to the scruffy log book with the cartoon on the homemade cover, which she now regards as a 'Draft'. She opens it at the beginning and finds that the first entry is for the 3rd of September 1939 which she knows is the day that Britain declared war on Germany. The flight is from RAF Ickenham in a Lysander and is obviously a precursor to those 1940 entries she has just looked at in the green book. The entries in both books include not only the duration of each flight but also the total flying hours progressively accumulated by Colin. The draft log says that Colin had flown 826 hours and 40 minutes by the 3rd of September 1939. Fiona examines the green book again. Yes! Exactly the same number of accumulated hours are recorded for that date, but the green book starts right back in 1935 when Colin, it states, started his flying training at a place called RAF Digby which it records as being in Lincolnshire. So earlier guesses were right, the draft book was intended just to record Colin's wartime flying with its entries to be periodically copied into the green book. Perhaps the green book was kept in a place of safety, with his parents possibly?

She turns the draft book's pages to the 24th of April 1940. There, as in the green book, are Colin's flights as a passenger to Namsos but no flights are recorded from that date until the 15th of September when he flies at RAF Speke in a Hawker Hurricane. A quick bit of mental arithmetic shows that about 40 hours of flying, over the period from the 24th of April to the 15th of September, are missing from the draft book. She takes the pencil in her hand and starts to write figures onto the note pad. She compares the final entries in both log books. The green book's last entry is for the 31st of May 1945, shortly after the war in Europe ended, a flight in a Spitfire over the south of England, bringing the total tally of Colin's flying hours to 2,562. The last entry in the draft log is dated the 10th of July that year, another Spitfire flight. Fiona realises that this was probably Colin's final flight as a pilot before his death as a passenger a few days later. But the total flying hours recorded in the draft log for the 31st of May 1945 are identical to those of the green log. She works backwards through both books recording dates and totals on her note pad. They all match until she reaches the 30th of June 1941 where the draft book total is twenty minutes less than that of the green book at the same date. During each month that she works backwards towards the summer of 1940 the difference between the two books increases until by the 15th of September 1940 it has reached forty-three hours.

For a moment she is non-plussed, then the penny drops, it's not the flying hour totals that are important but the individual entries themselves. More figures are jotted onto the note pad and it all becomes obvious. Between the 15th of September 1940 and the 30th of June 1941 almost every flight in the green book is recorded as 20 minutes shorter than the equivalent entry in the other book, and these minutes are used to compile the flying hours for 25 flights recorded in the green book between the 1st of July and the 15th of September 1940, flights which are not recorded in the draft book. So which is the correct record? Surely it's the draft which is actually the RAF's formal record of his flying because it contains certificates of accuracy by his superiors? The green book is the 'Fair Copy' to be shown to non-service people. But why did Colin practice what is clearly a deceit? To invent those 25 flights? And whom would have benefitted from it?

She has done enough for one session she thinks and takes herself off to her local gym for an hour's workout before meeting Meredith & Co for lunch in the newly opened vegetarian restaurant. Clichéd 'Ladies who Lunch' she admits to herself, but then there is curry out with Martin this evening and probably sex afterwards. 'I love my days off', she purrs to herself. 'I'll tell him about the log books during dinner.'

--///

Over shared chicken tandoori and beef vindaloo dishes, Martin listens to Fiona's description of how she found the discrepancies between the two log books. But when she tries to bring him into an analysis of Colin's motives he resists.

"Darling, I don't know why he should have altered the flying hour totals in the log books. It's so long ago, why are you bothering?"

Her eyes open wide and her nostrils flare a little. She can see him thinking, 'Uh Oh - trouble! That was silly of me.'

But she knows well her own 'getting wound up' signs, takes a deep breath and speaks softly but deliberately, "Have you been paying attention at all? It's not the totals that are important but the fact that he invented 25 flights over a period during which he doesn't appear to have done any flying at all."

"That's if you take the scrappy book with the home made cover to be the true record? You said that it doesn't start until September 1939 and he had been flying for years before then."

"Yes, 826 hours' worth. But it's clear from the handwriting and ink used that the green book was compiled in lumps from a draft and the 'scrappy book' was that draft."

"You don't know that. Perhaps there was yet a third log book? There would have to have been an earlier 'scrappy' log book recording all his pre-war flying as it happened."

Fiona considered Martin's question. He had a point. Albeit he was wrong, she was sure, but he had a point. A little lawyers' guile was required. A small concession now for a big victory later. "You could be right, I don't know, we just don't know. Perhaps we could ask Mary?"

Martin replies forcibly. "Absolutely not. Are we trying to make out that Colin may have done something over a few weeks in the late summer of 1940 that he felt necessary to cover up by inventing flying that never took place, something that she wasn't to know about even though they were close to becoming engaged? Are you suggesting that we tell her that, and without knowing the full facts?"

"No, no, of course not. Sorry."

She puts down her fork and moves her right hand three inches towards him across the table's surface. His free right hand matches her move and his finger briefly stroke hers. "Sorry, too," he smiles.

Later that evening in the steamy atmosphere of their bedroom laced with a scent of vindaloo, after a silent minute of recuperation, Fiona sighs, "Maybe that did it."

"Did it for me!" Martin replies.

"That's not what I meant you fat pig," she says trying to heave him off her body with one hand while digging a finger nail into his glans with the other.

"That hurt!" he squeaks, rolling off her onto his back.

"Serves you right for letting off in the middle of everything."

"Letting off! What sort of prudish schoolgirl talk is that?" And affecting a broad Scottish accent not very convincingly, "Call a fart a fart, woman. And you kept burping."

He sees her hand making towards his penis again and swats it away, then takes it gently in his hand and kisses the finger tips. "But not bad for a fat old pig then?"

"No, not bad at all."

A drowsy contentment intervenes for a few minutes, then he speaks. "And talking of curries, if that's what we were, I've got to head off to Singapore in a couple of weeks' time to help our insurers do a pre-commissioning inspection on our oil rig that's being built there. Remember, I had to go a year ago when the structure had been completed before the equipment was installed?"

"How long will you be away?"

"About two weeks I think. Look I'll have to fly through Heathrow so why don't you meet me there when I get back and we can drive down to Westgate together for a few days, if you can get time off?"

"Oh, time off is no problem. I'm already owed about six weeks of annual holiday thanks to having to work all hours on that terrible North Sea helicopter crash two years ago. And at the weekends while you are away perhaps I'll drive over to Fort William to visit Mum & Dad."

Martin grunts his agreement, turns over and goes to sleep. Fiona stays awake for a while formulating a plan in her head.

The following Monday morning Fiona corrals the newest intern, a lanky youth in an ill-fitting black suit, in the corridor outside her office.

"Andy," she says with a smile. Andy has been at the law firm for nearly three months, still gets all the crappy jobs, and is totally besotted with Fiona. He turns and tries to stutter a greeting. She cuts him off.

"Andy, I'm doing some pro-bono work for a charity in my spare time and it would really be a great help to me, and them, if you could do a couple of tricky but really important jobs for me."

Andy nods his head enthusiastically. She knows that through that poor head the thought has passed, 'Perhaps, I'm going to get something worthwhile to do at last.'

"It's finding out two things and I don't know how you will start. You will have to use your undoubted sense of initiative... and it's sort of secret so no one else in the office must know what you are doing."

Andy is almost salivating.

"I need to know whether an RAF squadron is still in existence and, if so, it's address. Here, I've written the number on this piece of paper." She thrusts a piece of closely folded paper into his now clammy hands. "Number 325 Squadron."

Andy looks at Fiona blankly.

"Oh, it won't be that hard," she encourages. "Try the Ministry of Defence in London for a start. There is bound to be a PR or information department. The second task is to discover if a certain Norwegian lady is still alive, and if so where she lives. Her name is Ingrid Johansen, I think she is probably in Norway. You might try towns called Vemork, Rjukan, Lillehammer and Telemark. I've written it all down on that paper."

The blank look remains on Andy's face.

"Or you could speak to the Norwegian Embassy in Lon-

don, as a starter. She pats him on the shoulder, goes back into her office calling out, "By close of business tomorrow, please."

Andy is waiting outside Fiona's office as she comes into work at 9am the following morning.

"You're bright and early," she greets him.

"Well, I've got some news, here see this bit of paper–"

Fiona hustles him into her office and closes the door behind them. She sits down on a small sofa in front of her desk and beckons him to sit beside her. He timidly obeys.

"Right, you've got some news, quick work, well done. Just begin at the beginning."

Andy pushes the sheet of paper into her hand. "This is the address of Number 325 Squadron of the RAF. After a couple of false starts I got to the right office in the Ministry of Defence and was told by a nice man that the squadron was operating helicopters in Anglesey, that's Wales."

"I know where Anglesey is," Fiona can't help but remark.

"The man said that you could write to the Commanding Officer of the squadron if you wanted more information about it."

"Well, thank you Andy, that was well done. And Ingrid Johansen?"

He squirms a little. "I phoned up the Norwegian Embassy as you suggested and asked a man there how I could trace a lady called Ingrid Johansen who might be alive, and might be in one of those towns you listed. The man actually burst out laughing. He said that the name was common, that there would be literally thousands of women living in Norway with the same name. Then he did try to be helpful and said that if I could get hold of her age, profession, marital status perhaps, then he could possibly be able to recommend a private detective who could trace her."

"Ok, I see the problem. Do you have the name of this person that you spoke to in the embassy?"

"Yes, I've written it on that paper."

"Thank you again Andy. I'll take it all from here," Fiona

says, ushering him out of her office with a gentle hand on his shoulder.

"Is there anything else I can do for you?" he asks, a hopeful puppy-like expression in his eyes.

'If I think of anything I'll certainly come to you first, see you around."

Fiona takes a portable type writer from the bottom of one of her filing cabinets, lays it on her desk and begins to write a letter to the Commanding Officer of Number 325 Squadron RAF.

Dear Commanding Officer,

I am a lawyer working for the above legal company in Aberdeen. I am also the wife of Martin Mitchel who in turn is the son of a pilot, Colin Mitchel, who lost his life in an air crash just after the end of the Second World War. My husband knows very little about his father's life who, because of the exigencies of war time, hardly saw his infant son. I am trying to fill in the gaps as a sort of gift to Martin and wonder if you squadron records could be of help.

In 1940 Flight Lieutenant Colin Mitchel was serving with No. 325 Squadron flying Lysanders from RAF Ickenham. On or about 22 April 1940 he was selected to help build airfields in Norway for the RAF to help resist the invasion of that country by Germany. From a dairy kept by Colin we know exactly what he did in Norway and how he got back to the UK at the beginning of June 1940. We also know that he was flying Hurricanes out of RAF Speke (now Liverpool airport I believe) in Mid-September of that year, so presumably no longer with No. 325 Squadron.

Does any documentation that you might still have indicate if he returned to your squadron after his time in Norway i.e. June, July and August 1940? I would be most grateful for any relevant information you might have on my father-in-law.

Yours Faithfully.
Fiona Buchanan

She has no qualms about the invention of marriage, signs the letter, puts it in an envelope which she addresses by hand, and leaves the office building to send it express at the nearby post office. She congratulates herself that she is well past the point in her career when she has to ask permission to leave the office, or even tell anyone what she is doing. She lingers over a mid-morning coffee, deciding her next step towards solving the riddle of Colin's missing months.

Back in her office, she makes a few notes on her pad then phones the number Andy has given her for the Norwegian Embassy. She speaks to a man whom she takes to be the same person that spoke with Andy the previous day. She explains that she is Andy's boss and apologises for his unpreparedness for his call of yesterday enquiring about Ingrid Johansen. She goes on,

"The Ingrid Johansen that I am looking for would be at least 60 years of age now and possibly considerably older. She was born in or near Telemark, possibly a place called Rjukan, and worked up until early 1940 at the Vemork power station. She escaped from Norway at the end of May 1940 and ended up with the British Special Operations Executive. She –"

Her phone correspondent interrupts her, his English is flawless. "You have my interest Miss Buchanan, but I think you should stop talking to me now, and restart with one of our military attachés. I'll see who is available if you don't mind holding for a minute or two."

Fiona waits for about three minutes.

"Good Morning, Miss Buchanan, or is it Mrs? I am Colonel Solberg." A film-star-like male voice, again with near accent free English, coos in her ear. "I gather you are seeking information about one Ingrid Johansen who was a member of the SOE. I will be pleased to help you as much as I can but first a few more details about her. I've only had the briefest outline from our PR Officer who you were just speaking with and I need to know what is your interest in this lady."

"Well, Ingrid Johansen, let's just call her Ingrid from now on, is mentioned in my late father-in law's diary covering the time that he was trying to build airfields for the RAF in Norway. Specifically Namsos and Bodø in April and May

1940. According to the diary and other sources I have already spoken to, Ingrid had brought a load of heavy water with her all the way from Vemork to Bodø where she asked my father–in –law, Flight Lieutenant Colin Mitchel, to help her move the stuff to Britain. As you know, I'm certain, things did not go well for the British and French adventure in Norway while the Germans were invading. Apparently, Colin and Ingrid escaped together from Tromso and somehow made their way together to Scotland where she was recruited –"

"Into the SOE."

"Yes, so I've been told."

Colonel Solberg's voice becomes a little brusquer. "Well, that should all help in finding her, if she is still alive, but I still need to understand why you want to connect with her. I assume that is what you want, to meet up with her perhaps?"

"Yes, I would like to meet her but it is my husband, Martin, who I think would really like to talk about his father with her. Martin was only three years old when his father was killed in a flying accident just after the war ended and he was away most of the time in the war, so they never really saw much of each other. In fact, Martin has no memory of his father at all. He wants to know who his father was and more particularly he wants to know how he and Ingrid survived the sinking of the British aircraft carrier supposedly taking them home from Norway. That's the reason I'm seeking Ingrid."

"The Glorious? They survived the sinking of the Glorious?" The smooth military voice had turned incredulous.

"Apparently so."

A moment's silence, then, "You have persuaded me, Miss Buchanan." The smooth tones had returned. "I shall take pleasure in putting you in contact with Ingrid Johansen. That is assuming that she is still alive and wants to speak to you and your husband. Her story, and that of your late father-in-law is intriguing. Let me know your telephone number and I'll get back as soon as I have some news."

After the call, Fiona feels well satisfied. 'And just a little white lie again about Martin and I being married, but I won't

*tell him anything that I've been doing until I've got some news
one way or the other.'*

--///

*Exactly a week later, Monday 9am, Fiona enters her office and
flips through the post that has already been put into her in
basket, just as she does first thing every working day. There is
an envelope in it bearing the acronym for 'On Her Majesty's
Service' imprinted above her address, the post mark is
Anglesey. Using the paperknife from the pen tray at the front of
her desk, she slits the envelope open. The single sheet letter
inside is from No. 325 Squadron' RAF Valley, Anglesey.*

Dear Mrs Buchanan

   The Commanding Officer No. 325 Squadron RAF has asked me
to reply to your letter in which you enquired about Flight Lieutenant
Colin Mitchell. I am the Squadron Adjutant and the keeping of
squadron records falls to me.
   The Squadron log book, a sort of diary, records all significant
occurrences including, and in particular, all flights. This log book, of
which there are several volumes, is kept in the squadron's registry
and dates back to the very formation of the squadron in 1916. It is
therefore possible to see who was flying during the period which you
are interested in. I have to report that although Flight Lieutenant
Mitchell was a very active pilot up until 22 April 1940, and indeed
was a flight commander (one of three), there are no records of him
flying with No. 325 Squadron after that date. There is a note in the
log that on 23 April he was detached to the Air Ministry. I have found
no mention of him again in any other squadron documents dating
back to the period, however, many such records would by now be in
Ministry of Defence archives somewhere else.
   In conclusion, in my opinion he left No. 325 Squadron on or
about 23 April 1940 and never returned.

   Yours Faithfully
   W E Cooper
   Warrant Officer

'That confirms it,' thinks Fiona. 'He was somewhere else for nearly four months after getting back from Norway. Even allowing for a decent recovery period after his sinking ship ordeal, he must have been doing something in this time. Something to do with the SOE? Something to do with Ingrid? Something that he wanted erased from his records? So next move, Ingrid?'

And as if by design her telephone rings and the honey tones of Colonel Solberg greet her.

"Ms Buchanan, good morning, Colonel Solberg of the Norwegian Embassy in London here; I hope this is not too early for you."

"Not at all, I was hoping that you would call soon."

"Well, I have news for you about our friend Ingrid Johansen. It turns out that she is a very interesting woman indeed, known as bit of a war hero, and alive and well and living in... can you guess?"

"Telemark?"

"No, No, Bodø! Where she met your Father-in-Law! Bodø is now a very different place from when he was there. Obviously, all the damage caused by the Germans has disappeared and the town is now much larger and more important than it was then. His little airstrip has developed into not only a major Norwegian and NATO air base but also a quite busy regional airport. And new town infrastructure is being built the whole time. I should imagine it is now rather a nice place to live. Anyway, I got a pal in our Ministry of Defence to investigate for you. It wasn't hard to find her as she was mentioned in our records as having been a member of the SOE and working among our partisans during the occupation, and she gets a pension for her service to her country. I actually spoke to her this last weekend."

Fiona can hardly control her impatience. "And will she speak to me?"

"Oh yes, she is very keen to speak with the wife of the son of Flight Lieutenant Colin Mitchel. I have her address and telephone number in Bodø here."

Fiona writes down the number and address, repeats it back for certainty and, after a few pleasantries and thanks, the phone conversation is over.

Fiona clasps her hands together to stop them from shaking and tries without success to decide what to do next. She busies herself with legal work, goes to the reception area and makes herself a coffee. After drinking it, and trying to pass a bit more time with routine administration, it is 11am. She phones Meredith.

"Hi Meredith, it's Fiona, I need a diversion from work. Are you game for an early, liquid lunch at that over trendy tapas bar we were at two weeks ago?"

The right answer comes, and she is off.

Chapter 11

The moment that I came in through the front door at a little after 6pm I knew something was in the air, in fact the clues were very obvious. Fiona greeted me with two martinis, one for her and the other thrust into the hand of mine that had just deposited my brief case on the lobby floor. Added to that she was dressed in a blue, Japanese print, silk dressing gown tied loosely, very loosely, with a red sash. That she also had a demanding look in her green eyes coupled with her pussy cat pout reinforced these clues. She affected a Mae West drawl, "Had a hard day lover man? Fancy a hard night?"

I pretended not to notice the intimation. "Average day, trip to Singapore confirmed, I'll be off a week today, Monday, so I'll probably leave Sunday and overnight in London. How many of those have you had?"

"Of these, these weeny marteenies? Only this one."

"I don't believe you, you're half pissed."

"Now that's a highly insulting remark. If I were to be pissed it wouldn't be just half. No, I've had a good day, I had lunch with Meredith, by the way she says that as I've only just stopped taking the pill I'm not going to get pregnant just yet. We had a couple of glasses of wine. I managed to work as normal the whole afternoon and I've been back here about an hour during which time I've had a shower, made myself desirable for you, practised mixing and tasting perfect martinis for you, and here you are. Everything I've done in the last hour is all for you. I've even got a couple of steaks defrosted. Make love to me and I'll tell you about my exciting morning." She put one foot on the seat of a chair and, as she had intended, the folds in her dressing gown fell away and I could see just how naked she was underneath it.

"I'll take a shower first"

"No need."

"Yes, a shower first, you know the rules. We both shower or we both don't shower, no mix and match."

"Ok, you've got five minutes or I start without you."

Twenty minutes later she was lying flat on her back beside me on the bed. She, like me, was totally naked. She was smiling and about to doze off. I tried to keep myself awake. I looked at the whiteness of her skin, skin which she sheltered assiduously from the sun. 'Redheads burn' she used to say when I first suggested going away somewhere sunny together. 'I can never tan, anyway a tan would hide those freckles that you admire so much. Aberdeen with its rain and fogs is a great place for redhead skin.'

I don't know how much Aberdeen is to do with it, but the alabaster lustre of her body is a continual wonder to me. I ran the back of my left index finger nail slowly up the crease between her pubis and thigh.

"That's nice," she murmured with a slight wriggle of her bum. She stretched her legs and flexed her ankles.

I decided to tease her, knowing full well that I never get the better of her verbally. "Do you know that you have knobbly knees?" I said with a small degree of truth.

"Don't get me onto your bodily faults," she replied. "We will be here all night if I list them all, or shall I just concentrate on that ever-expanding roll around your stomach and don't tell me again that it's resting muscle."

I decided to change the subject. "Do you know that we

have made love every night since returning from Westgate?"

'Mmm, yes, and Sunday morning."

"And you are not even fertile according to Meredith. What the hell does she need to know about taking the pill."

"She's a biologist."

'Well I don't know if I can keep it up."

'You couldn't last Sunday morning."

"Right, just for that I'll get up and make dinner although I know that you would you prefer to lie in your pit for the rest of the evening."

She emerged, dressed, as I put the steaks on the grill. The salad was on the table and the fried potatoes were keeping warm. We take it in turns, approximately, to cook meals but she is much more adventurous than I am… and better.

I offered a glass of red wine to match mine from the bottle we opened the previous night and settled down to eat and talk.

I started. "You had a good day you said, and I guessed you had because success always makes you randy."

"Am I that easy to read?"

'Only when sex is involved."

"Well, I've found about the 1940 missing weeks in your father's flying log book."

"How?"

"I discovered that his old squadron, in 1940 that is, Number 325 is still flying, in Anglesey of all places at RAF Valley, helicopters apparently. Anyway, I wrote to the person in charge, the Commanding Officer is the correct title, and got a reply from a guy who works for him."

"When was all this?"

"Just last week. I got the reply today. Anyway this 'guy', who goes by the title of Squadron Adjutant, says that there is no record of Colin flying with the squadron after 22 April 1940, but he did find a note saying that on or around that date Colin was 'detached to the Ministry of Defence'. There is no further mention of him after that in any existing squadron records."

A self-satisfied smile came over Fiona's face. "That was

rather clever of me, wasn't it?"

I agreed, although I didn't think it was really any great achievement, but she liked praise. "So, what have you concluded?" I asked.

"That Colin for some reason practiced a bit of deception. The flying log that I suppose is the one that he would permit people to read, the green leather volume, shows him flying Lysanders with 325 Squadron at a time in 1940 when we now know he wasn't. Perhaps he was going to destroy the other log book but hadn't done so by the time of his death. Maybe he wanted to cover something up, maybe he wanted to eradicate the memory of what really happened over those ten weeks or so, and maybe a combination of both."

"I still think it's not stuff we should discuss with Mary," I replied. "Although I'll tell Ian next time we go to The Courts. If she does know what happened then she has kept it all quiet, and thus she has her own reasons for doing so which we should respect. And if she doesn't know, then what would we gain by telling her? We could seriously upset her if there is something nasty lurking in Colin's history."

"Yep, I agree and she's your Mum in any case so I leave it to you and Ian to decide. I promise I'll say nothing. But in return…"

Lawyers are excellent at bargaining.

"…I'd like to see if I can contact that Norwegian lady, Ingrid, I feel that she might know something."

"Well, if she is still alive of course"

"Yes, of course and we don't know that, also of course."

"But lay off until I leave for Singapore. It will stop you being bored while I'm away."

'What on earth makes you think I'm bored while you are away? There is always Andy sniffing round my skirts at work and Meredith might make another pass at me."

"Meredith?"

"Oh, well before you were on the scene she and I were quite cosy, almost an item.

"Have you -?

"Emotionally certainly, physically not, but I've been tempted in the past. But now you are all I need. You are an entirely satisfactory lover. Quite good really."

"Really?"

"Yes, really. Even after these eight years I still adore you."

"And I, you."

Chapter 12

*F*iona feels a little uncomfortable that she has not told Martin the full story of her day's accomplishments, that she has already discovered where Ingrid lives and that she has full intention to contact her, but the feeling lasts just five minutes. This uncomfortableness is replaced by a frustration that she has agreed not to proceed further with Ingrid until Martin has left for Singapore.

The week passes slowly for her. She works hard, until after 6pm most evenings, to get ahead of herself in case she decides to make a sudden dash to Bodø. She allows herself to explore how she might make the journey there from Aberdeen. She puts a plastic ruler over a small scale European atlas and calculates that Bodø is about 800 miles directly north east from Aberdeen, about twice as far as London. It ought to be an easy trip, she thinks.

But her local travel agent soon dispels any idea of easiness. No ferries operate to Bodø from anywhere in Britain, and to go by air would necessitate flights to London, then onto Oslo with an overnight stop before catching an internal flight up to Bodø.

"And train or road between Oslo and Bodø would take

about 18 hours," the agent adds. "You are looking at four days of travel to get to and from Bodø to Aberdeen. Of course, you could turn it into a holiday and take the coastal ferry service from Bergen. One ship leaves every day to travel right up the coast to the Russian border almost, but that would mean arriving in Bodø three days out of Bergen."

Fiona is disappointed but far from discouraged. Somehow she will get to see Ingrid. Martin will be away for two weeks, she could surely get there and back well within that timescale.

The Saturday night before he leaves they have a particularly interesting and satisfying sexual session... love making? Yes, but great passion besides.

"You see," Martin says, "at my age if you rest me for a couple of days I'm better able to satisfy your needs. Like a thoroughbred race horse."

"Or donkey," she replies.

"Now you are equating me to a beast of burden, actually that's not so inaccurate, rather how I feel at times."

She kicks him on the shin.

--///

The following Monday morning she closes the door of her office and dials the Bodø telephone number that the Norwegian military attaché had given to her. "Ingrid Johansen? It's Colin Mitchel's daughter-in law calling."

"Oh, hello, Fiona, this is Ingrid. I have been expecting your call."

"Yes, I should have phoned sooner but was very tied up at work, I'm sorry. I also had to talk things over with my husband."

"And he knows you are phoning me?"

"Oh, yes, but he is away in Singapore so was happy for me to call you."

Fiona thinks, 'It's funny how the little white lies mount up, one leading to another, at what point are they no longer white?'

"Are you still there Fiona? The line is not too good."

"Yes, yes still here... in Aberdeen."

"Aberdeen. A nice city, I was there many years ago. Lots of big stone houses and weather no better than on the Norwegian coast."

"And where are you talking from? Colonel Solberg the Norwegian military attaché in London who gave me your number said you live in Bodø."

"Yes, that's right, I'm talking to you from my home in Bodø. You were lucky to catch me in, it's a day off for me. I don't work full time anymore."

Ingrid's voice exudes strength and confidence; this does not sound like an old lady speaking, Fiona thinks.

"Your English is near perfect," Fiona remarks. "I suppose you learned it when you were in Scotland during the war"

"Do I have a Scottish accent?"

"Not that I can detect, but you must have used English often since then to be still so fluent."

"Oh yes, I use it regularly. Now there is so much I want to talk about, this phone call could become very expensive and there are some things that are perhaps better not discussed on a phone line. The very charming Colonel said that perhaps we could meet up?"

"Yes, I would really like to do that. I have been investigating travel from here to Bodø, but it's difficult."

"Then I have a solution."

Fiona thinks that this lady sounds as if she has a solution to everything. A touch of 'headmistress' about her perhaps. Maybe that is what she is?

Ingrid continues, "I have to be in Oslo next week to attend to some family business. When we meet I'll explain why I live in Bodø rather than down south where I come from. Do you think you can get to Oslo?"

"Yes, I know I can. What day will be best for you?

"Wednesday, Thursday or Friday, any of those would suit me fine. Could you book into a hotel, at the airport or *downtown? I'm afraid I can't offer you any accommodation of my own as I will be staying with an elderly aunt."*

"I'll talk to my travel agent and get things going, then phone you again?"

"I'll be leaving Bodø tomorrow so I'd better give you my aunt's telephone number."

Fiona writes down the number. "I don't think I would be able to make Wednesday, but Thursday or Friday should be possible."

"OK then, we will meet and speak on one or both of those days. Phone my aunt's place tomorrow evening if you can, I'm sorry it's all a bit tight."

The phone call ends. Fiona sits at her desk. 'This is when I should smoke a cigarette,' she thinks, but she has never smoked. She pulls open a drawer in her desk, takes out a half bottle of Remy and a shot glass, fills the glass, and downs the contents in one gulp. 'That's a dangerous habit to fall into,' she thinks glancing at her watch which shows 10am. She wipes the glass with a tissue and replaces it and the bottle in the drawer. She collects her rain coat from the hat stand in the corner of her office, it was drizzling when she came into work, and walks to the receptionist whom she asks to take any phone messages while she is out with her travel agent. The usual, efficient lady receptionist is off for the day and Andy has been detailed to substitute for her. He is not happy.

"Alright for some," he mumbles. "Going anywhere nice?"

"I don't really know as I haven't been there before, but I thought a short break in Oslo would be interesting." Then she is gone.

--///

The travel agent finds flights from Aberdeen to Oslo via London's Heathrow airport such that Fiona can depart early on Thursday morning, two days hence, and be back home on Saturday evening having stayed two nights at the 'Grand

Hotel' in Oslo. "I've never booked anyone to Oslo before," the agent says. "Let me know how it goes."

Fiona telephones Ingrid to let her know that they can meet in Oslo on Friday morning.

--///

Fiona is tired as she trundles off the SAS plane that has brought her and her trolley suitcase from London to Oslo's Fornebu Airport. The same suitcase that she takes with her to court stuffed with legal papers. Her hotel is in the centre of Oslo, she thinks, but she hasn't seen a map of the city. She goes to the airport information desk in the three-story high building and gazes in admiration at the huge oblong mural stretching the whole height of the atrium which seemingly depicts a person, male or female, it's not obvious despite its nudity, entangled half way up a tree which in turn hovers over a dove. There are two other smaller figures depicted clearly as male and female. The one vertical panel dissolves and morphs into other murals all around the atrium, the whole place is one huge art gallery. The atrium seems to serve as the arrivals and departures hall of the airport. Set in amongst its murals, although it's really the other way round, are huge expanses of windows, stainless steel and beautiful wood work. This building, she decides, is just what she would expect from a Scandinavian nation and puts the terminal she has left behind at Heathrow to shame. She regards the main mural again and decides that the large figure is female on account of the one breast showing and bulky thighs. A young, very blonde woman behind the counter of the information desk breaks Fiona's reverie.

"It's by a well-known artist called Kai Fjell," she says. "With help from Snorre Anderson, and is called Arrival & Departure. Some people think the style is reminiscent of Edvard Munch."

"Thank you," says Fiona. It's very striking. I need to get to the Grand Hotel in Oslo, how could I best do that?"

"You could take a taxi, or sometimes the hotel sends out a limo. Have you booked one with the hotel?"

"No, I didn't know I could, or rather my travel agent in Aberdeen didn't know."

"So you are from Aberdeen. We get people in the oil business there sometimes. Scotland has oil, doesn't it, like Norway."

"Yes, that's right." Then Fiona realises that she should have guessed the oil connection and found another travel agent with more nouse. 'There might even have been direct charter flights here from Aberdeen,' she mentally scolds the agent.

The information desk lady continues, "My suggestion is the airport shuttle bus, it leaves from just outside of here every twenty minutes for the city centre, which is less than ten kilometres away, and it will take you right outside the Grand Hotel. I am sure that you will like it. It's quite magnificent, old and full of history, and huge."

Fiona's stomach is grumbling, she hasn't had a proper meal since leaving Heathrow where she endured nearly four hours of waiting for her Oslo flight and was driven to eat a badly prepared and worse served omelette. 'I should have eaten the SAS meal on the flight instead of drinking those two lagers and then dozing,' she thinks.

"Can I get a meal here?"

"Of course," the blonde lady replies, and points over Fiona's shoulder. "Just behind you is a very good restaurant and bar where you can get all sorts of meals including, of course, our own Norwegian specialities. The service is quite quick if you wish. The downtown shuttle leaves on the hour and then every twenty minutes."

Fiona thanks her, changes a hundred pounds into kroner, and settles into the restaurant behind her. She eats an excellent gravlax based salad followed by a sort of Danish Pastry, 'the Norwegian equivalent' she thinks. A glass of German hock completes the meal. She is well satisfied but taken aback by the

135

size of the bill.

She has but five minutes to wait in the late sunshine until the shuttle bus comes by the entrance to the terminal, and less than fifteen minutes later she is greeted by a uniformed concierge who welcomes her to the hotel and Oslo.

"And Norway," Fiona adds.

"Your first time Madam?"

Fiona nods at him as she gapes at the hotel's opulent entrance lobby. She mentally forgives her travel agent but realises that this is going to be an expensive two night's stay. Thankfully she carries a solid Amex credit card with her. She approaches the long reception desk and notices an array of clocks on the wall behind it displaying times in various cities of the world. The largest clock is Oslo time and it shows 9:20pm, an hour ahead of Aberdeen. She resets her watch as the young male receptionist, who has welcomed her with a warm smile and is extremely good looking, records the details of her passport, takes an imprint of her credit card and hands her the key to her room. As he describes the various bars, restaurants and other hotel amenities available to her she is aware that he is eying her up. As he looks fifteen years her junior she takes this as a compliment, but is careful not to extend her own smile directly to him, 'No complications needed here,' she thinks.

Her room is large, elegantly furnished in what could definitely be described as 'Grand Hotel' style rather than the Scandinavian Modern that she had half expected. She ponders whether to try phoning Ingrid at her aunt whom, she assumes, is probably rather old, but decides to disturb neither until the morning. Her bag arrives five minutes later. The porter pulls the curtains closed across the windows, remarking that the sun will rise very early and will wake her up without them drawn together. He shows her how to adjust the room's heating and turn on the television which faces the king-sized bed. He departs without any indication of expecting a tip.

The bathroom is huge with every amenity she could wish. She decides to soak in the magnificent bath rather than have a quick shower, selects some smellies from the shelf over the hand basin and immerses herself in fragrance for twenty minutes. She puts on the bathrobe with the Grand Hotel monogram, lies down on the bed and falls asleep very soon after. At midnight she is wide awake, she turns on the television but finds nothing that either holds her interest or that she can understand. There is a pile of life style magazines on a small table between two arm chairs and a comprehensive tourist guide to Oslo. She reads them all before falling asleep once more.

Fiona wakes early, the digital clock on the bedside table reads 6am. Her body clock believes it's just 5am. She draws back the curtains and the sun light streams in. She is on the third floor and easily visible to a curious passer-by below who is staring up at her and at her nudity. She hastily steps back two paces then thinks, 'Sod it, this is Scandinavia' and resumes her place at the window albeit with one hand veiling her pubis and the other arm hiding her nipples. 'My Botticelli Venus pose,' she muses. 'And I hope you like it'.

A quick splash around in the bathroom and she is out walking around the park outside the hotel. She walks for about an hour pausing at a small, but busy café where she indulges in an open sandwich, orange juice and coffee for breakfast. It is good, but expensive once again and she realises that her hundred pounds worth of kroner is not going to last very long.

Back in her hotel room, she rings the number she has for the old aunt. Ingrid answers the phone immediately and recognises Fiona's voice before she has completed her first two words. They agree to meet at the café within the hotel at 10am. The café is called, very appropriately, the 'Grand Café'. It is an opulent place with high ceilings and is decorated with murals and hanging pictures. There are tables at which one can be convivial and booths where one can be private. Fiona gets there early and chooses one of the booths which has a clear view to the hotel lobby from where she expects Ingrid to appear. She anticipates her guest to be soberly dressed, in a suit perhaps with sensible shoes, possibly hatted. The school *mistress image that she imagined when first they spoke on the telephone. But the lady that walks straight up to her is nothing like that. The age looks right, early sixties perhaps, the hair is close cropped and totally white, the face is thin and finely boned, the body looks athletic and is clothed in smart blue jeans, a maroon windcheater and expensive looking training shoes. Her right hand is held out and the smiling lips simply say, "Fiona, I'm Ingrid. It's so nice to see you at last."*

Ingrid's Story

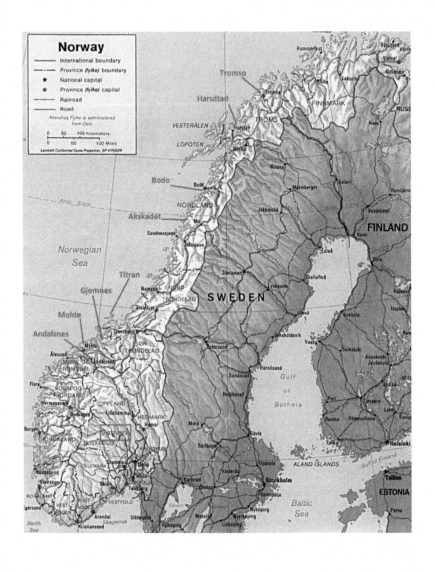

Norway

- International boundary
- Province *(fylke)* boundary
- ★ National capital
- ⊛ Province *(fylke)* capital
- Railroad
- Road

Akershus Fylke is administered from Oslo

0 50 100 Kilometers
0 50 100 Miles

Lambert Conformal Conic Projection, SP 47N62N

Hammerfest   Båtsfjord Vardø
                         Vadsø
Tromso   Kirkenes
          Alta Lakselv
    Harstad
         FINNMARK   RUSS

VESTERÅLEN   TROMS   Ivalo

LOFOTEN   Narvik

              Kiruna

Bodo   Bodø   Malmberget   Kolari   Kamijärvi
     NORDLAND
                                    Rovaniemi
Akskadet   Jokkmokk
         Mo   Kemi   FINLAND
    Sandnessjøen
         Moskeen   Storuman   Luleå
                                    Oulu
Norwegian   Skellefteå
    Sea
    Titran   Stornman   Lycksele
  Gjemnes   Namsos NORD
              Steinkjer TRØNDELAG   S W E D E N   Kokkola
                                              Kajaani
  Molde   Örnsköldsvik Vaasa   Seinäjoki
Andalsnes   Östersund   Äänekoski
         Trondheim   Jyväskyla
   Ålesund   Åndalsnes   Härnösand
    MØRE OG ROMSDAL   Sundsvall   Gulf
   Flora   SOGN OG   of
         FJORDANE   Hudiksvall   Bothnia   Pori   Tampere
  Hermansverk   OPPLAND   Rauma Hämeenlinna
         Gudvangen Lillehammer
Bergen   HEDMARK   Gävle   Helsinki
    HORDALAND BUSKERUD   Mora
              Hamar
         VESTFOLD   Borlänge   Turku
    TELEMARK Drammen Oslo   ALAND ISLANDS   Gulf of Finland
  Haugesund   Uppsala
Stavanger   Karlstad   Västerås   Tallinn
  ROGALAND   Skien Tønsberg Örebro   Stockholm
         VEST- VESTFOLD   Södertälje   ESTONIA
Egersund   AGDER   Nyköping   Baltic   Pärnu
    Arendal Uddevalla   Motala Norrköping   Sea
North   Kristiansand Skagerrak Falköping Linköping
Sea

Chapter 13

*A*s Ingrid walks the two kilometres from her aunt's house to the Grand Hotel, all the thoughts that had crowded her mind since that first phone call two weeks ago from the Colonel in London, concatenate into a jumble of scarcely resolved questions. What should she tell the woman that she is about to meet? There are some things that she wants to tell this daughter-in-law of Colin, others that she is ambivalent about, and yet others that surely should never be revealed to her or to Colin's son. Even where to begin is a problem, and where to end is an even bigger one. And how much would this woman, Fiona, want to know? Even that she is Scottish could present a problem, given all that happened in Scotland forty years ago.

Ingrid has already decided that the events preceding her arrival in Bodø could probably be skated over quite quickly. Fiona would not really be interested in the tedious journey from Vemork with that damned barrel. She hadn't thought of that journey for many, many years, but the phone call from Fiona just four days previously had brought it all flooding back. During a sleepless Monday night, she seemingly retraced every step, every lorry journey, every boat trip.

She had known heavy water was important, although then she didn't really know why. Working on the maintenance of the Vemork electrolysers brought her into contact with scientists and engineers that tried to explain to her what nuclear fission was all about. Then the French came at the beginning of April 1940 and were allowed to take 185 kilograms of the water 'on loan', as the plant boss Axel Aubert had put it, to keep it out of the hands of advancing Germans. This loan was supposedly of all the heavy water stored at Vemork at that time and no more production was planned. The critical importance of the heavy water thus became very apparent to Ingrid and she knew that there was still a quantity of the liquid within the electrolytic distilling apparatus itself. When Norway was invaded on the 9th of April she decided that her act of defiance towards the invaders would be to get all of that liquid, and herself, to Britain. She drained all the liquid that she could find into thermos flasks which she took back to the house in nearby Rjukan where she lived with her parents. She cycled back and forth between Rjukan and Vemork at the beginning and end of each day and at every lunch time with two full flasks. She told her parents what she was doing. They tried to dissuade her but soon gave in. They had been unable to get her to do anything she didn't want to since she turned sixteen and they knew that other young people were trying to get to Britain to help the struggle against the Nazis. They and her younger brother made it their mission to find more empty thermoses for her.

In a week, she managed to fill thirty-two flasks with about one litre each of heavy water. She tried to conceal what she was doing from her fellow workers, but she guessed that what she was doing was an open secret. She packed all the flasks into a matrix of cardboard and straw within an empty fertiliser storage drum with a sealable lid. This she decided to take up North, supposedly away from the Germans who, she assumed, would advance up Norway from the south. The loaded storage drum now weighed about 50 kilograms. It rolled fairly easily but was almost beyond her strength to lift by herself, even when using the cats-cradle of rope that she wove around it. She was 23 years of age, had no boyfriend and no idea of what to do next except to get away from the incoming Nazis.

On the evening of the 19th of April an acquaintance of Ingrid's father accosted her while she was cycling home from work. She had seen him in Telemark, she thought, and he looked to be about thirty years old. He called himself Peter and told her that he knew that she had a precious cargo that she wanted to get to the British. He told her that the British were on the coast about 500 kilometres north at a place called Andalsnes. He said that he and a few other men were setting out for Andalsnes in an old truck to fight with the British and would take her and her cargo with them, but they had to leave that evening. They would collect her at 10pm and travel in the dark. She should bring warm clothes with her, food for three days and the load which Ingrid had by now explained was liquid in a drum.

"Label it as Sperm Whale Oil," Peter told her. "I've been whaling and I know how valuable that stuff is for clocks and things."

Ingrid's parents were dismayed at the haste of her departure and tried once again to persuade her not to leave, with the same lack of success as before. Her father painted the drum as suggested by Peter while Ingrid packed a rucksack and changed into her cross-country ski clothing, warm and waterproof. Her mother made up a package of food. The atmosphere in the house was sombre, tearful, but determined. The two parents took pride that their daughter was going to resist the Nazis, although they fully realised that it might be years before they saw her again, if at all. But they also knew that several other families in their area were facing the same dilemma.

Ingrid sat in the cab of the lorry, three abreast with Peter in the driver's seat on one side and another man on the other side of her, Peter's younger brother. There were three more youngish men behind the cab sheltering under a canvas tilt who had been instructed by Peter to guard Ingrid's whale oil.

"We are all fishermen," Peter told her. "Often we work the same trawler, and we don't want to be around when the Germans arrive."

The old truck laboured up through the mountains and groaned down the descents. They stopped every two or three hours and refuelled about halfway. During two of these stops Peter heaved a suitcase sized radio out from the back of the lorry, connected it to the vehicle's battery and listened intently through earphones. He told Ingrid that he had 'borrowed' the radio from his boss's fishing boat.

After about twenty hours of travel they neared their destination and were stopped by a group of Norwegian soldiers who, after a brief questioning, were persuaded that the men in the lorry wanted to join the British troops to help guide them, and to fight if given arms. They also swallowed Ingrid's story that her drum contained very important war material that had to be kept out of German hands and taken safely to Britain if Norway fell.

"Go to the railway station," the young officer seemingly in charge of the ten soldiers said. "There is a lot of material there in big boxes which is being taken up north, armaments I think, and possibly to England. There are many British and Norwegian soldiers there guarding the stuff so it must be a very important shipment."

They arrived at the station at about 8pm to find a closely guarded train which they were not allowed to approach. They spent five days talking to Norwegian officers, to British officers, and to their troops. They lived in the lorry outside of the town of Andalsnes, watched the German bombers bomb the troop camps and the docks, and learned the truth. The train contained over fifty thousand kilograms of gold which had been stored in vaults in Oslo and which represented the Norwegian state treasury. It had been whisked away from Oslo just as the Germans arrived and then taken by truck to Lillehammer. There it had been transferred to a train which then made for Andalsnes where the British had agreed to evacuate it to Britain. The gold was to be divided among three warships to spread the risk of loss by sinking.

Ingrid watched the British cruiser HMS Galatea depart the port on the 25th April. She talked to some of the soldiers that had spent three days loading about 200 crates from the train onto the ship, and tried unsuccessfully to get herself and her drum included in the ship's cargo. German air raids on Andalsnes and the imminent arrival of German troops prevented the other two warships from docking, so the remaining crates of gold were put onto a convoy of about twenty-five trucks and moved up the coast to the port of Molde. A short journey by sea, but about 100 kilometres by road. Peter followed this convoy in the lorry with Ingrid. His brother and the other men had decided to join up with local Norwegian partisans who were trying to delay the German advance.

Molde was being bombed as the gold and Ingrid arrived. The following day loading commenced of about one half of the gold onto the British cruiser HMS Glasgow, but gold was not the only cargo destined for this ship. To Ingrid's amazement King Hakon of Norway and almost all the members of the Norwegian Government were also waiting to be taken on board. They had only just escaped from the clutches of the Nazis in Oslo. Despite some pleading, Ingrid soon realised that there was no chance of her and her precious drum being given space on the Glasgow for its 1,000 kilometres voyage north to Tromso. The plan was for a provisional Norwegian government to be established at Tromso to counter the puppet regime in Oslo set up by the Germans with their traitorous Norwegian, Quisling.

On the 29th of April, German bombing of Molde became so severe that HMS Glasgow and its precious cargos could no longer be risked. The warship set sail for Tromso where it arrived safely two days later. About eighteen tons of gold had been left behind in Molde, most of which was loaded onto a Norwegian coastal steamer, the Driva, before it, too, had to leave the port to escape bombing. The remaining gold, some 30 crates, was to be taken by truck about 150 kilometres north to the town of Gjemnes near to Trondheim, and there to be loaded onto the Driva, once it had arrived from Molde, for onward shipment to Tromso. Again, Peter and Ingrid followed the gold by road. They realised that the rendezvous with the Driva was going to be their final chance for them to get to Britain. The men involved in guarding the gold convoy had become used to their presence. They admired their persistence and agreed to help them get onto the Driva one way or another.

But the Driva never made it to Gjemnes. Having left Molde it was attacked by German aircraft and had to be beached to avoid sinking. Five small, local fishing vessels were sent to collect the gold, and all of them eventually arrived safely at Gjemnes.

Ingrid solicited all five of the captains of the fishing boats for space but was told that they were going only about a further 100 kilometres up the coast to a remote village called Titran which is on the island of Froya to the west of Trondheim. There they were to meet with two larger fishing boats which would finally take the gold up to Tromso. Ingrid knew she had to get on one or other of those larger boats, but if she couldn't first be taken on one of these five smaller vessels at Gjemnes then Peter would have to risk the truck on what was described as very poor road, possibly impassable, to Titran.

She cajoled and begged the more sympathetic of the five captains until one eventually agreed to take her, Peter and the drum as deck cargo. They and the remaining gold arrived at Titran on the 3rd of May where the two large boats were waiting and not much else. It was no more than a hamlet, mainly used seasonally as a camp for fishermen following herring shoals and home to a monument commemorating a maritime disaster that occurred there in 1899 killing about 140 fishermen.

The gold was successfully transferred from the small boats onto the two large boats which set off for Tromso the next day, but no amount of begging had persuaded either of the captains to take Ingrid and Peter. One of them did suggest that they try to get to Namsos, another 200 kilometres up the coast, where British and French troops had landed. One of the captains of the five small boats volunteered to take them to Namsos, but Peter had been monitoring Norwegian partisan radio broadcasts and heard that the Allies were that very day abandoning their toe-hold there because of severe bombing and advancing German land forces. Ingrid was in despair. They were stuck it seemed; there were German troops somewhere between Titran and their intended destination of Tromso and they had no means of transport. The captain that had wanted to help them said that he would sail up towards Namsos to try and find some other boat, perhaps even a British warship, which might take them either to England or Tromso. He showed them the stone barns that were used by visiting fishermen where they could bed down, and introduced them to a family that agreed to help them with food.

Three days later another fishing boat arrived carrying some fifteen Norwegian soldiers and partisans. They had escaped from Namsos and come to Titran because, they had heard, it was not under immediate threat from the Germans. They said that they were going to wait there until either they received instructions on where to go next or the arrival of the German troops forced them to move on. The boat had a powerful radio receiver-transmitter which was being used to maintain contact with other Norwegian forces. Ingrid decided to make one last toss of the dice and explain to the group's leader, although no-one wore any kind of rank badges, the importance of the drum of supposedly sperm whale oil that she and Peter had brought so far from its origin. The leader cottoned on, had a series of radio conversations, then told Ingrid and Peter that he had been instructed to get them to the British, at Tromso if possible. He had also to take his own men northwards to meet up with other Norwegian forces that were still fighting. The boat, called 'Kirsten', set off on 14 May.

Four days later the Kirsten pulled into a sheltered bay near to the tiny port of Agskadet. All the soldiers prepared to go ashore. Their leader said that they were going to join up with Norwegian forces in the area which were trying to delay the Germans who were steadily advancing northwards. He added that there were Allied troops at Bodø about 75 kilometres north as the crow flies, or double that by road. Ingrid and Peter could accompany his party if they wished, but the Kirtsten's captain was going no further north as he had heard that his family's town was now under German control and he wanted to get back to them. Ingrid and Peter made the only choice they could, and hefting the drum between them trudged up a track away from the coast.

--///

Ingrid enters the Grand Hotel, Oslo. She has been there several times before and makes straight for the café. She recognises Fiona immediately from her clothes which, in some difficult to define way, were not what a Norwegian would wear at this time of the year. She is amused at the position Fiona has taken up. A clear view of the entrance to the café and shielded by her corner seat from any approach from behind, the sort of position that an SOE operative might take up, she thinks. All the possible greetings that she had rehearsed during her walk evaporate and she can think of no more appropriate greeting than, 'It's so nice to see you at last', then wonders for a moment why she had added the final two words.

Chapter 14

*F*iona stands to shake hands with Ingrid saying, *"And I'm very pleased to see you too."* They both sit down smiling at each other, a moment's awkwardness.

Ingrid says, *"Shall we order coffee and a cake each?"*

"Yes certainly." Fiona gives a little wave to a waiter who glides over to the seated pair and takes the order.

"Although there are things that I would like to ask you about your husband and his family, I know that you contacted me to learn more about the time, the short time, that Colin. Oh my goodness! I've barely spoken that name out loud in forty years. That Colin and I spent together, so perhaps it would be best if I started off."

"Yes," replies Fiona. *"When we read Colin's wartime dairy we came across your name, in the entry dated the 25ᵗʰ of May 1940. He simply wrote that you came to him in Bodø, that you had just arrived from Harstad with some RAF men and that you had a barrel of valuable sperm whale oil that you wanted to get to England. Your name doesn't figure again in the diary, and its last entry, for the 8ᵗʰ of June, simply says, heading home."*

"Well, the first thing is for me to confess that I told a little

lie to Colin. I hadn't come with the RAF party from Harstad which is north of Bodø. We, that is Peter and I, more about him later, sort of infiltrated the RAF boys so that we could move into Bodø without being questioned. Peter and I had actually brought the barrel overland from a seaside village called Agskaret which is about 150 kilometres south of Bodø by road, although we found a more direct track, much shorter but very hilly. And we had brought the barrel a lot further than that before then."

"We have been told by a British man, Rupert Noakes, a civil servant, I suppose you might call him –"

Ingrid breaks in. "Ah! Mr Noakes, not your usual civil servant, somebody whom I got to know quite well but to whom I never quite took."

"Me neither. But it was he that told us how London got wind of your barrel of heavy water joining the convoy of Norwegian gold at Lillehammer."

"To be accurate we didn't join the gold convoy as it passed Lillehammer, but at a place called Andalsnes where the gold was to be transferred to ships to take it north up to Tromso along with the Norwegian King and Government. But German bombing allowed only one ship to be loaded with about one third of the gold. Peter and I followed the rest in a road convoy until we met up with more boats that were supposed to get us to Tromso. In the event the gold did get to Tromso and was conveyed to Britain by sea along with King and Government, but we were off loaded at Agskaret to allow some troops with which we were travelling to join up with the Norwegian forces fighting the Germans around Bodø. These other troops were in contact with the British and they told me that I had to get the barrel to the British Air Force contingent who were trying to build an airfield at Bodø. We were to contact a Wing Commander Sexton, who was in charge of the Air Force personnel there, or his deputy, Flight Lieutenant Mitchel. And this I and Peter did. We had help with transport some of the way but mainly we walked and carried the barrel."

"How long did the journey take?" Asks Fiona.

"Well we left my home on 19 April, arrived in Agskaret on 18 May, so that was a month all told. Then a further week to make the journey to Bodø by foot, by which time both Peter and I hated that bloody barrel, but we had brought it so far that we were not going to give up on it. We sort of constructed a rope sling to hang it from a long pole, carrying it we must have looked like a pair of oxen yoked together."

"That's an incredible story."

"Oh! It gets even less credible. What I've described to you was the easy bit."

The waiter sets a china coffee pot on their table together with milk, sugar and a selection of assorted small cakes. He asks if he should pour the coffee. Ingrid speaks in Norwegian to say that they will pour it themselves, which they do. Fiona signs the bill with her room number.

"Before I continue with my story," Ingrid begins to speak again. *"I'd like to understand why you wanted to find out about this woman, me, who just gets one short mention in Colin's diary."*

"Well, it started out because Martin and I, and I have to confess we are not actually married, but we've been together for eight years now, so de-facto married, and as we are trying for our first child, very much de-facto."

"Martin? That's your man's name, Colin's son?"

"Yes. Martin Mitchel. He's a very nice man, an oil exploration engineer, clever, and tolerant of me."

"And you, what are you?"

"Oh, I'm a lawyer. I work for an organisation specialising in company law. It sounds boring but in fact can be quite exciting as our principal business is with oil exploration."

"And do you love Martin?"

"Yes, very much." An unformed sexual thought including a naked image of Martin produces the little smile that so turns her man on. Ingrid notices it.

"Yes, I can see that you love him. So, you are a happy, contented couple?" Half statement, half question.

"Yes, very."

Fiona senses that a bond has been created between the two of them. 'Ingrid is good at handling people and situations,' she thinks. 'I may have to be careful.' She continues. "Colin was awarded a British decoration called the Order of the British Empire, usually just called the OBE."

"Yes, I'm familiar with it. I think Mr Noakes told me. He also contacted me soon after Colin was killed, he seems always to have been in our backgrounds, mine anyway."

"Well, it's not the sort of award a young pilot in the RAF would get. We were curious so we did some investigating. Eventually we were told about the extraction of heavy water from Norway just prior to the invasion by the Germans and that Colin had had a part in the story through his partnership with you, the name in his diary, the lady with the barrel of so called whale oil. So his role with the barrel, it seems, was rewarded with an OBE. But then we, actually me with my lawyer's mind, found some anomalies with his war records, specifically his flying log books. They seem to indicate that after getting back to Britain from Norway, which I now know was with you and that you both somehow survived a sinking warship, he was doing something for several weeks that he tried to conceal. Finding out what that was should be the last missing jigsaw piece."

"Yes, a lawyer's mind." *The coffee has been drunk and a tart or two eaten. Ingrid stands.* "The next part of the story of me, Colin and the barrel will be quite hard for me to relate. I don't think I can do it while being subject to your courtroom gaze. Let's walk outside, there are very nice parks around the hotel. We shall walk side by side, like a couple. I think I would prefer that."

Fiona stands to show her agreement. "Will I need a coat?"

"Oh, I don't think so. It's a beautiful summer morning outside. We can head up towards the royal palace and explore its grounds."

They turn right outside the hotel and after 200 meters or so enter the palace park. They admire the outside of the palace, and then begin again to walk and to talk.

"So, on the 25th May 1940, after a week of mainly walking, although we twice got short lifts in farmers' horse and wagons, Peter and I arrived at the seemingly chaotic military camp that had formed around the poor broken town of Bodø. I had seen the German Luftwaffe in action as I had made my way up the coast to Agskaret but nothing had prepared me for what I saw when I first entered Bodø. The destruction was indescribable. Peter and I sought out Wing Commander Sexton who didn't seem very interested in my story about my mission, but he acknowledged that he had heard from London that I was coming and told me that Colin was to be in charge of my drum of whale oil. He clearly knew nothing of its true contents.

We found Colin exactly where I expected, on the still being constructed airfield. He agreed to the drum being stored in one of the underground bomb shelters. I said that I had some things to do but that I would be back in a day or two. The very next day three old British biplane fighters arrived at the airstrip and did their best to defend the town from the Luftwaffe, and met with some success. The three pilots all died later during the war, there is a memorial to their bravery in Bodø just where the old airstrip, Colin's airstrip, was built.

Peter had friends on the outskirts of Bodø who had agreed to put him and me up for a few days. I introduced myself to a Norwegian officer who, after checking my story, told me to lie low until the British had decided whether to stay in Bodø or abandon it as they had Namsos. Peter, in the meantime, left me on about 1 June. I had become fond of him. We had seen things over the five weeks we had been together that we had never thought possible, and we had become sporadic lovers. He had decided to join up with some partisans and made off into the mountains. I met up with him after the war, in Bodø where he had found a job on a fishing boat, and we got married. But he had been a prisoner of the Nazis for over three years and his health was broken. He died in 1955 and I never married again. But, I stayed in Bodø."

The two women walk slowly. Fiona comments on the

buildings and the parks occasionally when Ingrid rests from speaking to draw breath or to consider what she should reveal next.

"Anyway," Ingrid goes on. "Towards the end of May it seemed obvious that the British and the French were going to pull out. There was a great deal of shipping activity and lots of attention from the Luftwaffe. The airstrip was under repeated attack, but seeing the damaged buildings in and around the town I could think of no better place to safeguard the drum than the underground shelter it was already in. I tried to find Colin but without success, somebody told me that he had taken his men up into the hills for safety from the bombing.

I finally caught up with him again on the last day of May. He had now moved his men into a partly damaged warehouse by the dock side awaiting orders to embark one of the warships waiting to remove all the troops back to England. By this time, it had become common knowledge that the British were also evacuating all their forces out of France. So basically, with the then non-aggression pact between Russia and Germany still in force, Britain appeared to be all that remained to face off against Hitler. Opinion within the local Bodø people was quite divided. There were those who had witnessed the destruction of their town and wanted no more fighting, the Germans were coming, so let them come and there were others that were determined to keep on fighting either in Norway or, more feasibly perhaps, from British soil. I was one of the latter, and I found several men who had the same view.

Colin had just received a message from Britain. He showed it to me written on what he called a Signals Pad. His prime duty now was to get me and my barrel to the UK, and as discretely at possible. He and I were to attempt to get to Narvik where space would be available for us, and the barrel, still no mention of heavy water, on a troop ship waiting there. I should perhaps remind you that all this happened in the middle of the year and we were well above the Arctic Circle so the sun scarcely set at night. This meant that troop evacuation had almost limitless daylight hours, an advantage to the British for ease of operations but a disadvantage because of the Luftwaffe's daylight bombing raids. The light did make ship navigation along the Norwegian coastline much easier for the Norwegian and British shipping.

Colin had two options. He could wait until we were allocated space in a warship going up to the coast to Narvik, of which there were very few, or I could try to find a Norwegian boat, perhaps a fishing vessel, which would take us. I turned to Peter for help the day before he departed and he came up trumps. Small fishing boats, which we Norwegians called 'Skoyter' but the Brits called 'Puffers' because of the 'puffing' noise their engines made, were already in action around the coast taking stranded groups of soldiers to evacuation centres and generally making themselves useful to the British Navy. Peter introduced Colin and me to the crew of three, all rather pirate like, who agreed to set off for Narvik with us in two days' time. Peter said that the crew were probably involved in smuggling, or guerrilla operations against the Germans, or both. There were, he said, unlikely to be any other passengers than ourselves. And so it proved to be. Just before midnight on the 2nd of June, Colin and I carried the barrel aboard and make ourselves comfortable in the small crew room that was used for resting and meals.

The captain, whose name I cannot remember, said that the boat should take about a day to make the journey to Narvik, keeping very close to the coast line on our right to avoid detection by the Luftwaffe. The journey was, in fact, very pleasant. A long day's cruise in fact, in fine weather and calm seas with breath-taking views of the Norwegian mainland mountains and fiords, and no sight of German aircraft. I had never been this far north before and Colin became less of a military officer and more of a companion now that he was away from Bodø. He knew virtually no words of Norwegian and in those days my English was very basic, just three years at high school, but we reached an accord. He would aim to get the barrel and myself to England, he with me if possible, although I think he wasn't too concerned about the barrel, which by now was distinctly scruffy but seemed sound."

Fiona breaks in, "But your English is now perfect, how has that happened?"

"I spent about three years in Britain, Scotland and England, after I had made the crossing that I'm about to tell you about. And for many years I have been working for the Bodø tourist office, mainly guiding the English and American visitors that spill off the passenger ships that often visit, and I also spend time in the local tourism office as an English-speaking guide, so I get plenty of practice. Anyway, back to the little puffer boat.

With the Narvik fiord appearing into sight, and about three hours to landing, or so Colin and I thought, the Captain called out loudly for all on the boat to hear. He said that he had just had a message on the boat's radio to say that we were to sail past Narvik and make for Harstad which is the far side of the large island which appeared to bar our way. 'There is a passage through the islands, they are called the Loftens and Harstad is just on the other side. There are more troops to be evacuated from there so we should find berths for you, Ingrid and your British companion.'

Colin got a bit agitated, but could only exercise his frustration through me as none of the boat's crew spoke any English at all. He explained that his orders were to get to Narvik where ship's space had already been allocated to us. I just reminded him that the whole of my journey from my home had been full of changed plans and uncertain outcomes. I reassured him that everything would work out in the end and that we would be in Britain after just a few days.

We arrived at Harstad on the morning of the 4th of June and our little craft jostled its way through a mixture of other puffers and naval warships to a small empty space at the quayside. The captain told us that he would try to hang onto the space until either he could use the boat to help the evacuation, or until he saw some other way that he could hinder the Germans, in the meantime Colin and I were welcome to continue using the crew room as our base. The town was larger than I imagined and although I saw some bomb damage, the destruction was nothing like I had seen at Bodø. Looking around the harbour, we saw men in their hundreds lining up to await embarkation on the ships which then headed out towards the western horizon and out of our sight.

Colin straightened up his uniform as best he could and made off towards what appeared to be some form of military organisation headquarters. I, meanwhile, went with one of the crew members to see what we could find in the town. Colin reappeared at midday just I was helping the crew prepare a mountain of sandwiches that would see us all through the next couple of days. We had managed to find bread, tinned beef and milk. Colin admitted that he had managed to scrounge a lunch of sorts at one of the several military feeding stations and had news for me and the barrel. We would be moving out of Harstad and on our way to Britain on the 7th of June, where we should arrive in the north of Scotland after a further two days.

There were just two more days for Colin and me to wait, and wait we did, passing much of the time on our puffer where we washed our, by now, very grimy clothes. Colin also spent time with the British troops. I think that he would have liked to have joined with them completely. Perhaps attaching himself onto the two RAF fighter squadrons that were based some distance away and tasked to keep the Luftwaffe from Harstad, Narvik and the several other small ports where troops were mustering prior to evacuation. I saw him gazing in admiration at the British Hurricane fighters that sometimes flew overhead. I asked him if those were the sort of aircraft that he had been flying in Britain but he said he had had a rather boring job flying a battlefield observation plane and he had never been anyway near a battlefield in it. "But one day," he said, "I'll move onto Hurricanes and maybe even Spitfires." I had no idea what a Spitfire was, but I could see that the prospect excited him.

He told me that we would be ferried out to one of the warships, a destroyer probably, which would then take us way out to sea where we would be transferred onto a waiting troopship for the final leg of our journey. He added that he was a bit concerned about taking a woman, a civilian, on this journey. An army officer had expressed to him that the presence of a female among the troops might affect discipline. They might have more concern about protecting me than going about their duties if the ships came under attack, which the officer thought was a very distinct possibility.

'Do you think you could disguise yourself as a man', he asked me. 'You are already wearing trousers and a ski jacket, you are tall and your hair isn't very long, it wouldn't need much to change your appearance.

Initially I bristled a bit at the suggestion but then considered that such a change would be just one more bump on my journey and all part of the adventure. I told him that I would cut my hair very short, wear the knitted balaclava that I had in my rucksack and smear a little engine grease on my face. And call me 'Ing' not 'Ingrid'', I concluded.

Early on the morning of the 7th I emerged from the toilet compartment of the boat disguised at best I could as a young male. Colin was pleased with my look and the crew joked that I could have a permanent place with them on the boat instead of heading off to Scotland. The captain indicated that it was time for him to do some war work so would take his boat out to the destroyer to which we had been allocated. Colin and I put sandwiches and flasks of water into my rucksack and his duffle bag which was also stuffed with all his belongings. The destroyer, I can't recall its name if I ever knew it, was only a couple of hundred meters off shore. Early the previous day I had watched it embark a large batch of troops and take them way beyond the horizon, now the ship was back and already being loaded again. It looked enormous as we approached but Colin remarked that destroyers were actually quite small as warships went. We took our place in a small queue of other boats that contained troops and soon it was Colin's and my turn to climb aboard a rope ladder that hung from the deck high above us. I refused to move until I first saw the barrel gently hauled on board by two sailors using a long, stout rope. Once on the deck a naval officer greeted Colin to say that he knew the importance of the barrel and his companion; me. He offered to let us sit in the Officers' Wardroom if we wished but the barrel would have to stay on deck. I replied, using as husky a voice as possible, that I would stay on deck next to the barrel, we were not to be separated.

"You will be at sea for several hours, are you sure that you want to out in the open? It may get a little rough once we are away from the harbour."

"I'll be fine," I replied.

"Okay, then I suggest you sit down by that tube over there. It brings up warm air from the engine room so will help to keep you more comfortable if you sit with your back against it. What about you Flight Lieutenant?"

Colin said that he would stay with me.

It took about six hours for our destroyer to reach a convoy of troop ships huddled well beyond the Harstad horizon. In that time Colin twice left me and my barrel. On the first occasion he came back with two bottles of beer that he had been given in the wardroom and also pointed out where the nearest toilet was, or as he called it, the 'heads'. The second time he returned full of excitement. He had been on the destroyer's bridge when the Captain said that after unloading troops onto his designated troopship, he had to meet the aircraft carrier HMS Glorious which was a little further away. He needed to collect a spare radio from her to replace a broken one in his ship. He told Colin that the Glorious would set off with two accompanying destroyers direct for Scotland and the big British Navy base at Scapa Flow. It would be there very quickly, not much more than a day sailing. 'Would Colin, his companion and the whale oil barrel, like to transfer onto the Glorious?' he had asked. He wetted Colin's appetite by reminding him that the Glorious was full of Naval aircrew who might also be joined by the remnants on the RAF contingent as they abandoned mainland Norway.

"I told him yes," Colin said to me.

I was fine with the decision. I had to look after the barrel and his job was to get us to Britain, how he did it was up to him.

Our destroyer came alongside one of the troop ships and the couple of hundred troops we were transporting were quickly transferred, then we headed away from the convoy and after about a further hour the huge shape of the Glorious appeared over the horizon. Colin said our destroyer was making at least 30 knots and the distance to Glorious swiftly closed. We were both standing up peering over the gunwales. I was almost overwhelmed by the looming shape filling our field of view. Colin became very animated. I was seeing a rather different aspect of the character, the rather formal attitude that he had been using towards me was now being replaced with a desire to bring me into his excitement.

"She was originally built as a battleship during the last war. Launched in 1915 I think. Then ten years or so later, she was converted into the aircraft carrier that you are seeing now. Imagine the top bit, the 'flight deck', being removed and you can get an idea of the original design of the vessel. Of course, all the big guns were taken off her during the conversion. The main flight deck was sort of laid on top of what was left of the main structure which it why she now looks rather top heavy. And there was enough space left over to accommodate another flight deck for take offs only at the front end of the ship under the main deck. She is a significant vessel and of major importance to the Royal Navy. She can carry nearly 50 aircraft, some of which can be stored in hangars under the main deck, and she weighs about 25,000 thousand tons I believe. She is nearly 800 feet long, about 250 metres, and has a top speed of over 30 knots, the same as this destroyer. She needs all that speed to help get her aircraft into the air."

"Where did you learn all that?" I asked.

"In the wardroom, drinking my first beer."

We were alongside the Glorious by now, our destroyer keeping perfect pace. I was wondering how we were going to transfer from the small ship to the one now so completely dwarfing us alongside. A sailor came up to Colin and saluted him. "Ever been in a boson's chair?" He asked.

Colin replied "No."

"What about you mate?" He said, looking rather in disgust at my scruffy appearance. I shook my head.

"Right then, you are about to have an interesting experience, but we will send this barrel over first to show how it is done."

The sailor helped me carry the barrel to near the ships centre and facing the Glorious. The faded looking rank braids on Colin's uniform rendered him, in the sailors' eyes at least, too precious and I do know the various meanings of that word, to risk carrying loads. We were just in time to see two other sailors haul a crate towards them from Glorious. A thick rope had been slung across the gap that separated the two ships and the crate was suspended from a pulley riding on the rope. Sailors from both ships were controlling the progress of the crate by means of other ropes reaching from it to each ship. The crate was unhitched from the rope and the barrel attached, swinging wildly in the wind although swiftly brought under control by the two teams of sailors. My heart was in my mouth for the whole process as the relative movement between the two ships caused the barrel to pitch up and down and the main rope became slack and then tightened again. But it traversed safely above the water between the two vessels and was carefully removed from its suspension. It was put gently on to the Glorious deck situated less than half way up the side of the bigger ship.

Our sailor friend looked at me and said that I would be the next across. I couldn't imagine how I would make the crossing. Was I to hang from that pulley like the barrel while I was hauled across the foaming gap between the two ships? The sailor caught my dismayed reaction, grinned, and then said that I would have a nice chair to sit in. The chair, the Bosun's chair, not much more that a sling really, was attached to the main rope joining the two ships. I climbed into it, a safety strap was lashed around my upper body and before I could really think about what was going to happen I found myself suspended between the two ships and bouncing up and down as the barrel had done. But I was quickly across, out of the chair which was then pulled back to the destroyer and joined by Colin only a couple of minutes later. Finally, our luggage packs arrived by the same means. The Glorious sailors cast all the ropes of their vessel which were promptly retrieved by the destroyer which was already pulling away from us and putting on speed.

A sailor who appeared to be in charge of the bosun's chair party, a petty officer I suppose, welcomed Colin and me on board with "I am glad that's over, we were sittings ducks for any German submarine while steaming so slow and straight. Now we have got to hang around until your land based planes arrive."

"Oh they are not mine," replied Colin. "Are you saying that the RAF are going to put down Hurricane fighters onto the flight deck here? I don't think that it's ever been done before. Those aircraft don't have any tail hooks to slow them down."

"Well, if your RAF needs the fighters and I can only imagine that it does, then the only thing is to put them onto that great piece of steel sheeting above our heads."

I noticed that we were positioned well to the aft of the ship's hull, sort of under the main flight deck but by the side of the hangar which was shielded from our sight by part of the ship's structure.

"I've got to go now," the Petty Officer concluded. "The ship is picking up steam so I think the Captain is looking for maximum speed because we are expecting to fly aircraft on and off the ship for the remainder of the day. Try to make yourself comfortable round here for a while then I'll send someone to show when you can get food and to find you a billet although it may have to be mattresses inside one of the hangars. Maybe for you, sir, there may be room in the Officers' Wardroom, although don't count on it as there will be a stream of pilots needing homes shortly." As he wandered off we could sense the ship's speed building up and the straining noise of the engine room.

It was now early evening of the 7th of June although, of course, the sun was still well up in the sky. While away from me Colin had found out where we could get some food and where we could have a wash. We decided that the barrel could spare its human companions for an hour or so while we looked after ourselves. We found the mess deck serving adequate food complete with tables and chairs to sit at and we relaxed talking to several different sailors and an officer or two who had decided that their wardroom food was usually inferior to that supplied for the non-commissioned ranks. Despite its huge size the ship seemed full of people. We were told that there was a total of at least 1,500 crew and passengers all itching to get back to Britain and away from the lurking German Navy. However, the ship could not get on its way until the last Hurricanes of the RAF's Number 46 Squadron had landed. After then, we were assured, a full day of hard sailing should see us safely in Scapa Flow, or a bit longer if the captain tried to preserve fuel or had to zig-zag his course to avoid submarines.

At about 7pm we heard aircraft engines that sounded quite different from those of the RN aircraft that had been occasionally taking off and landing during the afternoon. "Merlins," said Colin. "Here come the Hurricanes from Bardufoss, Number 46 Squadron." And there above us were three of these aircraft, all of which landed safely.

"I don't think that has ever been done before," Colin said in admiration. "They are not designed to land on aircraft carriers. They have got no tail hooks to grab cables to slow themselves down, but they all made it, and there should be more to come yet." Colin rushed up to a nearby ladder, climbed up above me and disappeared. I knew that he would be chatting to the RAF pilots for a while and I was content to stay where I was with the barrel. He returned after about half an hour full of details of how the landings were made and adding that another seven Hurricanes were expected later.

But the next to arrive, at about midnight, were actually ten Gladiators. The same sort of biplane that I had seen trying to defend Bodø. The seven expected Hurricanes arrived shortly afterwards, again all aircraft landed safely and we immediately sensed Glorious turning to a south westerly heading for the Orkney Islands and the great harbour of Scapa Flow.

The weather was good so Colin and I decided to remain on deck with the barrel near to where we had first come aboard. Colin put on a flying jacket that he took from his kit bag and I found a thick skiing jumper in my ruck sack. We were comfortable enough sleeping half sitting up with the barrel as support and we slept for eight hours non-stop. When we woke our ship was zig-zagging about her course to Scapa in fine, calm weather. During that day, the 8th of June, Colin and I took it in turns to find food, water and use the ablutions. Every now and again we could see two warships moving around us. I recognised them as destroyers and a sailor told me that they were our anti-submarine escorts, HMS Acasta and Ardent. At other times they positioned themselves either side of our bow. The ship had an almost holiday air about it, the sailors were going home and they were pleased.

I had been trying to decide whether to tell Colin the truth about the contents of my barrel. As we settled down in our area of deck space in the early afternoon looking through the guard rails at the very gently rolling sea, I determined that his devoted attention to his task of getting me and the barrel to Britain deserved the truth. Of course, I was then no more a student of nuclear physics than I am now, my professional training after leaving high school was essentially that of a laboratory technician. I knew heavy water was something needed in nuclear research, although I didn't have any idea of what nuclear research really was, but the passing over of the power station's stock to the French soldiers meant that it was in some way important, although for what I had no idea. I just knew that the little cache that I had discovered had to be kept out of German hands, and this knowledge was reinforced by the attention that the British had been paying to my journey up the Norwegian coast and onto this great warship. And that is essentially what I related to Colin. He too, seemed to understand the significance of the barrel's contents and was, I think, rather relieved that he was not just guarding a foreign girl with a pile of whale oil but was now on what he saw as a worthwhile mission.

By about 4.30 that afternoon we were perhaps halfway into our journey to Scapa and making about 18 knots, or so a sailor had recently told us. Suddenly the ship healed over in a violent change of course and immediately afterwards I saw three large splashes in the sea not far from away followed by three explosions. Loudspeakers burst into life and sailors started running past us putting on life jackets. I couldn't make out most of what was being broadcast but Colin said that action stations had been called and the sailors were all going to their appointed battle positions. "The ship is under attack!" he shouted. He rushed off and came back a few minutes later with two life jackets which we put on over our clothes. "There is nothing else for us to do except keep out of the way of the crew who all know what they are doing. We may be involved in a fight of some kind. Look, our two escorts are going full speed and heading away, they must have seen something. Keep your head down".

I could feel the Glorious putting on speed. A couple of minutes later I heard something like an express train passing over the ship and heard explosions straddling us in the sea. A moment later a third salvo hit the ship, but I never heard the explosion. I must have momentarily passed out because the next thing I knew I was being engulfed by water. My life jacket brought me quickly to the surface and I could see the barrel bobbing nearby, and there was Colin outlined in flames diving from the ship and calling, "Ingrid, Ingrid."

Chapter 15

*I*ngrid stops her story. Fiona says, "Oh my God".
The two women are now well beyond the royal residence,
in a pedestrian precinct with smart shops and cafes
spilling out onto the pavement.

"I could do with a bit of a break from talking. We could
have a light lunch at one of these cafes, they are all good,"
Ingrid suggests.

Fiona thinks that an excellent idea, she could do with a
drink as well.

"This one is famous for its smoked salmon and Norwegian
smoked salmon is the best in the world. Do you like salmon?"

Fiona nods. They sit down. A smiling waitress brings them
menus and asks if they would like something to drink. Fiona
asks for a local lager. Ingrid chooses the same and orders two
smoked salmon, open-topped sandwiches.

Fiona agrees that her sandwich is excellent. A sauce
makes the fish much sharper than she might get in Aberdeen,
but she won't be drawn on which is the better smoked salmon,
Norwegian or Scottish.

During the meal they stop talking about the war and
briefly talk about their personnel lives. Fiona with her parents

in Fort William, her upbringing with her siblings, how Martin came into her life, her job. Ingrid talks of her younger brother who stayed with her parents at she set off for Britain, and now works as an architect in Sweden, her parents still living in Rjukan, hale and hearty in their eighties, and her mother's sister living in Oslo in a retirement home which has a second bedroom for guests and where Ingrid is now staying.

They order coffees. Once they arrive Ingrid starts to speak again of Colin and HMS Glorious.

"Colin reached me and, as the wake from the stern of Glorious approached us, shouted, "Swim away, swim away from the ship or its propellers will get us."

I was, still am, a good swimmer and I swum for my life. Colin stayed by my shoulder, urging me on. We were rocked, tossed and covered by the wake several times but, for a time at least, we were safe. Curiously, the barrel had been washed along with us and was bobbing in the now smoother water not twenty metres away. A good third of its diameter was above water thanks to the air in the packing around the water bottles which, I remembered, filled well over half of its internal space. The sling of knotted ropes that had been used for its transport all that way up the Norwegian coast was still intact. We clung to the ropes so that the combination of the floating barrel and our life jackets kept our heads above water. It appeared that we were not in any immediate danger of drowning, but the coldness of the water soaking through our clothing was another matter.

When you are up to your neck in sea water your horizon is very limited, no more than a hundred or so meters when lifted by a wave. The Glorious had disappeared from view after just a few minutes at full steam although we could hear its engines a little longer. Then we were alone. My watch had stopped at forty minutes past four. Colin's, which was an RAF issue waterproof device, continued working. When it indicated forty-six minutes past four we heard heavy shell fire which continued for about another hour at gradually decreasing volume as the Glorious moved further away from us. Colin said that she could be 50 kilometres away from where we were floating if she were still making full speed.

We had no idea of what had happened. Had Glorious with her great speed shaken off whatever had attacked her? Had the escort destroyers seen off the enemy? The idea that such a huge ship could be sunk never really occurred to us.

We had been in the water over an hour and were already very cold. Even in June the waters of the Norwegian coast remain swiftly lethal to swimmers.

The barrel seemed to be lower in the water. "I think it's leaking," I said.

I pressed an ear up against the side and heard the faint sound of broken glass. "And the glass flasks seemed to have broken. And all that's inside now is a mixture of brine and heavy water."

Colin's teeth were starting to chatter, the cold water seemed to be affecting him more than me probably because I was quite plump in those days, but he managed to spurt out, "It's not surprising that the flasks have cracked open from the fall from the ship's deck. The barrel could easily have hit you on the head and I would clinging onto this useless object by myself. So we now have no purpose for being here freezing to death. Of course, if you look towards the sun it's really quite a pleasant day for a dip."

"What are we going to do?" I asked.

"We are going to sing and tread water to keep the circulation going in our legs. The life jackets will keep us floating if the barrel disappears. And we are to pray to whatever gods we believe in to send a passing boat."

So we sung, alternatively, one song by me then one song by him. I sung nursery rhymes and folk songs, all in Norwegian of course, and what he sung in a very bad voice was almost indecipherable to me. He told me they were dirty rugby songs. We kept this up for another hour or so and I could see that Colin was fading. Although I was very cold, I appeared to be in better shape than him. I kept telling him to move his legs. I cuddled him to share my warmth. I kicked him to make him continue to move.

Time passed on, he lost consciousness and I started to lose strength. I drifted into a sort of reverie, moving in and out of dozes, my parents' images filled my mind and I accepted the inevitability of dying. The barrel started to sink completely, to join whatever lay beneath us, and for what seemed to be the first time in many days, I let it go.

Shortly afterwards, in a period of semi-consciousness, I became aware of a faint throbbing noise that I took to be my pulse trying to flush warmer blood about my body. The noise grew louder and my brain roused itself to tell me that there was a boat approaching with the unique sound of a puffer. Adrenalin kicked in and with the last of my strength I waved and waved, and shouted and shouted. I could see a little fishing boat seeming to come before me just before I lost consciousness.

Sometime later I awoke in a tiny, but warm, cabin. All my clothes had been removed and I was wrapped in blankets. Colin lay beside me, similarly swaddled. A Norwegian male voice softly spoke, "We hadn't realised you are a woman, but we had to get those clothes off you."

I tried to sit up but my body couldn't obey. I felt numb, paralysed even, perhaps I had been hurt into getting onto this boat, perhaps my back was broken, but I could feel no pain. I tried to wiggle my fingers and my toes, and they moved! I realised that I was suffering no more than the after effects of my cold immersion and that I should recover. I called Colin's name but got no response. His eyes were tightly closed but I could see the rise and fall of his chest and knew that he was breathing.

The man spoke again, "My name is Bengt, there are three other men on board and we are heading to Torshavn in the Faroe Islands where we want to offer our services to the British. We set out from Bodø two days ago."

I knew that the British had occupied the Faroes back in April when the Germans invaded Denmark, the Faroes of course being an integral part of Denmark.

"We only have another 150 kilometres to go so even in this old slow boat another twelve hours should see us there. Here, I have a mug of chocolate for you to drink. I realise that you are Norwegian but who is this man? He is suffering from severe shock I should think. He was dressed as a British pilot before we stripped off his clothes. Were you shot down or something?"

I simply told Bengt that Colin and I had both been in Bodø and were being conveyed to Britain in a warship which came under attack and caused us to be blown into the sea. "The ship went on at full speed still under attack leaving us behind to fend for ourselves. I think that happened at about half past four and I know we were in the water for at least two hours."

"More like three, it was well past seven when we saw you. We had actually been keeping a close watch out for the floating mines that we were told the Germans had been laying from their submarines, and you have been asleep here for another three hours. It is nearly ten o'clock now.

Two other young men squeezed in to the cabin and asked me how I was feeling. 'You are both very lucky,' was the main and repeated comment.

Colin woke up. I explained to him what had happened to us and that we were on a boat heading towards the Faroes. None of the crew spoke any more than a few words of English but they listened intently to what I was saying. Colin seemed in a worse way than me and had difficulty in getting down any of the soup and bread that Bengt offered.

"It's about all we have left," he said. "It will help warm you up inside."

We approached Torshavn at about midday on the 9th of June. Our clothes had been hung out to dry on a line suspended between funnel and mast and although stiff with salt, they were better than arriving in port dressed only in blankets. Colin had recovered somewhat and managed to stand next to me on deck. The harbour was full of fishing boats, some flying Norwegian flags others Danish, and there was also a collection of smallish warships, mine sweepers and a destroyer or two. As we pulled in towards a spare space on the quay side I reflected on all that had happened to Colin and me in the past twenty hours. I said to him, "We were very, very lucky."

He murmured "Yes," and put his arm around my shoulders, just in time to provide comfort as I burst into tears.

"I'm sorry, I'm sorry," I sobbed to him, but he replied, "No need to be sorry, you were the stronger. I don't think I would have survived without you."

"But without me you would never have been on that ship with my accursed barrel. It was all hopeless, it was damned, a wild goose chase."

Two men were waiting on the dock side, one Danish, or more probably Faroese, dressed as a civilian and the other a British army Major. I could make myself understood in Danish just as the civilian could get by with a smattering of Norwegian. I threw off any pretence at being male. I started to tell him about what had happened to us but the Major brusquely butted in with questions to Colin. Colin just told him that we had been on HMS Glorious and then found ourselves in the sea when the ship came under attack, until picked up by the fishing boat.

The major said that nothing had been reported about the Glorious having been under attack, but then added, "We don't actually get much in the way of war news up here. Look, you both look all in. Come up to our HQ and I'll get a doctor to have a look at you. It is only a short walk, can you manage?"

The civilian was talking to Bengt, I think he was something like the Harbour Master and was checking papers from the crew. I butted in to thank the three fishermen for having rescued Colin and me. I think I gave them all a kiss.

We walked slowly about a hundred meters to the army HQ which turned out to be an old warehouse full of British soldiers and local civilians, all apparently on good terms with each other. We were seated and very shortly an army doctor came to look at us, check our temperatures and our breathing I think. He said that we should both stay in bed for a day or two and undergo observation then, if we were generally OK, we would need a couple of weeks of convalescence in a TB sanatorium perhaps, or someplace similar. He would get us temporarily into the building in Torshavn now requisitioned as a military hospital, but we needed to get to the British mainland as soon as possible.

The doctor headed off to arrange space for us in the hospital. Colin spoke to the Major who had met us at the quayside. He asked that a message be sent to Rupert Noakes to tell him that he and I were safe in the Faroes but the barrel had been lost. The major looked nonplussed. Colin took his wallet from his uniform jacket. In it he found the message he had received at Bodø which had sent both of us on our mission. He carefully extracted the still very wet piece of paper and gently unfolded it.

"Look," he said. "You will find the address of the message centre for Squadron Leader Noakes at the heading of this piece of paper. Say something about our retrieval from the sea and our need to recuperate, and please just say that the barrel is lost. He will know what I mean." The Major agreed to try his best.

Shortly afterwards an army car took Colin and me away to the hospital where individual rooms had been found for each of us. The doctor reappeared and gave me a sleeping draft, Colin got the same I believe. I didn't wake until the following morning when I found an army nurse fussing over me. She brought in a tray with tea and toast as breakfast. By mid-morning I was feeling much better and, after making myself as tidy as I could, I went in search of Colin. He, too, was dressed and out of bed but had been forbidden to leave the hospital building. We talked of what the future might be holding in store for us. He just wanted to return to flying but in something more interesting than the Lysanders that he had told me about. For myself I had no clue. Perhaps, I wondered aloud to him, I could somehow get attached to those Norwegian forces now sheltering in Britain. My knowledge of the area around Telemark was good, perhaps I could draw maps or do something similar to help.

We pottered around the hospital for the rest of the day, taking lunch in a little common room set aside for walking patients and then sitting there flicking through a few old books and magazines, all in Danish, that were scattered around. In between we dozed off. In the late afternoon the Major who had met us off the boat walked in.

"I'm sorry that I haven't brought you news sooner, but there is a terrible flap going on. The Germans are claiming to have sunk the Glorious but no one really knows where yet. The Navy and Air Force are conducting searches but no survivors, other than yourselves that is, have yet been picked up. With so many high priority messages being sent and received Torshavn is becoming one of the main centres for coordinating the search. I didn't manage to get your message off to Squadron Leader Noakes until lunch time today. I mentioned about you getting blown off the Glorious at the first attack and that you needed a period of convalescence, and I didn't forget about 'No Barrel'. I have just had a reply. You must be rather important people. You are to go away from here as soon as possible and be taken to Scotland. We have engaged the fishing boat than rescued you for the task, and you are leaving here at 10pm tonight. Something to do with tides the skipper told me. I asked him for the precise position of where he picked you up so I could pass it to the search organisation but he said they had just been following the sun, which to them was to set over the Faroes. In truth, he wasn't able to help much."

We set off as planned. Bengt seemed upbeat that he was heading to Britain under instruction from the British military. He and his crew were helping the war effort, striking a blow however indirect against the German invasion of their homes. And I and Colin felt the same. He would go back to flying and I? Well, I had absolutely no idea, but the fact that Noakes had so quickly removed us from Torshavn indicated that he perhaps had some role for me. The boat, Bengt said, had nearly 600 kilometres to cover with the bulk of the voyage directly due south across open sea and the remainder hugging the west coast of Scotland. We were going to a small port named Mallaig and wouldn't be there until about thirty hours after departing. The army had supplied the ship with packed field rations which were adequate if not exactly exciting although the crew, unlike Colin and me, were delighted to find that the packs contained cigarettes.

The weather stayed fine. The journey was uneventful and, when we reached the tip of Scotland, very beautiful. We all stayed in good spirits and arrived in Mallaig just after we had eaten breakfast on the 12th of June. Rupert Noakes was waiting at the quayside. He told Bengt that he would be contacted with new instructions in a day or two and to remain in port until then, and he took us in his chauffeured army saloon for about half an hour's drive to a place he called 'Arisaig'.

I told him a potted version of my travel with the barrel up to Bodø, then Colin and I took it in turns to relate our sea journey.

"You were incredibly lucky," Noakes said. "Not only in getting picked out of the water before you both died from exposure, but in not staying on the Glorious."

Colin and I looked at each other in puzzlement, he went on. "It took two days for the survivors to be found and then not by the Air Force or Navy but by Norwegian fishing boats making for the Faroes, like your Bengt. These survivors have just arrived at Torshavn. There are less than forty, and some have died in the hospital already.

"Forty!" we both gasped in unison.

"Yes, out of more than fifteen hundred if the crew of the two destroyers are counted. They were both sunk too with very high casualties. One left only a single survivor."

"Maybe some more will still be with found and rescued," I said, trying to shake off the notion of such appalling loss of life.

"I think not," replied Noakes. "The area was apparently littered with bodies. There is no one left alive."

We sat in silence in the car until we turned on to a private drive guarded by two soldiers who waved our car through, and pulled up at a big building called, appropriately enough 'Arisaig House'.

"Now this place is rather special. You will be looked after here until you are completely recovered then you, Ingrid, will probably remain here if you wish and you, Colin, will wait for the RAF to summon you, they know you are here. This place is soon to be part of the Special Operations Executive, I'll explain about that later, but from right now whatever you see, hear or do here is absolutely top secret."

--///

Ingrid stops talking. The coffees are well finished and they have outstayed their welcome at the café.

"So that's the story? Yours and Colin's. Thank you so much for entrusting it to me. I'm sure that Martin will be as enthralled as I am."

"Yes, of course you must tell Martin everything that I have told you. And if you are still interested then there is a bit more to come about Arisaig. I'm talked out now and must in any case get home to Aunty, but if you like we could have a drink tonight in your hotel? Perhaps before you have your supper? I will be eating early to keep Aunty company but could come along afterwards. How about 7pm?"

"Yes, I would like that very much," replies Fiona. "Are we on your route back to your aunt's place? If so, I can easily find my own way back to my hotel."

Ingrid says that her Aunty lives quite close. They confirm the 7pm meeting and depart.

Chapter 16

*B*ack in her hotel room, Fiona pulls her legal pad and pen from out of her suitcase and writes for three hours, putting down all of Ingrid's story. She often pauses and tries to imagine what the journey must have been like for Ingrid and, later in the story, for Colin. The air raids during her month long journey up the coast from Vemork to the bombed out town of Bodø, and all that time driven by her obsession to deliver a barrel of heavy water to Britain. The near-death experience in the sea while the damaged Glorious sailed off to her fate and the loss of the barrel, how would Ingrid have felt about that? Then her arrival in a remote part of Scotland, with rudimentary knowledge of English, to be told that she could have a role with the Special Operations Executive, the famous, or was it infamous, SOE.

Fiona knows something about the SOE. Where she was brought up, and where her parents live, is on the outskirts of the West Scottish town of Fort William about 120 miles north by road from Glasgow. The whole area around that town was the training ground for the British Commandoes in the Second World War and rehearsals for the D-Day landings. As a school girl she visited several of the memorials and other places of historic interest from that time. And no more than 60 miles to the west is the peninsular facing the small islands of Rum and Eigg, with the fishing port of Mallaig at is northern tip from where ferries to the Western Isles depart. She has made the crossing from Mallaig to Skye several times, and in spending time in the peninsular has learned of its part in the training of members of the SOE. The whole area down to Fort William was militarised during the war; local residents had to carry special identity cards and seek permission to travel, which caused some resentment. She even knows about Arisaig, not so much for its wartime role but as the departure point from mainland Scotland for 'Bonny Prince Charlie' after he and his highland army were defeated by the English at the Battle of Culloden on the other side of Scotland, marking the end of the 'Jacobite Rebellion.'

She rests for a while on her bed and wakes from a doze to see that it is past 6.30pm. Food will have to wait she realises, until after her drinks with Ingrid. She takes a quick shower and freshens up her appearance and is in the hotel bar sitting at a small table precisely at 7pm. Ingrid joins her just two minutes later.

"You are very punctual," Fiona remarks. "Did you walk here again?"

Ingrid confirms that she did. Fiona orders a gin and tonic from the hovering waiter while Ingrid chooses a vodka martini.

They chat about nothing in particular while the drinks are being prepared, although Fiona does confirm that she will be leaving on the 9am flight back to London next morning so will have to get up quite early.

'Skol' and 'Cheers' are declared and after each taking a sizeable pull of their drinks. Ingrid starts to talk about Arisaig.

"How much about Arisaig do you want to hear? There is the war stuff of course, but there is also the time that Colin and I spent together."

"I would like very much like to hear about your war experiences, but anything about Colin would be very important *to Martin and to me."*

"Well let's just see how it goes then, one thing will proba-bly follow another and some things I have never spoken about before."

Ingrid gazes into space for a moment or two and Fiona realises she is having difficulty in finding the right content and tone for what she is about to say.

"There was a great deal of military personnel in and around Arisaig House. Colin had no trouble in accepting this but I was quite concerned. If Noakes had a role for me here then what on earth could it be? I was an untrained and in many ways naive foreign civilian. But the tragedy of the loss of the Glorious and the retreat out of France overshadowed our presence such that to begin with, we were little noticed.

Part of the house was being used as a sort of sick quarters or sanatorium. Colin was put in a ward with, I think, three other men all of whom were recovering from the sort of injuries you get through accidents. Broken bones mainly I seem to remember. As the only woman, apart from two army nurses who had met Colin and me as we got out of Noake's car, I was given a spacious room of my own, a sort of bed-sitter, and told by one of the nurses that it would be my permanent quarters during my time at Arisaig. I was to make myself at home as best I could. Laid out on the bed was a selection of clothes from undergarments to overalls and including duffle jackets and pull overs. I was told to take whatever would fit me and leave the rest outside my door in the hallway. Then the nurse, I just can't remember her name at present, showed me around most of the rest of the house. Central to the stone building was a large entrance hall which led off to rooms right and left. These included a library, another big room that was called the 'hall', a drawing room, dining room, smoking room and 'business room' which contained a small bar. There were also several other smaller rooms scattered around. The second and third floors were comprised of multiple bedrooms and a few separate bath rooms. My room was on the third floor where I was lucky to have a bathroom next door that was shared with just the two nurses. My guide told me that much of the first floor was going to be used for training and some of the students would be accommodated in the upstairs bedrooms, but that was all to come later. She also lectured me to avoid any physical stress over the next few days as I regained my strength and not to leave the grounds of the house until the resident doctor had given me the all clear. She added that Colin had been given exactly the same instructions.

I met up with Colin at about 6pm that evening when I decided to try to get a pre-supper drink from the bar. We had just helped ourselves to a of bottle beer each and recorded the transactions in the 'Honour Book', to be settled at the end of each month, when Noakes arrived and bade us sit down with him.

After asking if we were comfortably accommodated, he started to tell us about Arisaig House and the SOE.

"It not official yet but this place is about to become a sort of coordination and training centre for the Special Operations Executive, although that name is not yet official. With the war going so badly for us, Churchill needs to be able to show the British population that the country can strike back against Germany. So, after a great deal of conflicting advice, and downright hostility from some quarters, he has decided that a couple of existing covert organisations, that have achieved nothing of note so far in this war while acting independently, are going to be amalgamated and placed within a new structure. They will be designed specifically to harry the Germans on the soils they occupy, and to give nascent partisans the training and tools to 'set Europe ablaze' as he has put it. The SOE, as it will be called I'm sure, will be placed under a coalition Government minister and will report directly to Churchill. In addition to the SOE, the whole area of the loch side of Loch Morar, that's the large stretch of water a little to the north of here, will have a training area for what might be termed as 'unconventional' operations. Sabotage, attacks on port facilities, seaborne landings, all that sort of thing. Soon there will be hundreds of men billeted around here, thousands maybe, and all out of range of German bombers. One principal objective will be to prevent your old power station at Vemork from producing heavy water. Do you know what that is Colin?'

Colin replied that I had given him a heads-up on the product, that it seems necessary to the production of some form of advanced power systems or weapons.

"That's all you need to know, now forget about it. And you Ingrid don't fret too much about losing that barrel of yours. It would be nice for our boffins to be able to play with it here, but the important thing is that you denied it from the Germans."

"Which I could have done by just pouring it on the floor."

"Well that's one way of putting it, but it doesn't reflect your efforts to get it to us, along with Colin that is. And now that you *are* here I would like you to consider working for the SOE. I just mentioned Vemork, it must be prevented from producing heavy water for the Germans. It will therefore become a prime target for sabotage and your knowledge of the plant layout and the countryside around it will be invaluable for helping to train those saboteurs. You would be put into Women's Army uniform as a junior officer and receive the appropriate pay for the duration of your stay here. We will also try to get a message to your parents that you are safe."

I didn't need to think twice. I agreed. He shook my hand and welcomed me as one of the first recruits to the SOE. Then he turned to Colin.

"The RAF has agreed to 14 days of sick leave starting tomorrow, more if you should need it, but you seem to be getting over your experience pretty well. You are also going to be taken off flying Lysanders and moved onto fighters. However, for several more weeks there is apparently no suitable place available for a conversion course, so the RAF is content for you to be seconded to me, here at Arisaig House."

"Do I get a choice?"

"Not really, no. You don't have the advantage of being a

civilian like Ingrid and being able to choose your destiny."

"Then I'll stay as long as it takes for me to be recalled to flying."

"Let's go and have supper then. At present the food here is not too bad."

--///

"Colin stayed with me at Arisaig house for the best part of three months. The first two weeks we spent a lot of time together, walking the spectacular scenery surrounding us, getting to know each other properly, with him coaching me in English and me getting used to it spoken with the local Scottish accent.

The SOE officially came into being in July 1940 although preliminary work towards its formation was already being done well before then. I got involved in the preparation of three attacks on the heavy water plant and a myriad of other associated jobs.

The first attack on Vemork was in fact not mounted by SOE agents but by the 1st Airborne Division of the British Army in November 1942, nevertheless I was heavily involved in the mission's planning and imparting local knowledge to the force. It was to be an airborne landing using gliders, but all of the aircraft crashed, killing some of the soldiers and enabling the capture of others that were executed by order of Hitler. These were people I had met, briefed and trained. They were my first personal experience of loss of lives and is was not to be the last.

Well before this failed raid, the Germans had greatly increased the production of heavy water both at Vemork and at a new facility in Rjukan, my home town. This increase seriously worried British scientists who were now becoming aware of the possibilities of a nuclear bomb and assumed that the Nazis were trying to build one.

At about the same time as the failed airborne raid, four

Norwegian SOE saboteurs were dropped by parachute into a mountainous area some distance from Vemork. There they holed up for the winter until joined by six more in February 1943. This action had actually been planned in London where I had to travel several times for their preparation, thus I knew all of the participants. Somehow detailed plans of the Vemork plant had been spirited to London by my old boss there. The attack took place at the end of that month and was completely successful with all the saboteurs managing to escape from the thousands of German soldiers sent to search for them. About half of the SOE boys made it to Sweden while the reminder went to ground in Norway and continued working under the directions of the SOE. I met them there later on.

The Germans rebuilt what had been destroyed and about six months after the raid the plant was up and running again. So, in November 1943, the RAF and Americans set up a large bombing raid as it was believed that security at Vemork would have been so tightened by the Germans that sabotage on the ground would almost certainly fail. Most of the bombs missed the target and some hit Norwegian civilians, killing over twenty of them. There was a bit of an uproar from the Norwegian Government in Exile over these killings and I, of course, was anxious about my parents. However, radio messages from local SOE operatives reported them to be unscathed. But the bombs that had hit the plant did the trick and this time the Germans decided not to rebuild, most of the stored heavy water was also destroyed.

--///

"So that was the end of the production of heavy water for the Germans then," Fiona comments, her first words since Ingrid had started speaking. "I need another drink and so, I should think, do you after that story." A hand wave to the barman and two more drinks swiftly appear.

"Yes, but it was not quite the end of SOE involvement in

Norwegian heavy water. SOE London heard that the Germans were going to ship out half-finished heavy water from the undestroyed areas of the plant and take it to Germany. This was in February 1944 and part of the journey involved the crossing of Lake Tinnsjo by ferry with two trucks loaded with the heavy water. Three local SOE agents attached a time bomb to the ferry which sunk within a few minutes of the bomb exploding, sending all the heavy water to the deepest part of the lake and killing 14 civilians and a handful of German soldiers as well. And that really was the last chapter of the Norwegian heavy water saga."

"And was that the end of your involvement?" Fiona asks

"No, not really, not at all really. I had been pressing for some time to go back to Norway and do something practical against the German occupation with the SOE agents or partisans already there, but was always turned down. However, as 1944 moved on, things were building up in Britain towards a landing in France by the massed American, British and French forces, D-Day. It was thought that local disruption in the Nazi occupied countries such as the Netherlands, Balkans, Denmark, Norway and many others would hold down German forces that could otherwise to be moved to reinforce France against the Allied landings. I was selected to go into Norway as a clandestine radio operator and underwent appropriate training around Arisaig. In July 1944 I was parachuted into the Lillehammer area of Norway, which was, of course, well known to me. I joined a group of partisans who were harrying the local German forces and manned my radio until the war's end when the Germans were still in Norway. Spending much of my time with my radio holed up in remote mountain huts, I personally didn't see much action although I was able to get to my parent's house a couple of times."

"You have an incredible life. Your parents and you must be very proud."

"Not really. I did what I could, I was never under fire, I was never captured or tortured by the Germans as many of my compatriots were. I survived the war and it was all a very long *time ago. I moved on leaving it all behind many years ago."*

"And Peter? Was that his name? The man who got you to Bodø. Did you say you married him?"

"Peter came out of jail as the war ended. He had spent three years locked up in a Norwegian prison run on behalf of the Nazis. He wasn't tortured or anything as he was regarded as an agitator, a distinct nuisance to the authorities really but not a saboteur. But the conditions inside the jail were not good and he had contracted TB. We got married in 1946 and less than ten years later he was dead."

"No children?"

"No, Peter and I had no children."

"It is getting on a bit and I need to get something to eat at the restaurant here, will you join me?"

"Thank you, no. I have eaten and I must now get back to my aunt. You leave early tomorrow, so we have to say goodbye now."

"Yes, thank you so much for agreeing to meet with me. You have filled in so many gaps, but it has to be goodbye, for now at least."

"Will you tell your man, Martin about my time with Colin?"

"Yes, yes of course, that was the main point for me coming here. Although he will be equally fascinated by your wartime history."

"Then there is one thing more that you show know about Colin and me." There was a catch in her voice and her eyes turned weepy. *"In the three months we were together we got very close. We became lovers in fact. It was one of the best periods of my life. I knew it couldn't last. I never saw him again. It was one of those very many wartime romances, something that just occurred as the world was seeming to fall apart. A fling is how it could best be described in modern terms. It was a gift to each other."*

The two women stand up. Ingrid asks if they will meet again.

"I certainly hope so. I would like to bring Martin next

time. He may have more questions to ask of you."

"Yes, I would really like to meet him, Colin's son, Martin. Why don't we meet up in Bodø?"

"Well, air connections between there and Britain are poor. That's why it was so lucky that you had to get here to Oslo to see your aunt."

"Come by boat then, and spend some time seeing the Norwegian coast and its multitude of little islands and small communities."

"You mean like on a cruise liner?"

"No, not at all like a cruise liner. Every day a sort of mail boat sets out from Bergen and over a week it travels up to the furthermost tip of Norway, right on the Russian border and back again. It calls at many ports along its way, some big some tiny, delivering equipment, stores and passengers. Every one of these ports receives two ships each day, one going northwards and the other going south. They are quite big and very comfortable vessels and you can get off at all the ports for a quick walk around. You can even make a layover and catch a following vessel. You and Martin could start at Bergen, which is probably more easily accessible by air than Bodø, and then get off at Bodø for a night or two once the ship arrives, then either go back to Bergen or continue for the whole round trip. I'm sure that Martin, and you, would be interested in the monument at Bodø to the three RAF Gladiator pilots and I can show you where Colin's landing strip was and the place where the barrel was kept. The shipping company is called 'Hurtigruten', I believe, and I'm sure that there will be a brochure at the lobby desk."

They walk to the lobby and at the concierge desk find a brochure for Hurtigruten.

"Oh!" exclaims Fiona. "This must be the outfit that my rather incompetent travel agent in Aberdeen told me about. We dismissed the idea for this trip because I would have been in transit for at least four days. But coming with Martin for our next visit it would probably be just the thing."

They kiss each other on the cheeks and Ingrid disappears

in to the still bright daylight outside. It's nearing 9pm, Fiona goes into the restaurant and reads the brochure while she eats a variety of small open sandwiches. By midday local time the following day she is back at London airport, and four hours later walks through the front door of the Aberdeen house.

Chapter 17

I phoned Fiona from Singapore on the Saturday. During our usual opening enquiries about how we each were, I sensed a kind of reticence in her speech and voice. I asked her if she was tired after a difficult week at work.

"No, I am not tired. In fact I've been off work all this week."

"Have you been sick or something? You just now said that you were fine."

"Not sick. I've been in Oslo, seeing Ingrid."

"Ingrid, in Norway? You said that you wouldn't arrange that until after I returned. That's so bad! How did you arrange it all so quickly?"

"Well, I fibbed to you a bit. I have to confess that I actually did some homework before you left for Singapore and had been given a phone number for her in Bodø via the Norwegian Embassy in London. Bodø is where she lives and there is a story to that as well. So all I had to do once you were on your way was to give her a call and arrange to meet in Oslo, which I did and we have done."

I paused for the moment as I took in what she had said. It was a typical Fiona thing, get right on with what you have to do and sort out any problems later. It was one of her most endearing traits and the sort of aspect of her character that I had grown to love. "OK, that was a fib, it will mean punishment when I get back. That should be sometime late'ish next Saturday. What's she like?"

"She is in her mid-sixties I would guess, good looking, obviously Scandinavian and very fit. A thoroughly nice woman and seemingly very interested in you. We have made a tentative arrangement to all get together sometime. Look I'll tell you everything next weekend. You will be proud of your father although he was lucky to be around to sire you."

I was a little disappointed that she would not yet tell me more over the phone about Ingrid and her story about Colin, but I realised that she had made up her mind and would not now be moved by me. We changed the conversation to my stay in Singapore. The work was going well and I was finding Singapore a pleasure. The orderliness and penchant for cleanliness I admired and the few somewhat draconian laws didn't bother me at all.

We concluded with our usual mutual expressions of love.

I was as good as my word, as were the airlines and I was back in Aberdeen by late Sunday afternoon. I had looked forward to being with her again almost from the time I had left Aberdeen two weeks earlier. Her smile was as welcoming as always and the tightness of her embrace just inside of our doorway promised a pleasant and interesting bedtime. But first of all, she had to tell me about her trip to Norway and her time with Ingrid. We sat down at our kitchen table with cups of tea and a couple of biscuits, and she began, occasionally referring to notes from her legal pad.

She told the story well and I soon became very caught up in the providential escape from the Glorious, the few survivors from such a huge ship, and Ingrid and Colin miraculously among them. An hour or so passed as she talked and I made comment or asked questions, then Ingrid's tale was told and it was time for martinis.

Fiona makes superb martinis, and as I savoured my first

sips I pondered my father, Colin.

"Ingrid seems to have rather skated over the time they had together in Scotland. Did you say the place was called Arisaig?"

"The house where she stayed until getting dropped into Norway in 1944 was called Arisaig, but the whole surrounding countryside and the loch were full of the SOE, Commandos and the like. It was a huge training area. I know that from living in Fort William as a child. The whole area reeks of military history and not just the Second World War but centuries of Highland uprisings and Jacobite rebellions. But you are right, she didn't go into much detail about her time spent with Colin. But I think that she was getting tired of speaking, of bringing up long buried but emotional memories, by the time she got to that final part of the story. And of course, it was just the beginning of her career with the SOE which must have been a very significant time for her. Imagine dropping by parachute into Nazi occupied Norway and successfully hiding out until the end of the war! She said that she and Colin had some sort of fling in those three months of Scottish summer. She actually used the term 'lovers' to describe what happened between them, perhaps she held, still holds, a candle for him? Maybe that is why she is so interested in you."

"Maybe," I agreed. "But he had no sooner left her in Arisaig in September than he was back in England and as I am sure you have already worked out, sleeping with Mary and getting her pregnant. And another curious thing is that it all took place while the Battle of Britain was in full swing. Surely he would have wanted to join in that?"

"But he wasn't a fighter pilot, he couldn't have participated in the shooting down of German bombers without proper training which, if I remember right from his logbook, he did get a few months later. No, that's not quite right, I remember now, his first flight in a fighter was from Liverpool, Speke the place was called, and it was in a Hurricane. He was being trained there, and it was on the 15th of September. So, he must have left Arisaig and Ingrid before that date."

I never cease to admire Fiona's almost photographic memory and powers of recall and then there is her ability to draw opinions and conclusions from a seemingly nebulous collections of facts and fancies.

She continued, "So, they arrived at Arisaig on the 12th of June, and he was away by, let's say a week before that first Hurricane flight, the 8th of September. But suppose he went down to London or wherever to see Mary for a few days before going to Speke. I'm sure that must have happened. For God's sake, she was pregnant by the end of September. It must have been around about the beginning of September when he and Ingrid parted company, mid-June and through July and August. Just ten or eleven weeks together. Then almost straight into the arms of your Mother. It all adds up. Bit of a devil wasn't he?"

I agreed.

I suppose the time was about two the following morning. We had gone to bed at ten the night before, immediately made love, and by half past the hour I was sound asleep. But the jet lag caught up with me and now I was wide awake and bored. Fiona had moved slightly away from me and was lying on her back with just a sheet covering her naked body; she appeared sound asleep. I thought about how much this person by my side meant to me and for a while about her desire for a child. I was hoping that things would work soon for her and she would not suffer a long wait or, worse, eventual disappointment. Of course, I had no idea if I was potent. What if it were me that prevented her from having a child? Well, there were ways, some better that others, to counter that, I knew. But my need for a child, son or daughter, perhaps both, was not driven by the imperatives that she seemed to have. I could live without offspring but how would a barren marriage affect her? One thing I did know, pregnant or not, Fiona and I should marry when I reached forty as we had long agreed. Although there was no good reason not to do it sooner. I think she rationalised that by that time we would have been together nearly ten years, more than enough to identify our relationship as permanent. In truth, I think I was ready for marriage at the end of our first year together but she was not. I suppose with her lawyer's mind she had to be completely sure of herself.

I rolled half over towards her and traced around the outline of her nearer nipple. I gently pulled back the sheet and could see the nipple become hard with a hue near that of her hair. Her right hand flew up and brushed me away.

"Bugger off," she murmured. "I'm asleep," and she turned her back towards me. I gently kissed the nape of her neck, rolled onto my back and continued with my sense of ennui.

My thoughts turned to Ingrid and Colin. Fiona had estimated that after the near drowning experience they had spent ten or so weeks together on the shores of a remote Scottish Loch, coupling. Then he was off to fly Hurricanes and to see his supposed girlfriend, my mother, whom he promptly made pregnant. I could not decide whether this was a reasonable course of action for somebody who had barely escaped death or, instead, reflected a major flaw in his character. But I had never experienced terror or the prospect of imminent death. Perhaps it was just as both Ingrid and Mary had both said; 'These things just happened in wartime.'

These reflections on Colin and Ingrid gave way to questions about Mary. What had she known about Colin's time in Scotland? Did he ever tell her about Ingrid? What really was their relationship? Would the marriage have lasted after the '100 days' that Mary had said they spent together during the war? I had absolutely no idea of what the answers to these questions might be, and I realised that my growing familiarity with Colin had suffered a significant setback and with it doubts about my mother's earlier life and even, perhaps, her character. But I was sure that Fiona would take a more rational approach when I spoke to her in the morning.

And then there was Ian. What should he be told of the affair, because that is what I was starting to regard it as, between our father and his Norwegian lover? Everything surely, but could the story affect his already fragile health?

Again, I would rely on Fiona's guidance.

My thoughts became more muddled and incoherent as sleep finally claimed me. Fiona woke me at nine in the morning with a cup of coffee and a kiss. She was fully clothed and looked as if she had been up for a while.

Over breakfast I described to Fiona as best I could what had been churning around in my brain during the night. She listened sympathetically and then made the sort of pronouncement that only she could fashion.

"The process we have to follow it really quite straightforward. Firstly, you have to have a one-on-one with Ian to tell him the whole Ingrid-Colin story as we know it. I'll tag along if you like, but it would be better if you two are by yourselves as I have a tendency to talk over you."

"That's true, but I could describe it as a tendency to dominate conversation."

She ignored my jibe. "And as part of this chat you have to ask him how much he thinks Mary should be told. My gut feeling is that she should be told nothing of what happened in Scotland. We hardly know the story ourselves, do we? We do know that she was aware of what Colin did in Norway, and his escape, and his survival of the Glorious sinking. She told us herself and was most put out when we intimated that we had knowledge that she did not have. What would be the advantage of any of us exposing her to what we know of Colin's escape from Norway? He must surely have given her some inkling of what he had gone through when they met again that September? In fact, she said that he did. And as for Colin's peccadillo, that surely must be a taboo subject, although, again, she may have been told by him or otherwise have found out. It was all 35 years ago, for goodness sake. Keep it off limits to her."

"OK, you are totally correct as usual, thanks. I'll slip down to Westgate in a fortnight's time. Out Friday night and back Sunday evening, I can't take any more time off work right now, I'll need two weeks to write my report on my rig inspection in Singapore."

"Then I'll leave you to visit Ian by yourself, and I'll make a date with Meredith. But I do think you should consider going to see Ingrid in Bodø. She seemed to have a great interest in you and I know that you would like her. It would increase your sense of relationship with your father."

I flew down to London two weeks later by myself and spent much of the weekend relating to Ian the story of Ingrid's and Colin's time together. He listened intently and posed few questions because, I assume, he knew that I wouldn't have the answers, realising that I was telling him absolutely all that I knew. Then I told him about Fiona's analysis of the discrepancies with Colin's two flying log books. How it seemed that the final version of his flying record, that in the green leather-bound volume, detailed flying in the late summer of 1940 which seemed never to have taken place.

"So he was trying to hide something," Ian commented when I finished. "And would have succeeded had he not died before destroying the war time draft log book. Something that happened in July and August 1940, time with the SOE? Or time with Ingrid? Or something else? And who was he hiding it from? Surely it must have been Mary? In which case it had to be his short-lived relationship with Ingrid and its immediate juxtaposition with the resumption of his place in her arms. Which immediately resulted in me. Or rather my conception out of wedlock."

"Yes, Fiona had worked that out too."

The conclusion that I and Fiona had derived did not seem to bother Ian all. "I'm still the son of Mary and Colin, and when and where I started is of absolutely no concern to me."

I could see that his mind was as bright as ever. He told me that his specialist has said that his MD was in a period of remission and that he might not experience any further physical deterioration for some time, a year or two perhaps, judging from his own knowledge of the disease.

Ian was in total agreement with Fiona's recommendation not to tell Mary anything about what had she had discovered. But he pressed me to go to Bodø and seek out Ingrid myself. I said that I would, perhaps in the coming autumn.

Fiona and I decided to take Ingrid's advice and combine a visit to her with a voyage up the whole Norwegian coast on a Hurtigruten ship. The pressure of work on both of us, combined with an already booked skiing holiday in France during the winter, Fiona being rather good, me being rather bad, meant that we couldn't find time until May the following year, 1981.

During this time however, we did make a trip to Arisaig which is only a short and beautiful drive from Fiona's parents' place in Fort William. We drove up to Arisaig House, now operating as a hotel and which nestled into an idyllic setting just a couple of hundred yards from a deserted shore line. I was all for going inside and asking about the buildings' wartime history but Fiona persuaded me otherwise.

"I want to go inside too, but I think we should wait until we hear more from Ingrid when we see her." She argued. "Otherwise we will be sought of pre-empting her, seemingly knowing more about the place than she tells us, or wants to tell us. Then we can come back here after our Norway trip and have a good poke around based on what we then know."

I agreed. But we did visit a small museum in the local village and learned the outline history of what the SOE had been up to in the area. Arisaig was a very important place, but there were several other local 'houses' that were also occupied by the SOE. Apparently, it was not only the remoteness of the peninsular that made it attractive for clandestine purposes. The railway that ran all the way from Glasgow to Mallaig, with a stop at Arisaig village, was not only useful for the movement of personnel, it was also used to train those personnel how to blow-up railway lines once in Europe.

Fiona kept in touch with Ingrid during this period and the older woman seemed to relish the opportunity to meet with me. She was most excited when she was told that we were both going to travel the whole way from Bergen to Kirkenes by a Hurtigruten ship in May. We would break our trip in Bodø to see her and then all three of us could catch another north bound ship two or three days later.

We went to France to ski in January and when we returned to Aberdeen we decided on the dates for our Hurtigruten booking. We phoned Ingrid to confirm that our visit would fit in with her work or holiday schedules. Her suggestion was that we spend only one day and night in Bodø then she would join with us for the remainder of the journey to Kirkenes.

"I have never been much further up the coast than Bodø since wartime," she said. "And the ship will pass all the places that I stayed as I made it up to Bodø and, with Colin, beyond. Let me book you into a nice hotel here for the one night."

Fiona and I readily agreed with her suggestion. Flights and the ships were booked and on the 15th of May we departed Aberdeen for our flights to Bergen via London. Fiona had still not fallen pregnant despite both of our best efforts. We agreed that on our return home we would seek some expert counselling.

--///

Our ship was waiting at the docks when we arrived in Bergen for the evening departure. It was bigger than I had imagined and looked a little like the sort of cross-channel ferry used to transport cars and people between Britain and France. But the passengers, about 250 of them, were not as important, I think, as the cargo that I saw being loaded directly into the ship through the large doors in its side. Fork lift trucks hustled in and out with pallets of wares bound for the little towns and villages at which we would berth every few hours of our journey. Cars and other vehicles were also loaded by simply driving through the loading doors.

The ship had none of the facilities of a cruise liner. Its main purpose was clearly to provide transport up and down the

Norwegian coast, but our cabin was comfortable and quite spacious with direct views to the sea and coastline. A large saloon doubled as a dining room, with buffet style meals that were delicious, and a lounge from which to view the passing scenery. There were a couple of cosy bars and a limited amount of external deck space for walking or just viewing.

We were scheduled to take a little under three days to reach Bodø. The weather was generally good with already very long daylight hours, and the ship either stayed close to the picturesque and increasingly rugged main coast, or weaved its way between islands. The journey was a complete delight. Cargo was taken on and off at each port we stopped, sometimes for less than an hour. This process was an interesting sight in itself. Fiona recalled some of the places that Ingrid has mentioned. Andalsnes, Molde and Trondheim where the stop was about three hours giving us plenty of time to leave the ship and explore the town. We sailed past Namsos which was a little disappointing, but we had several ports of call before we reached Bodø at lunchtime on the 18th of May. We had crossed the Arctic Circle earlier that day when the Captain dressed up and performed a little pantomime with members of the crew. The occasion was marked with a certificate for each passenger that wanted one. Fiona and I took ours although many of the other passengers declined, probably because they had seen it all before as regular Hurtigruten users.

Ingrid was waiting on the quayside as we disembarked with our luggage. She gave Fiona a big hug, shook my hand, looked into my face intensely for a moment, then gave me my own hug. She looked as Fiona had described on my return from Singapore. Quite tall, maybe 5' 9", fit and healthy appearance. She probably still skied in the winter and hiked in the summer. Short cropped grey hair with a hint that it once had been blonde, and wearing smart jeans with a windcheater, all in blue. She gushed a little as she welcomed us and, seemingly, had trouble taking her eyes off me. I assumed she was comparing my likeness with that of Colin as she remembered him.

"Yes," she said in confirmation of my thoughts. "I do see a family likeness although, of course, he was many years younger than you are now when last I saw him. I have my little car here. Why don't you put your luggage into it and then we can have a short run around before going to a nice café for lunch. You can't book into your hotel until two o'clock in any case. We can explore what remains of Colin's old airstrip, visit the aviation exhibits there, not many as yet and because the whole area is now principally a Norwegian Air Force base and is strategically very important to NATO, we are limited as to where we can go. But just near there, however, is something that I really want you to see first."

We climbed into her Saab and she drove through the centre of the town which was much larger than I had imagined with many new buildings, some quite tall.

"This is much bigger than I thought from Colin's narrative," I said.

"It would be very much larger still if it were not for the huge airbase just coming into sight. It alone is much bigger than the wartime town ever was and, because of its position, effectively comprising the whole of a large peninsula and engulfing the little airstrip that Colin helped build, the town was not able to expand to the south. All its post-war buildings are now behind us. The town was completely rebuilt after the war. Indeed, a year after its devastation in 1940, after which there was scarcely a building left standing, although casualties were actually remarkably low, the Swedes built about 100 small houses for the homeless families. I'm not sure why they did that, possibly some guilt trip about staying out of the war while their Scandinavian neighbours were overrun and, of course, supplying iron to the Nazi war machine. Anyway, the area is still known as 'Little Sweden'. Bodø now also encompasses all the neighbouring villages and is the centre of government administration for much of the surrounding countryside. It's an important place now, and I've seen all the changes. I'll take you for a drive around tomorrow if you like, before our ship leaves at 4pm."

Ingrid continued to drive until the huge air base with its impregnable looking wire fencing filled our view. There was, however, an entrance for commercial travellers. Still almost in the shadow of the military complex, she stopped the car and bade us follow her to a simple carved, white stone obelisk which bore a lengthy, vertical inscription carved at head height.

"This is what I wanted you to see first of all," Ingrid explained. "It is a monument to the three RAF Gladiator pilots who tried so gallantly to defend the town from the Luftwaffe as they operated out of Colin's airstrip. It was erected four years ago with a great deal of ceremony and speeches."

I was surprised to see that the inscription was in English, with the badge of the British Royal Air Force as its heading. It read

FLT LT C.B. HULL RAF - Died 7 September 1940
PO J. FALKSON RAF - Died 8 June 1940
LT A LYDEKKER RN - Died 15 November 1942

ON 26th OF MAY 1940
3 GLOUCESTER GLADIATOR FIGHTER AIRCRAFT OF
THE NO.263 SQUADRON
LANDED ON A TEMPORARY AIR STRIP NEAR BODØ.
UNFALTERINGLY THE PILOTS OF THESE AIRCRAFT
CHALLENGED A
NUMERICALLY SUPERIOR ADVERSARY AND
INFLICTED
GREAT LOSS UPON THE ENEMY.
LATER THEY GAVE THEIR LIVES FOR FREEDOM.
THIS MEMORIAL IS ERRECTED IN THEIR HONOUR.

Fiona and I read the inscription in silence, then held that silence for a little longer.

Ingrid was the first to speak. "Did you know that they had all died after their time at Bodø?"

"Yes," replied Fiona. "Yes, we were told that when we first

198

set out to find out more about Colin and his time in Norway. But I don't think either of us realised they had died so soon."

"Both Hull and Lydekker were wounded during their combats with the German aircraft, Hull quite badly. He recovered after being evacuated back to Britain and took part in the Battle of Britain. He had been promoted to Squadron Leader meanwhile, but was shot down and died over the River Thames estuary, I believe.

Lydekker was actually a British Royal Navy Pilot. He re-joined the Navy after returning to Britain but lost his life when the aircraft carrier he was serving in was sunk by a German submarine.

But poor young Falkson, only twenty years old I believe, landed his Gladiator onto the Glorious while Colin and I were on it, and lost his life when it sunk.

And although Colin's name is not on this memorial, his part in building the airstrip from which the three young pilots operated is well known among the older people here, many of whom helped in its construction. Mr Wick, the local civil engineer who worked with Colin, is still alive and well, I think. It's ironic, a tragedy really, that Colin survived the war yet was killed within a few months of its end."

"Yes," agreed Fiona. "And we know from his log book and medals that he was flying in combat for most of the war."

We gazed in silence at the memorial a little longer. Each with our own thoughts. I wanted to know what was going through Ingrid's mind. I supposed that she had been at the dedication of the monument and had probably gazed at it many times since, but not with Colin's son by her side. I thought I could see a reddening of her eyes. She looked away, then peered into the small bag hanging over one shoulder from which she pulled a blue covered leaflet.

"Here," she said. "Here is a copy of the dedication pro-ceedings. It's in both Norwegian and English and contains the transcript of the speeches. I've my own copy, so please keep it."

I quickly glanced through it, and passed it to Fiona who

put in in her bag saying, "I'll read it later, and thank you very much. I'm sure that Martin's mother will be interested as well."

"Now," continued Ingrid. "With your backs to the airport and facing towards the town, look towards the edge of this green area."

Fiona and I turned around.

"Can you see that ditch there? Let's walk towards it."

We were soon gazing into the bottom of a muddy ditch.

"This," said Ingrid pointing along the excavation. "This is where your father sheltered in the midst of the worst German onslaught of Bodø. That was on the 27th of May. Mr Wick was with him."

Fiona broke in. "Yes, I remember. It's in his diary. He said he had never ever prayed so much. He saw the hospital and most of the town destroyed before his eyes."

"Yes, Colin told me about it while we were waiting to board a ship at Harstad. I didn't know he had written a diary."

"It covers the time he was in Namsos, then evacuated, then what happened in Bodø. It contains nothing else, nothing about his journey back to Britain, no other war memoirs, so it is clear that his time in Norway was very important to him."

"Do I figure in the diary?"

"Only the one mention, when you brought him the barrel of supposedly whale oil for protection. I've brought a copy of the diary for you, if you want it, that is. It's in my suitcase in the car."

"Thank you, but I'm not sure I need to be reminded about what happened to him, and Bodø, and Namsos. It's all a long time ago and I have my own memories of what he told me himself all those years ago. I don't think I want to go through it all again, but if I change my mind over the next few days that we are all together, I'll let you know."

"We understand," replied Fiona.

We got back into the car and drove a short way into town, near the quayside where Ingrid had booked us a table for lunch in a cafe. We ate a light, sandwich style meal of the type typical to the buffet in our Hurtigruten ship. Ingrid and Fiona seem to be bonding well and, even though Ingrid often looked at me and smiled, she directed most of the conversation to Fiona, drawing out details of her family history, education and job. I switched off and gazed out of the windows of the café which faced out to the quay side and the open sea beyond. All the buildings looked new and substantial but I tried to imagine the sights my father had seen here in 1940. The warships, puffers and other boats milling around trying to evade German bombs. The lightly built quayside buildings had been destroyed with myriads of troops seeking cover as they awaited evacuation. The noise, hubris, terror and death. And to my side and surrounding the café I imagined a totally destroyed town. I was brought out of my reverie by Ingrid suggesting that she run us to the hotel and meet up for supper there at 7pm. I heard Fiona agreeing as she flashed a 'pay attention' look at me.

The hotel was about three city blocks away from our lunch café, and it was near 3pm when we entered our small but comfortably equipped room. We unpacked the minimum of things needed to see us through one night, undressed and made love.

"From Norway, with love," murmured Fiona.

"Isn't it good, Norwegian wood?" I replied until drifting off to sleep.

We were up and showered two hours later and took a walk around the town centre. As if by some magnetic force, we found we were once again at the quay side. We sat down on a bench and looked at the ships, some tied up and others waiting out in the sea.

"You were thinking about this area in 1940 while we were having lunch, weren't you?" She asked.

"Yes," I replied. "I was trying to imagine how it was for Colin, Ingrid and everyone else. She seemed much more interested in you than me at lunch, so I allowed myself to day dream."

"Oh, I wouldn't be fooled by that. She is a pretty sharp

cookie. I think she wanted me not to feel left out so she concentrated on me first. But I think that she will be quizzing you this evening. It's a sort of lawyer's court room trick."

"What do you think of her?"

"Hard to make out. Either the time she and Colin were in Scotland together was just an opportunity for a roll in the hay for both of them, a sort of celebration of their successfully coming through a perilous time perhaps, or it was something much more profound. For her at least. If so, she is hiding it all from us at present and likely to continue so, I would guess. Let's wait and see if she opens up more tonight over dinner."

The hotel had a cosy bar and a good looking restaurant with an extensive menu. After Ingrid arrived, promptly at 7pm, she agreed to my suggestion that we should eat there and not venture outside again that evening. I explained that we had already explored most of Bodø's central district before meeting her and that it would be pleasant and interesting if we could all spend time together touring the surrounding countryside the next day, before we joined the ship for the remainder of our voyage up north.

After a couple of cocktails each we sat down in the restaurant and were treated to an excellent fish-centred meal.

Fiona led the early conversation trying to stimulate Ingrid into telling us more about her life.

--///

When the war ended there was a great deal of soul searching among some Norwegians trying to justify how they had spent their time under German occupation. Ingrid had, of course, nothing to be regretful about and there were others who had adopted various degrees of non-cooperation raging from sabotage, through defiance to non-cooperation. But, there were also a very few others who had showed enthusiasm for the Nazi environment. Norwegian law was altered to allow the execution of their puppet leader, Quisling, by firing squad, *about four months after the defeat of Germany. But, as Ingrid explained, much of Norway presents a hostile environment for human habitation so most Norwegians just got on with their lives at best they could under the Germans.*

There were not the wholesale reprisals of the French experience against known or suspected collaborators, and there were enough home-grown heroes to satisfy most consciences. Peter counted as one of these, as did Ingrid of course. Sadly Peter's reward for being a thorn in the Nazi side was three years in jail and eventually a fatal case of tuberculosis.

After emerging from her hiding places at war's end Ingrid returned to her parents' home and was able to take up her old job at the power station. She and Peter got married in the summer of 1946 and soon moved to an apartment in Bodø where he had found a permanent post on a large fishing vessel. Ingrid was regarded as something of a celebrity there and with her excellent English soon found part-time work in the planning of Bodø's recovery. They had five, maybe six, good years together before increasing ill health prevented Peter from working any longer, and soon afterwards Ingrid had to give up her work to nurse him. To begin with they strived hard for children, but without success. Later they realised the care needed for Peter would be incompatible with the nurturing of children so they took the decision to remain childless.

After Peter had died, Ingrid was able to concentrate more on her career and eventually became one of the first members of the area's developing tourism industry, an association that had continued to this day.

--///

Fiona and I found Ingrid's story and her lively manner of telling it interesting but we realised, both at the same time I think, that nothing more was ever going to come out of her time in Scotland with Colin. Then she started to speak directly to and about me, just as Fiona had predicted she might.

"I think that you have both heard enough of me and my little life by now, and Fiona told me much about her history at lunchtime, so I would really like to hear about you and your family, Martin."

"Well," I started. "There are really two things of overwhelming importance to me right now. The first is Fiona and the second is our relationship. We are trying for a baby and intend to get married when I am forty."

"So that must be very close now, this year in fact."

"No, 1982, just over a year to go. It's my brother who is forty this year."

"Your brother! I didn't know that you had a brother, an older brother?"

"Yes, Ian."

Ingrid immediately repeated, "Ian, Ian?"

"Ian," I confirmed. "He is exactly a year older than me. We are very alike to look at, often taken as twins when we were children and teenagers."

Ingrid's voice changed from surprised to eagerness. "And where does he live, is he married, what sort of job does he have?"

So I told her about Ian.

"Never married, great job, and carried the burden of Muscular Dystrophy since he was thirty."

"Muscular Dystrophy? I've heard of it although I do not know much about it. It's crippling, isn't it?"

I found her use of the word 'crippling' rather distasteful, but she had guessed right, for crippling is exactly what MD is. "Yes, he is what one might describe as 'crippled'. His mind is at sharp as ever, but he can barely walk any longer and needs help for all those things that we take for granted."

Fiona was staring into her glass of wine. She knew that everything about Ian had to come from me.

Ingrid continued, though I could detect a huskiness in her voice, "But where does he live? How does he live? Who looks after him?"

I told her about the family house in Westgate on Sea. How Mary attended to those needs of his that he permitted her to. How I, often with Fiona, went to see him every month if possible.

"Ian is proud, but he can't walk more than a step or two and most physical things are beyond his capabilities."

"And what is going to happen to him? What does having Muscular Dystrophy actually mean?"

I didn't mean to be so brutal, but I couldn't help myself. "He is going to die."

I could see the look of shock that immediately enveloped her face, and I saw Fiona's disapproval and felt her hard, under-the-table kick of my shin.

"I'm sorry, I shouldn't have said that so bluntly. But I have watched his progressive deterioration over the last ten years and it's been a harrowing experience for me, Fiona and our mother, Mary. He has a rare variant of MD, that's what we call Muscular Dystrophy, that affects older men, always men. Other more usual types of MD affect younger people and kill them off earlier."

"So Ian is older than you?"

"Yes, as I said, almost exactly a year. His birthday is in June as is mine, but I was born in 1942 and he in 1941."

I could see Fiona getting uncomfortable about the way my conversation with Ingrid was going. She was probably thinking that Ingrid could add nine months to September 1940 just as easily as she had done and come to the same conclusion about what Mary and Colin had been up to then. Ingrid's next question could very well to be ask when Mary and Colin got married. She jumped in and tried to close down the topic gently.

"We, Martin and I, see as much of Ian as we can. Mary, of course, looks after him marvellously and it's not as if he needs feeding or help with his personal... his personal hygiene, if you know what I mean. He is in remission now, not meaning that he is getting better of course but that his physical deterioration has stopped temporarily. There has been no change with him for quite a while, has there Martin?"

"Yes, yes, not for quite a while," I agreed, hoping that I would not have to define 'quite a while.'

"So," Fiona went quickly on giving Ingrid no chance to speak. "He could live for years yet. He is a very entertaining man to be with and we all just love his company. He never appears unhappy. He is very stoic."

"Stoic?" asked Ingrid. "That's not an English word that I've heard off."

"It sort of means brave, accepting of one's problems without complaint, cheerful in the face of adversity. Yes, 'stoic' is exactly what he is. Perhaps, one day, you could come to England to meet him? We have already told him your story which he has found extremely interesting, as do Martin and I of course."

"Yes, maybe. I would like to, although I don't really do foreign travel these days. In fact, I've never been away from Norway since I returned in 1944. Stay at home really, and I like to be immediately available to my parents and my aunt in Oslo."

"Well, maybe one day. But tell us about your parents."

The conversation throughout the remainder of our meal was directed towards Ingrid's family and life in Norway in general. I talked about the discovery of North Sea Oil about which she, because of its enormous potential for the Norwegian economy and social provisions, was well informed. She excused herself at about 9pm after arranging to meet at ten the following morning. Fiona and I had a night cap in the hotel bar and headed to bed.

"Have we learned anything new?" she posed when we had finished reading in bed and turned off the lights.

"Well, lots about lots of things, some very interesting, to me at least, but nothing of course about what we really wanted to know. Nothing about Scotland and Arisaig."

"There may be nothing much really, just a short time of intimacy. And however much we might continue probing, the truth would only hurt Mary and probably Ingrid as well. We could never really use the story whatever it turns out to be. I say let's drop the subject, leave things as they are, and enjoy the rest of our trip up north with her."

"Agreed. Goodnight. I love you."

We had packed our bags and checked out of the hotel by the time Ingrid arrived to pick us up. The day was spent in driving north-westerly through Bodø and touring the surrounding countryside and villages. Fiona and I enjoyed the day and an amiable, near intimate, atmosphere developed between us and Ingrid. By the time we boarded our ship in early afternoon we regarded ourselves as old friends. The ship was very similar to the one we had been on the previous day. We had three days and nights to reach our final port of Kirkenes, right on the border with Russia.

The ship passed by numerous mountains, fiords and islands as it travelled north. The weather was generally good so we all three spent as much time as possible on deck. Ingrid became more and more pensive as we passed places that she had last seen from a small boat in 1940, with Colin at her side. Memories were clearly flooding back to her. We docked in two ports before we went to bed, and through the night we were woken by the ship's arrivals and departures from three more. Early next morning we dressed and went on deck to find Ingrid already there, she hadn't been to bed at all. She told us that we had passed Narvik in the dark so all she had seen were its lights.

"But soon," she said, "we will be stopping at Harstad for about an hour."

"Harstad," repeated Fiona.

"Yes, it's where Colin and I set off on our voyage to Scotland. The sort of beginning of our odyssey."

As we neared the port I could see the excitement building in Ingrid. "Over there," she pointed to a spot on the left side of the quay. "That's where our fishing boat stayed for four days while we waited for our passage to Britain. I wonder what happened to those three fishermen. I hoped that they survived the war. I suppose I should have tried to trace them. I remember the name of the boat, the Kirsten, and the skipper's first name was Bengt, but nothing else. It was there that I tried to pass myself of as a man. It was all such a long time ago," she sighed.

She moved quickly to the other side of the ship. Fiona and I followed. She stretched an arm out towards the horizon in the west. "And there, two hundred kilometres out across that sea, that's where we boarded the Glorious. And further on, much further on towards Scotland, that's where that great ship was sunk."

Our ship was scheduled to stay about one hour in the port of Harstad. Fiona and I debated whether to make a quick walk around the town, but we had already made a tour of Trondheim, where we had three hours walking around the very attractive university town that was, so our guide said, the third largest city in Norway. We had also had our time in Bodø, so we were ambivalent about disembarking the ship again. But in any case, Ingrid made up our minds for us by saying that she wished to take a little walk around the dock area, but by herself, if we would understand? We did understand. She came back looking quite pensive and took breakfast on her own.

The grandeur of the Norwegian coast line continued to awe us as the ship now passed by little ports that were not only new to Fiona and me but also to Ingrid. Our sense of comradery blossomed and by the time we reached the end of the voyage our feelings of friendship were palpable.

We arrived at Kirkenes just after breakfast. The three of us took a taxi to the airport where Ingrid's flight to Bodø was due to depart almost immediately.

We said good bye with sadness. Promises were made to keep in touch. Fiona and I invited Ingrid to come to visit us in Aberdeen or to Westgate to meet with Mary and Ian. She avoided addressing the invitation directly, just a muttering of, "Maybe, perhaps when you two finally get married, that would be a good time, perhaps you could come out here for your honeymoon and I could see you again then?"

Fiona and I left a bit later to Oslo and thence to Aberdeen

via London. It was a long and tedious journey back. We debated breaking off in London and going to Westgate to see Ian and tell him of our time in Norway.

"But what would we actually tell him?" queried Fiona. "Apart from the history of our week in Norway, we are going back without really knowing anything more than what we have always told him. Let's keep to our plan, go home, and try for babies."

I agreed.

Mary's Story

Chapter 18

1981 drifted towards 1982. Ian, but not Mary, was told the outline of our trip to Norway. The interaction with Ingrid was played down but the description of Bodø, its monument to the Gladiator pilots, the ditch used as a bomb shelter, and the other places we passed and visited from the ship all held his interest.

But 1982 began without Fiona being pregnant. A quite rudimentary check, I think, of my sperm count had been made some months previously and it seemed that all was well for my role in conception. She started to become worried about herself and to occasionally display an aggressive anger to me, and to her mother. She was always regretful and apologetic after each outburst, and they little bothered me because I had shared quarters with Sjouke in Rotterdam who had a wicked temper at times with a foul mouth, and who never apologised for anything, but nevertheless who was remembered kindly by me as an entertaining friend and lover. What concerned me much more was Fiona's growing habit of coming in from work and collapsing into uncontrollable tears. I'm not good with tears; I have little facility for consoling and she had always appeared so strong that I had never developed a knack for soothing her as she had never needed it.

Unknown to Fiona, I turned to Meredith for advice and was thoroughly told off. Now Meredith is quite stunningly beautiful, but beauty from a completely different mould to that of Fiona. Raven black, short hair in the style a flapper might have aspired to in the 1920s. Pale face with dark eyes, very tall, small breasts and the most perfectly proportioned legs that I have ever seen. I could understand that her looks and her unavailability could drive a man wild. So perfect is she to behold that I seemed always to have a silly smile on my face whenever I spoke with her. That smile turned to bewilderment when she addressed me furiously.

"You bloody men! Why the hell don't you look beyond your noses and listen to your partners instead of behaving like ignorant oafs. She's unhappy, how on earth can you not perceive that? She thinks that there is something wrong with her body, that she can't conceive. She has taken medical advice but been told that everything seems to be 'okay down there'. Get yourself to another doctor too, it's just as likely to be a problem with you, but you never thought of that did you? That little count of your sperms is not enough to detect more subtle problems. I don't mean your GP, whom I also use, but a gynaecologist, a fertility expert, someone who really knows how babies get conceived. Go together. What you both want has to be a team effort, a proper partnership."

I was completely nonplussed by the incongruous situation I found myself in. Being blasted by this picture of loveliness whose anger did not cloud her face but was plainly evident in the tone and content of her taking down of me. But she was correct and had opened my eyes to my selfishness, or perhaps it was really just typical male thoughtlessness. No matter what, the situation had to be put right.

So, in January of 1982 Fiona and I attended, as pair, a series of medical examinations and tests as well as receiving what was essentially marriage guidance. That we were trying to solve the problem together raised her spirits and cooled her temper. Eventually we were told that there no was no physical reason why we couldn't have children. She was healthy and fertile, and my sperms were capable of doing the trick. The lady fertility consultant advised us to stop trying so hard.

"I can tell that you both enjoy sex, stop making it hard work. A labour that has to be performed. Enjoy yourselves, you have plenty of time yet. You are only thirty-six Fiona and at the peak of your sexuality. Go have fun, reduce your alcohol consumption perhaps, and I'll take money that I will be seeing you with a swelling belly within a year."

We took her advice. In late May, Fiona cracked a bottle of Champagne and said, "I'm with your child, now make me the honest woman you promised. You have three weeks until your birthday. And the baby is due next January so I've only just started out on my journey."

"Yes, but first we must tell Mary."

"No! First we must tell my parents. I've already phoned them that we are coming this weekend. Mum might already suspect. That's three days away and I expect you to start on the wedding organisation right now. I think that we should have it at Westgate because Ian can't travel far. Registry office first then a dinner in a fancy restaurant. I'll leave you to choose where. We'll invite not more than twenty guests."

She had taken charge. That was no surprise and I was as pleased as she for the prospect of marriage and parenthood. Well, perhaps not quite as much, but very happy nonetheless.

By the time we set off to Fort William on Saturday morning I had the wedding date fixed and all arrangements in place bar asking Ian to be the best man. Three weeks was, however, too short a time for the civil legalities, but six worked just fine. Fiona was pleased enough with what I had done.

Her parents, George and Isla, were delighted with our news of marriage and the thought of another grandchild to join the two of Fiona's younger sister, Abigail, who lived locally and met us for drinks on Saturday evening. George and Isla readily agreed to travel down to Westgate as they were fully aware of Ian's condition. Abigail said that she and her husband would come down by train with them and then hire a car for the journey to Westgate. They would find somewhere to stay locally and leave the children with her mother-in-law.

The following weekend Fiona and I flew to London and took the train to Westgate. Our news was greeted with much the same enthusiasm exhibited by Fiona's parents. Ian, as I had expected, readily took on the best man duty. Abigail had already agreed to take on the equivalent role for Fiona. Mary said that she would arrange everything to do with the post-wedding celebratory dinner.

Back in our Aberdeen home Fiona started to blossom and her character reverted to her normal cheerful but feisty self. Each morning she took to walking around the bedroom in the nude, turning around in front of me and saying, "How do I look? How do I look? Any changes?" In the early weeks she would stick out her stomach and tease me with, "This is how it is going to look in a couple of months' time, and then I am going to turn into an elephant, and you won't love me anymore."

By the time of the wedding I could plainly see the changes in her body. She was carrying a little more weight on her face which, with her now almost permanent smile and bright blue eyes, rendered her even more attractive to me. She no longer stuck out her belly but instead took to sucking it in when in my view. I could see the changes in and around her nipples, darkening from the colour of her hair to a tan. "You're right about me going off you, you are losing the dimples in your bum cheeks and they are the only reason I fancied you in the first place, and you are getting hairy. Your crotch is becoming like Moses's burning bush." I dodged the magazine that she lobbed at my head.

"Have you looked at your body in the wardrobe mirror lately, at least I've got good reason for my, to me, very attractive changes. Meredith says so. You have no excuse for letting yourself go so much, I was seduced by an athlete but am now ogled by a satyr."

And that was usually enough banter to coax us back to bed.

The wedding went off smoothly. The following day we went to a good hotel in central London and saw all the sights that we had been promising ourselves for many years to visit but had never got around to. George and Isla also spent time in London and we met them a couple of times for meals. Abigail and her husband had to go back to their children the day after the wedding.

Fiona said that she had phoned Ingrid to say that we were getting married, that she was pregnant, and that we would we delighted if she would attend the wedding and meet Ian, but, while expressing delight at our news, she had declined the invite.

Back in Aberdeen, Fiona commandeered the second largest bed room and announced that it was to be the nursery. I enthusiastic joined in its complete redecoration and fitting out months before it needed to be ready. Then Fiona tackled me on the bathroom or, rather, bathrooms. I agreed that the single bathroom was small, basic and out of date but argued that it could be improved.

"No, that's not what I want," Fiona retorted. "We have talked about this all before. An en-suite bathroom for ourselves built into that corner of our bedroom."

I did have some memory of the past discussion at least a year or two previously, however I wasn't going to make it easy for her. "But I thought that we had agreed to knock our existing bathroom into the little bedroom next door and turn it all it one big spa-like edifice."

"Well now I would like the spa-type edifice to be our new en-suite. The existing bathroom may stay as it is until our child passes the messy stage."

"Around the age of 25 then?"

"Speaking from your own childhood experiences, are you? We've got plenty of money put by for just this eventuality. What are you quibbling about?"

I had lost as I knew I would, and in truth I fully supported her plans.

I changed the subject. "How much time are you going to

take off when the baby comes? Enough to see it through to school age?"

"Goodness no. The company has agreed that I will have three months off on full pay then, after that, up to another three months furlough without pay. I think they are being reasonable. I will go back to work after that, although maybe just part time to begin with."

"So it's going to be child minders and day care places?"

"And your time, and perhaps an au-pair girl. I really don't know, and I don't want to make up my mind until after the child is born."

--///

The new bathroom was a big success, and Fiona continued to grow and bloom. Prenatal check-ups all went well and everybody was looking forward to a safe delivery of our first baby. For the remainder of the year I travelled to Westgate each month as usual. Fiona came less often but did make the journey with me in late December, by then almost the last month of her pregnancy, to join me there for a pre-Christmas celebration. Mary had been knitting and buying things for her first grandchild and her results took us over the airline's free baggage allowance for our return journey.

That Christmas should have been a happy time, but the joy was overshadowed by a marked deterioration in Ian's health. He was constantly having to breathe oxygen from a bottle attached to his wheel chair, he found it difficult to talk more than a few words at a time and his face was the colour of whey. His hands had turned skeletal and his wrists bent so much that they were almost useless to him. Most of this deterioration had happened in just the preceding two months. His appearance made me near weep every time I looked at him.

"It appears that my remission is over," he whispered to me when we were alone. "And I've now reached where I would have been had there been no remission. The physical wasting shouldn't kill me just yet, but I believe my specialist who comes down from London regularly to see me, is concerned about my heart behaving erratically at times. He's given me some pills that seem to be helping. All the same, if we are going to have a heart-to-heart chat then I think now is the time."

We reminisced, recalling how inseparable we had been as children, how alike we had looked, how we could play at being twins and fool other people.

"I wish that we had been twins," I said, really without thinking.

"That could have been a hazardous choice for you. You could have ended up with what I have. Same egg splitting in half, seems to me that would raise the odds somewhat."

We talked about memories of our grandparents, Byron and Joan. We knew that we had had happy childhoods with great love and protection, all thanks to the extraordinary efforts that Mary had made for us in her role as a single mother.

"Did we miss having a father?" Ian asked me.

"Not me, no. I never saw the need for one. If a male was needed in our lives then Byron filled in perfectly."

"And Mary, did she miss having a husband to share our upbringing?"

"You know, I don't think so," I replied. "In fact, she may have been better off without Colin who seems have had a tendency towards being a rake. Then there is your illness of course –"

"You mean the MD that she passed to me. One has to wonder how she lives with that."

"Yes, yes. That's what I'm thinking of. It is unimaginable. And why you and not me?"

"I bear no grudge. No jealously… now at least. It was, and is, what it was. Be at peace over it, brother."

Ian was getting very tired and speaking with increasing difficulty. His eyes closed and he went gently to sleep.

Later, I turned to Fiona in our chaste Westgate bedroom.

"What do you think about Ian? I think he looks dreadful."

"Yes, he does. I've been talking to Mary. She says that her local doctor thinks she should be prepared for his death, probably in just the next few months. Eventually his lungs and chest will be unable to get enough air in to keep him going and he will go of asphyxiation. Every visit you make here, darling, you should regard as being the last that you see him alive. Including this one."

We returned to Aberdeen on the 20th of December. I knew that Fiona would not be going back to Westgate until well after the child was born, although I would make the journey every two weeks if I could.

But early on the morning of Thursday the 6th of January 1983, the day before my next planned visit, Mary phoned. She had found Ian dead in his bed. The doctor had just made a preliminary examination of him and believed that he had suffered a massive heart attack. I arrived in Westgate that evening. Mary was alone with Ian's body. She had refused to release it to an ambulance or undertaker until I could pay my last respects.

He was lying in his bed with a sheet draped over him. I pulled the sheet back a little so that I could see his face. He was in his pyjamas. His eyes and mouth were closed. I was struck by how tiny he looked. So thin, frail, nothing much more than a clothed skeleton. Curiously, his beard had stayed luxuriant all during his illness. Without it, I imagined, his head would have looked little more than a skull.

Mary pulled back a corner of the sheet to reveal his hand. "He was still warm when I found him, I thought that was he was just in a deep sleep or a coma of some sort. I massaged his hand, his chest, and slapped him gently around the face but there was no response. I knew then that he was dead but I called the ambulance in any case. The crew arrived within ten minutes and confirmed what I already knew. I called his local doctor who also came around quickly. Within one hour of me finding him it was all done and dusted, that's when I phoned you."

I clasped Ian's hand in one of mine and stroked it with my other. I was too choked for words for a minute or two. Then I spoke against the nascent sobs that were heaving to be let out from my chest. "We were so close, so close when we were young, and even now I feel as if something had died within me too. But you, Mary, you haven't been alone in this house all day with, with him?"

"No, I stayed here until mid-morning, until I knew that you would be arriving this evening, then I went for a long walk along the sea front. I haven't done that for ages. I sat down on a bench in the memorial gardens and looked at the sea, and thought of him, and you, and of Fiona and the baby. One life soon to be replaced by another. I cried a little, then made myself stop by thinking of all the good times we had had together. I thought of what he might have become had he not had his wretched disease, and I thought of the unfairness of life. I got back here in the early afternoon, and went into his bedroom to check if it had all been a bad dream. I got myself something to eat and then fell asleep in an armchair almost until the time you arrived. You know, for the last few years our relationship has almost become like mother and child again. There is so much he needs help with, and he only wants me to do it."

I noted the present tense that she had just unconsciously used and realised that it would be some time before she got used to saying 'had' in place of 'has'. I suspected it might be the same for me.

"But didn't you want somebody to be with you, to keep you company?"

"No, not really, not at all. The doctor's wife offered to be with me, which was nice of her, but she is busy with her three children and better spending her time looking after them than me, so I declined her offer saying that I was fine and that you would be down here soon. Several neighbours knocked on the door to see what the matter was. I suppose they had seen the ambulance outside. I simply told them that Ian had died. None were really surprised of course, they had seen how frail he had become and they went away. Except for one who left a plate of sandwiches and a bottle of wine on the doorstep a little while ago with a note saying that it's for our supper. Mrs Radison from three doors away I think, although she didn't sign her name. All nice people round here, they are all my friends, they would help if I needed it. I've been here for over forty years you know, far longer than anyone else in the Courts."

For the rest of the evening we tried to avoid the subject of Ian, without complete success. We went to bed early. My head buzzed trying to sort out all that needed to be done for Ian to have a funeral, and I imagined that similar thoughts would be keeping Mary awake.

Chapter 19

*M*ary has used up all of her nervous energy trying to deal with the immediacy of Ian's death. In her bed at 10pm she expects, and hopes, that she will close her eyes on this awful day and awake to find that is all a ghastly dream. But she knows it is not, and she knows that she will have little sleep this night and for many more nights to come until, she cannot say the words and the unspoken thoughts churn her brain, until Ian has been cremated. His wishes plainly stated on several occasions.

She thinks of his life, the healthy child so close to his younger brother. His career, so promising to begin with, such hope for recognition and advancement, then the diagnosis in the prime of his life with the dreadfully destructive disease and the inevitability of death dogging his shadow. Another few years while he fought to do his job, then the capitulation and slow, cruel descent into the imprisonment of his mind in a wasted, useless body. A body that in the end she had to tend just as she did when he was a baby.

She had never minded being Ian's nursemaid. She had thought of getting a carer of some sort to help her but she had not wanted another person to be washing him, wiping him, *dressing him, feeding him, and loving him. She had soon discovered that she could not manage the house, its garden and care for Ian all at the same time. She compromised by engaging a helper, Diana, whom by now she regarded as a close friend, to do most of the household chores. She came to the house regularly three times each week. Mary already paid a local man to cut the lawns and he had willingly taken on more of the gardening tasks as well as odd-jobs around the house. She was coping pretty well, she thinks, that is until his death.*

'Oh, my goodness,' it suddenly occurs to her. 'I will have to phone Diana tomorrow to tell her about Ian and ask her not to come for a while. But that's not right, Ian liked her, so maybe she should come here the day after tomorrow once the undertaker... Oh God! I need an undertaker, that's got to be arranged, Martin can do all that tomorrow.'

These thoughts spawn many others in Mary's listless mind... 'Cremation? No, the undertaker will fix that. A service... in a church? No, that would not have been Ian's choice, just something simple in the cemetery chapel. Presumably there is one at Margate cemetery. But why the cemetery at all? Perhaps the undertaker has its own chapel. I'll use that company on the outskirts of Margate, what are they called 'Somebody and Somebody'. No, 'Somebody and Son'. Yes, Joseph Smythe and son. They will do. I suppose a cremation is a pretty simple thing to arrange, I won't be trying to find a burial plot at least. The coffin should be plain, everything should be plain and simple. That was Ian's style.

And who is going to carry the coffin? Who will be the pall bearers? Most of our, that's mine and Ian's, friends are getting a bit old to carry round a coffin, and Martin has no one to call upon down here. The thought of some of the old crocks she knows trudging round Margate with a coffin on their shoulders lightens her mood for a moment. Anyway, undertakers use that sort of collapsible trolley these days, so no pall bearers needed.

But somebody has to give a speech, an elegy perhaps. I

don't think I'll be up to that. It would have to be Martin I suppose. And who should we ask to come to the funeral? How many of his old work colleagues would come? How many of them would want to come? How do I get to tell them in time? There must be a death notice. An obituary? No that's a step too far. I must find someone to contact all those work colleagues. His old boss perhaps... his number is probably in that Rolodex he keeps on his desk.'

The same thoughts and questions pound ceaselessly through her head over and over again as she tosses on her pillow. She prays that she may sleep and put this dreadful day, now yesterday, behind her. She turns her thoughts from Ian to herself. How would her life have been if Colin hadn't died? A father to the two boys, yet they never seemed to have needed one. They never missed him because they had never known him. Any guidance that might have been needed from a male figure was provided by her father, Byron, living across the road. But was any such guidance ever really needed?

'God, I hardly knew the man. A four-year marriage yet I would probably not reach fifty if I counted the number of times we made love, and the ridiculous thing is that he is, was, the only man who ever made love to me. And he wasn't particularly good, judging by what Cosmopolitan and the like describe as 'good'. Bedtime was always a bit of a charade for me. Not unpleasant and I wanted to please him, but a bit of a masquerade all the same. I know I never truly climaxed, my later life showed me that. My guess is that we would probably have parted company, and quite early on were it not for... I can't bring myself to say it or even to think it, so I've built a completely impregnable wall around what happened. And even then, our relationship scraping by perhaps, until Evelyn and then Pamela came into my life. And if it hadn't been those two, and the several other women who might have become enduring lovers but in fact passed in the night, or one or two nights, what then? How might he have accepted my preferred sexual taste? Not at all I suspect.

Poor Evelyn, she was so much in love with me. Of course,

that's why I bought the London flat so that we could spend the occasional night together. Then I ditched her for the love of my life, Pamela. She was everything I imagined that I could have been. Wealthy, a successful publisher, always beautifully dressed and groomed, and totally open with her sexuality. Her lesbianism was not her preferred sexual taste, it was her only taste, ever. We made such plans. To live together in London where I would have moved into that converted warehouse of hers by the Thames. I would have sold this house, Ian was to have my London flat and Martin, well he was away at sea and perfectly able to sort out his own living arrangements. But then Ian, poor Ian, developed MD. Of course, he was not badly stricken for several years and Pamela begged me to make the move from Westgate. But his doctor had told me about the inevitability of the course of the illness, how it could in the worst case be all be over in three years. I recognised that, sooner or later, I would become his nursemaid and there would be less and less time to indulge myself with Pamela. We tried to keep our relationship going but it became less and less tenuous, and then abrasive so that by the time Ian had to live here permanently, she was gone.'

She begs her brain to turn off and let her sleep, but without success. She goes over the same thoughts again and again in her mind and, as they become more and more jumbled and less and less coherent, the imagined words fail to coalesce and she is left with images. Ian as a baby, a toddler, a schoolboy, the prime of his twenties and his corpse, now in the bedroom right underneath where she now lays. She has difficulty in imagining Colin's face, for so many years she has tried to avoid ever thinking of him, but Martin's and Fiona's faces form a sort of circulating kaleidoscope in the telescope of her diminished consciousness and maybe their baby will look like Colin. She believes she may be dreaming, but by opening her eyes and seeing a glow underneath her bedroom door from the nightlight at the top of the stairs, she knows that she is not.

At six in the morning she hears Martin in the bathroom which lies between their bedrooms. She gets up, puts on her *dressing gown and goes downstairs to the kitchen to make a pot of tea. She resists the temptation to peek into Ian's room. She hears Martin coming down the stairs. She knows the reason that he is in the house and that he is coming downstairs to hug her and to stroke her head and the nape of her neck. Finally, she burst into tears, the thoughts of the night vanish and she is ready to work with Martin to bid farewell to her other son.*

Chapter 20

Mary looked terrible when we met in the kitchen that morning. I don't suppose I presented any better a picture.

"Martin, we have to get going on the arrangements right away," she began. "I've had lots of thoughts about what has to be done, but they got all muddled up while I was trying to get some sleep."

"I had a restless night as well. At one time I got up and made a short list, it's upstairs. It may not make a lot of sense in the cold light of morning, but it could be a starting point for us to put our heads together. The first thing –"

She cut me off, "The first thing is to get him out of this house and into the hands of an undertaker. There is one in Margate which I think we should use. Do you know that he wants... wanted, to be cremated?"

"Yes, I did know that. When I finish this tea I will go upstairs, have a shave and generally clean myself up."

At 8am I phoned Joseph Smythe & Son. I was surprised that the phone was answered immediately. I commented that I didn't expect them to be open at that time of day and was told that the funeral parlour's phone was automatically rerouted to the home of the person talking to me, who identified himself as the '& Son', Smythe Junior. He started to take charge of the funeral arrangements even as I told him about Ian's death and the address.

"We will be round at ten. Can you get a death certificate from the doctor before then?"

I said I would try.

"And Sir," he finished with. "There are lots of things to be done in this time of sadness for you and your mother. I will be bringing along a list of all the immediate and necessary arrangements for us to go through along with other things that you and Mrs Mitchel may want to consider. A cremation you say, so no burial plot which makes things easier and simpler."

Mary telephoned the doctor at precisely 9am. He had already prepared Ian's death certificate and just half an hour later his wife arrived with it.

"Philip and I are so sorry about Ian's death," she said. "He has been Ian's doctor since before he was diagnosed, over ten years."

"Yes, well before then." Mary agreed.

She left having hugged Mary and we waited for the undertaker to arrive.

Three men, suitably adorned in dark suits and white shirts, arrived in a closed black van at their promised time. Smythe Junior, who was very much in charge of the removal process, helped the other two transfer Ian onto a collapsible trolley and wheel him out to the van. The task was done with care and dignity in front of a distraught Mary.

"After tomorrow you will be able to come and see him in Margate at any time, and stay as long as you like." Smythe Junior told her with a compassion that seems genuine.

By the time the van bearing Ian had departed, the three men spread together across its bench front seat, all the funeral arrangements had essentially been made. A date for the cremation, six days' time, the use of the undertaker's own funeral parlour for a non-denominational service which was to include no religious elements apart from two hymns selected by Mary.

"Really they are for those coming who do appreciate the holy aspects," she rationalised.

The cremation to be witnessed only by immediate family and the recommendation of a venue for a small, post-funeral wake.

The rest of that morning Mary and I took it in turns to tell friends about Ian's death and funeral arrangements. I found Eugene Russel's phone number in Ian's Rolodex and called him. After expressing his sorrow and condolences, he said that he would come to the funeral with three or four others who had worked with Ian and who had remained in touch.

In the afternoon Fiona arrived in her car. She had driven the whole way down from Aberdeen by herself, staying the previous night in a roadside motel about halfway along the journey of 600 miles.

I and Mary both chided her for making such a long journey, by herself, in such a late stage of her pregnancy. "Suppose you had decided to give birth in Yorkshire, on Ilkley Moor, how would we or anyone else have known?" I said.

She just shrugged off our reproof saying that she could be more useful in Westgate helping us rather than being stuck feeling useless in Aberdeen. And useful she proved to be by overseeing, or taking over, almost all the domestic actions leading up to the funeral, and probably causing a nuisance to Joseph Smythe & Son. I was delighted to have her with me, of course.

The funeral was in most ways unremarkable I suppose, except for one thing. Some twenty-five people, including Eugene's party, saw Ian sent off with dignity and sadness. I, Mary and Fiona witnessed the cremation and in the preceding service in the undertaker's hall I gave a short address describing Ian's life and character. In doing so I stood by his coffin and faced my audience which was seated in pew-like settles between me and the entrance to the hall. As I paused, having asked everyone to silently recall their own memories of Ian, I saw a figure with slumped shoulders standing at the rear in partial shadow by a door which appeared half open. A scarf covered the head and I had my reading glasses on so I could not be certain of whom it might be. I finished my address and, as I walked back to my seat in the front row of chairs, I saw the figure turn away and slip out through the door. It was Ingrid, I was certain.

That evening Fiona admitted that she had telephoned Ingrid as soon as I had departed Aberdeen for Westgate.

"She had known he was ill, we told her all about it when we were with her either in Bodø or on that ship. She didn't seem surprised and made no indication at all that she would come over from Norway for the funeral. Are you sure it was her? It could have been one of the undertaker's staff, a secretary or whatever, checking where the service had got to."

"Not a secretary. It was Ingrid, I'm sure."

"Should I phone in a few days' time to ask her?"

"No, I think not. Had she wanted us to know about her presence then she would have been around when we came out of the hall and spoken to us, but she didn't. If it was her, then she had her own reasons for her discretion. Let's honour that."

Fiona nodded, then said, "How long shall we stay down here? As far as I am concerned I could start my maternity leave and take a couple of weeks to help Mary out, but how about you?"

"Oh, I'll be able to get time off really when I want. There is such a demand for naval engineers in and around Scotland for the oil industry that my firm will be quite accommodating to make sure that I don't head off to someone else. But the baby is due in just three weeks now. Perhaps we could stay here for another week." And that's is what we told Mary later that evening, the 14th of January.

On the 19th of January Fiona went into labour, and twenty-four hours later delivered a healthy baby girl, Catherine, in Margate hospital. A scrunched up little bundle weighing nearly seven pounds who I immediately thought was the image of her mother.

There were some complications in the birth requiring a bit

of patching up of Fiona, nothing too serious but she would have to stay a week in hospital. I took the opportunity to dash up to Aberdeen and back in one day to check in with my company, as I had suspected, my boss was understanding, and to collect two large suitcases full of baby kit. Enough for the month that we now planned to be in Westgate with Mary and Catherine.

--///

Mary is exhausted by the evening after the cremation of Ian and is sure that she will sleep tonight. She is glad, delighted in fact, that Fiona and Martin with stay with her for another week, there is so much to do in sorting out Ian's effects.

'They can help me so much, and keep me sane'. She would like them to stay longer but she fully understands the necessity of getting Fiona back to Aberdeen and her doctor.

Sleep does come but not before Mary lies awake trying to imagine what she should do with the rest of her life.

Should she leave Westgate, leave the memories behind, stop renting out the London flat and live in it herself? There is, of course, no chance of reviving a relationship with either Evelyn or Pamela. Her copy book is well and truly blotted with both of them. All her friends are in the local area, what would she do with herself in London? No satisfactory answer comes to her. Then how about moving up to Aberdeen to be near Martin and Fiona? With a new-born baby they might appreciate her as a local help. Of course her parents, George and Isla, is that their names, would also want to share their grandchild, but they live in Fort William which is on the opposite side of Scotland to Aberdeen. But then Martin, Fiona and Catherine would be the only people I would know there. It's the same problem as moving to London. There is really no sensible alternative to staying in this house. Maybe, just maybe they would move down here, move in with me. The place is big enough for the four of us although things need to be modernised a bit, and I'll be leaving the house to Martin in my will in any case. But now is not the time to broach the subject, she decides.

She wakes up early the next morning realising that she will now have to make decisions about what to do with Ian's possessions, his room, his memories. She goes into the bedroom. The bed is just as it was when Ian's body was removed by the undertakers, the sheet is pulled back and she can just make out the imprint of his body on the mattress. She strokes the mattress flat and raises a hand to her face. There is the scent of Ian of her fingers. She gathers up all the bed linen and takes it straight to the outside dustbin. The rubbish men will be along later this day on their usual weekly round.

She looks at his clothes hanging in the large wardroom which dominates one end of the room. Most of the jackets, coats and complete suits have not been used for years as he became smaller and unable to climb into them. They can go to the charity shops along with his shoes. Underwear, shirts, socks, ties, sweaters lie neatly in the drawer section of the wardrobe. She gathers them up and takes them all to the dustbin.

His large desk, high enough for him to get his wheel chair under, is covered with small objets-d'arts, writing utensils, a photo or two and the like. Martin and Fiona can have their pick, she decides. Drawers underneath contain documents he would have regarded as important, again Martin and Fiona can sort through those.

She goes into the adjacent bathroom. In addition to the usual men's toiletries, there are medicines and other things that reflect the final months of his life. A portable commode, antiseptics, cream to allay sores from prolonged sitting, incontinence pads. Ian would not have wanted Martin and Fiona to know about these things, so she gathers them all up in a large plastic bag which also goes to the dustbin. She hopes that somehow the bathroom will bear his scent, even a trace smell to bring back to her his time as a baby, but she only detects the faint odour of disinfectant. She realises that once

Martin and Fiona have done their work and departed next week, she will be left with little else but memories of Ian. And that begs the question of what she do with his suite, these two rooms of the Westgate house. It is too hard, and not the time, for her to answer that.

Over two days following the funeral Mary, Martin and Fiona work to sort out those of Ian's things that Mary has not already binned. His remaining clothes, and a lot more brick-a-brack besides, go to the Oxfam shop. Ian didn't really have a lot of other possessions. His car and sporting equipment have long since been disposed of, but there are a few very nice pieces of silver that he had collected over the years. Mary offers them to Martin who takes a Georgian wine jug but asks her to keep every other piece herself.

"He pursued a rather austere life," Martin remarks.

"Austere, maybe, but practical. He knew he was going to die at any time, what would have been the point of gathering lots of possessions?" Fiona remarks. "Is there a will? We really ought to look at that before we go much further in what we are doing."

"I am his executor," replies Martin. "But I have never seen the will so have no idea of what he wanted to do with his estate."

"I have the will," says Mary. "He gave it to me some time ago. He was going to tell me what is in it, but I stopped him. I didn't want to know."

She goes to her bedroom and comes back with a sealed envelope. "It's in here," she says handing it to Fiona. "Here, you are the lawyer, have a look at it."

Fiona carefully opens the envelope. The will is inside along with what appears to be a bank statement.

She examines the documents. "The will looks all fine and legal, properly witnessed and not so long ago either."

Mary remembers. "Yes, his bank manager and another man, probably a solicitor I think, came to see him about three months ago. It must have been all sorted out then."

Fiona looks at the other document. "Well, in a nutshell, he

has got about 150,000 pounds in the bank, quite a tidy sum seeing that he was unable to work for many years."

Mary is surprised that he had so much cash. "But I think he played the stock market a bit. He told me that he was selling everything up, liquidating is the word he used I think and putting everything into a bank savings account, which seems to be what he has done."

Fiona goes on, "And in simple terms there is a bequest to me of 10,000 pounds, which is very nice and the remainder is split between the two of you. I could handle the probate angle from my office in Aberdeen, but I think in fact it might be better getting it all sewn up locally, outside of the family so as to speak. We might speak to that bank manager and get the solicitor that came here with him to act on our, his, behalf."

Martin and Mary agree with Fiona's recommendation and make the necessary phone calls.

Then, with only two days left of their planned visit, Martin and Fiona become parents. They, and Mary, put Ian out of their minds while experiencing the surprise and euphoria of Catherine's birth. But circumstances alter cases and can provide different solutions.

'They now say they are going to stay here a month,' thinks Mary. 'They ought to move into the downstairs suite so Fiona doesn't have to keep trekking up and down stairs and I don't have to share my bathroom. A thing I find quite difficult for more than two or three days.'

And then a further thought strikes. 'What if they were to move here permanently? For Martin that would be like him moving back into the ancestral home, well, home for forty years at least. It's showing its age of course. Fiona would want the kitchen completely remodelled, everything would need to be redecorated. Perhaps it is time to get rid of all that wood panelling. And for space? Maybe we could build on a summer room to the lounge, or even a studio over the garage. The possibilities are endless and I'm sure Ian would be glad to know that his money would be used for such a worthwhile project.'

'Worthwhile for me that is,' she reflects. 'Let's see how things are for a while. They might even suggest it themselves.'

--///

After about two weeks of disturbed sleep and jostling between Fiona and me, with inputs from Mary about who does what and when for Catherine, we had some sort of routine sorted out. The satisfied adoration of Fiona for our child was palpable, and whenever I saw Catherine clasped to her breast an uncontrollable smile broke over my face. The house was full of love. I resolved over and over again to be the best husband and father I could be to them both.

"Give it another couple of months, Martin," she whispered to me in bed. "I'll be all sorted out down below by then. I'll put myself back on the pill, and we can resume where we left off, once we get back to Aberdeen that is. I love you as I always have done. I don't have to share my love between Catherine and you, it's new love for her that I feel and there is more than enough for us all."

We kissed long but chastely. It was enough.

Chapter 21

few days later, still at Westgate, I received a phone call. At first I thought it would be my company chasing me to return to Aberdeen, but it was Dr Phillip Barker, Ian's local doctor who had produced his death certificate and was now temporarily overseeing Fiona's and Catherine's progress. Mary regarded him as a family friend but my contact with him had only begun at the time of Ian's death, so I was a little surprised when he asked me to visit him in his surgery rather than continuing the conversation by phone.

"It's nothing to worry about. Of course you have never consulted me so I have no idea of your health except my impression that you are in pretty good shape. No, it's to do with Ian. I'll explain more when I see you."

I arranged to go to his surgery the next day at 10am. Despite the doctor's reassurance, the thought did cross my mind that the visit would involve Muscular Dystrophy. Was he going to give me some sort of warning that I could succumb to some variant of Ian's disease that only hits much later in life?

I simply told Fiona that Dr Barker wanted to discuss some aspect of Ian's disease with me. She was too tied up with Catherine to suggest that she could accompany me or even to speculate on why he might want to speak to me.

--///

Dr Barker, who I had of course met at Ian's funeral and later during a couple of his visits to see Fiona while she was in hospital, rose from the chair behind his desk, shook my hand and invited me to sit facing him. He settled back into his chair as I did mine. He was an earnest man, about forty or so, very bald but otherwise unremarkable. He had a friendly personality and was well regarded in Westgate, the sort of medic that anyone would be glad to have as the family doctor. He began by asking how Mary was coping with the death of Ian, and then how Catherine and Fiona were doing. My replies were reassuring on all counts.

"And you?"

"Oh, just the sleepless nights that I expected, but generally we are all managing pretty well. I am enjoying my new role as a father."

He opened a slim cardboard covered file that lay in front of him. "What do you actually know about Muscular Dystrophy, particularly the rare Becker's variety that Ian had?"

I told him what little I knew. The one in four chance of a child inheriting the flawed chromosome from a parent carrier, from one's mother only, I believed and that I seemed to have missed the bullet.

"In which case, as a male, you would have had either a one in two chance or an absolute certainty depending on which way one plays with the statistics."

I had taken a short course in statistics while at college and I remembered what the Consultant in Edinburgh had explained to me, so I was not certain that what Dr Barker had just said was right. He saw my doubting face and continued speaking.

"I have no real knowledge of the science of statistics although I do know that it is taking a much greater significance due to the emergence of the analysis and study of DNA. Do you know what DNA is?"

I replied that I did.

He reached into a drawer in his desk and pulled out an old copper penny. "I have a little demonstration of the problem with statistics which I can show you if you like. I normally use it to break the ice with uncommunicative children to get them to start opening up to me."

He flipped the coin onto the desk in front of me. It came up heads.

"Now," he continued. "What is the chance of this coin coming up either heads or tails when dropped like that?"

"One in two for either side."

"And why is that?"

I thought that he was taking the mickey out of me, but I went along with his game out of curiosity and because I knew the answer. "That coin, all coins, have only two states for rest, if one discounts landing on its edge. Heads or tails. Which can be one or the other but not both simultaneously."

"Well put, accurate and intuitive, so the coin has a 50 percent chance, probability if you like, of coming up heads and the same probability for coming up tails. So, half a chance for each. Each side has a one in two chance of coming up."

I nodded, a slight irritation was starting to emerge within me.

He went on, "Now if I toss it again what are the odds of it coming up heads again, or instead, coming up tails?"

"It's exactly the same. A one in two chance, heads or tails, just as before."

"Not a one in four for heads again, because it's just been heads? You just said that a tossed coin has a 50/50 chance of landing either heads or tails, each side having half a chance of landing face up, so if it tossed again wouldn't the chance of a second heads be ½ of ½ making 25 percent, or one in four?"

"No, it's one in two just the same. That coin has no memory of how it was tossed in the past."

"Yes, that seems to be the obvious and correct answer, but let's us now try a variation on our little experiment. Suppose you are in sort of a gambling joint, a poor man's casino perhaps. Suppose I'm the croupier and I toss this same coin several more times after its initial heads up position, a total of eight throws perhaps in all, and before each toss is made you have to bet a pound on how the coin lands. Would you put the pound on the second throw coming up either heads again or tails?"

I had to think for a moment. "It shouldn't matter, either state is equal. I'll put the pound on tails."

He laid a second penny, heads up, next to the first. "And it's come up heads again, and you have lost your pound. Now, how will you bet on the third throw?"

"I'll bet on tails again."

"Why?"

"Because it has already come up heads twice so it is now time for tails."

A third penny was laid heads up. "Heads again, and another pound down the drain. And for the fourth throw?"

"Tails."

"Why?"

"Because the chance of four heads in succession is getting pretty low."

"Yes, $\frac{1}{2}$ times $\frac{1}{2}$ times $\frac{1}{2}$ times $\frac{1}{2}$, which all comes to $1/16^{th}$. There is only a 1 in 16 chance, or 6.25 percent for the fourth head. You would probably have won a pound with 'tails' this time."

I smiled. I had reasoned correctly it seemed and the game, for which I could see no point and which seemed trivial, was over. Perhaps now we could get onto why I was sitting in this doctor's surgery. What was my being here to do with Ian's illness?

Dr Barker gave a little smile. "And how does the coin participate in the choice of heads or tails? It has no memory. How does it know that four consecutive heads are a bit much and it should next land as tails? And instead of using the same coin each time, how about if a new coin is introduced for each throw, would you still bet in the same way?"

All I could reply was, "It's not easy to rationalise when you put the problem like that."

"Yes, it's a conundrum. Simplistically, every throw has the same chance of landing heads or tails, but our intuition and proven fact, is that the probability of consecutive head or tails decreases with their accumulation, and it doesn't matter if one or several different coins are used. Suppose that these three coins here represent three brothers borne to a mother bearing the 'defective' Becker's Muscular Dystrophy chromosome. That they are all 'heads up' indicates that none of the boys have inherited the disease. Now, remember when you were choosing the fall of these coins, you selected 'tails' for the toss of the fourth coin because the probability of it landing 'heads', to make a succession of four 'heads up', seemed to you as extremely low, just 6.25 percent we calculated. So, if you were the fourth son what do you *really* think your chance of *not* inheriting the disease is? One in two? Or, as we just calculated for the forth tossed coin, one in sixteen which means there are fifteen chances in sixteen that you *will* get MD. And the bet is not for a pound, it's for a life."

"I don't know, I really don't know," I replied.

"And neither do I," said the doctor. "All I can say is that statistically a person might or might not get a disease. I cannot be more specific. I cannot tell him that he will actually get MD or not. Thus, what we, the medical world that is, has to do is to find an accurate way to predict if someone will get the disease without fudging around with statistics, and then find a way to prevent or cure it."

He took five more pennies from his drawer, dropped them loosely into his open left palm and added the three from the desk in front of him. He transferred all the coins to his left hand which he then clenched into a fist and placed knuckles down on the surface of his desk. He opened his hand and I heard the coins clink. He quickly removed his hand and all eight coins lay neatly on the surface. They were all heads up. "Just a little trick I learned years ago. Helps me to get those children to tell me what is really on their minds."

He replaced all of the coins into the drawer.

"Now, what has this to do with Becker's MD and Ian? We know already that the concept of a one-in-two chance of inheriting the disease for a male may or may not influence the chance of his younger male siblings also having the disease. So what is the mechanism that one brother gets the disease but the other, born of the same womb, egg bank and semen sack, does not? You say that you have some knowledge about DNA thanks, presumably, from the well-publicised but ground breaking work of the Cambridge Nobel prize winners Crick and Watson, and others. DNA holds an individual's genetic makeup, and is the genes that may or may not give you a nasty disease or physical abnormalities. Researchers all over the world are trying to discover which genes, let's call them a-typical genes, might give rise to the sort of diseases that are essentially impossible to cure and impossible to detect until the symptoms become manifest. Of course, a-typical genes could equally well be the source of mental or physical perfection. It may be all to do with statistics which, as we have shown, can be tricky. A particularly tough nut to crack is Muscular Dystrophy but, with new analytical equipment in development and a plethora of theories, there is now hope that at least the cause of the disease, and its many variants, may become known in the next few years. With this in mind, several laboratories are building libraries of interesting DNA. One such place is based in University College, London. Thanks to Ian's neurological consultant, Peter Schulz, the college has samples of Ian's DNA but what they want now is some of yours. They believe that once procedures have been developed, they will be able to compare the two samples, look for differences and then revisit the odds of avoiding or contracting Becker's and, perhaps, of many other intractable hereditary conditions. So, what Peter has asked me to do is to take a DNA sample from you and send it to him. Would you agree to that?"

I paused before replying, not because I was reluctant to give the sample, some sort of blood draw I assumed, but because I was trying to absorb the importance of what I had just been told. Could detection lead to a cure? That surely was the ultimate hope, but, alas, too late for Ian.

"Yes, of course I will give the sample. What does it involve, me giving blood?"

Dr Barker face spread into a smile which expressed 'Thank you'. "Yes, just a simple and small blood draw which I'll take from a vein in the crook of your left elbow and send straight to the University College staff."

The doctor removed the blood sample from my arm using a hypodermic and transferred it into a glass phial. As he was labelling the phial and I was pressing a cotton pad over my tiny puncture wound, he said he could not guarantee that I would ever hear from University College again, "I believe that they are collecting hundreds of different samples from siblings drawn from all over the population. Still, I guess no news would be good news, Eh?"

I told Fiona all about my meeting with Dr Barker, but I did it out of earshot of Mary so that she would not be drawn back into her grief for Ian.

--///

Four weeks after Catherine's birth, the Mitchel family set of for home in Fiona's car. I say Mitchel family advisedly because Fiona had not changed her name on marriage to me. Too many signs and document headings to be changed in her law office she claimed, but I knew it was really for pride in her own Scottish surname. Fiona Buchanan had a nice ring to it and a standing for what she had managed to achieve under its banner in her professional career. Of course, I wanted to get back to the house in Aberdeen, all now nicely fitted out for Catherine's presence, but I had a sense of guilt in leaving Mary so soon. She insisted, however, that she was ready to move on, whatever that meant, and that I should concentrate on Catherine, nurture her and enjoy her childhood, but bring her down to Westgate when we could. She said that she accepted that I would probably not be visiting as often as I had as Ian's life had drawn to its close.

"Every three months would be fine, with Fiona and Catherine if possible, but we can make lots of phone calls."

I went back to work while Catherine settled comfortably into motherhood. She said that she would take the remaining five months of maternity leave that her company had granted her although she might do some part-time work from home before then. As I might have expected, she started to get files and briefs from work well before the five months was up, and sometimes she would take Catherine into her office for an hour or two while she attended meetings. There were always trusted staff available to keep her entertained. I was contributing much more to Catherine's upbringing than I would have predicted a few months earlier. I was besotted with her as I was with Fiona, whose sexual appetite was now completely revived, and I was happy to do anything asked of me. Soon I didn't need asking at all. I knew what to do and when to do it. But, of course, I was only a part-time parent because I had to go into my office five days a week and occasionally I had to fly out to the northern islands for a couple of days to inspect an oil rig.

We didn't have Catherine christened, but Meredith, who immediately took on the role of favourite aunt, was delighted to be asked to be her de-facto Godmother. And as the months passed Catherine's burgeoning red hair and established blue eyes promised the child a remarkable resemblance to her mother.

Catherine was about five months old when Fiona said that she and I should have a serious talk about our future. She started off by saying how pleased, and surprised, she was that I had taken on tasks that perhaps more conventionally would have fallen to the mother. "Are you sure that you don't have any Scandinavian blood?" she teased. "You have become a very Modern Father."

I had no idea where this talk, all one sided so far, was leading.

"You know, or maybe you don't, that I rather like this part-time working arrangement that I've been doing. It seems to suit my law practice as well, although I would prefer it if I could go into the office a bit more often. I guess when the partnership opportunity comes up with the retirement of Hugh, then I had better be putting in a bit more time and commitment anyway."

'She's going to talk about child care or an au-pair,' I thought, but no.

"Darling, we share most of the looking after of Catherine, pity you can't breast feed too, and you do much of the house chores. So what would you say to you working part-time too? You are essentially a consultant anyway with your specialisation in rig inspection. It seems to me that apart from visiting the rigs you could do most of your work from home, and if you were sort of freelance you could control the amount of time you worked and spend more time during the day with Catherine. And we wouldn't have to have a nanny, or dump her at a day centre."

The idea had never occurred to me to leave the safety net of my company. But I knew that in fact we always used several part-timers, who went by the title of Consultants, in such areas as insurance assessors, corrosion experts, divers and the like. We would have more than enough income from two part-time jobs when the legacy from Ian was factored in, and I would be able to see Mary virtually whenever I liked. I was already feeling that I was neglecting her in favour of Catherine although I knew that she accepted this lopsided sharing of my responsibilities and time.

A few more minutes of discussion with Fiona, and I had agreed to pursue her suggestion. The company were quite enthusiastic when I broached the subject although they wanted me to be dedicated to them rather than seek a portfolio of clients. Their bait for my agreement to this stipulation was the offer to continue paying into my part of the company's pension fund. A new contract was drawn up for me to work 100 hours each calendar month and be on call for more if required. Thus, just two weeks after Fiona making her suggestion, our shared parenthood and part-time working regimes started.

We were all due to visit Mary a month later, but a few days before we set out I received another phone call from Dr Barker. He said that he had heard from Mary that I would be in Westgate the next weekend and staying for a few days. Could I pop into his surgery again for a chat?

"I want to emphasise you are not in danger of getting some nasty disease but something has come up in those DNA samples from you and your brother that you should know about. It might be better if you were discrete at this time, come by yourself I suggest and don't tell Mary. Any time after I've finished my rounds would be fine. How about after lunch Monday?"

I tried to extract more information from him but he was adamant that he was not going to pre-empt our meeting by telling me anymore.

"Don't worry, it's nothing to do with your wife, Fiona, or your lovely child. How is she doing by the way?"

I replied that Catherine was thriving and before I made any more comment he politely but firmly rung off with, "See you Monday pm then."

--///

I had told Fiona that my appointment was just a follow-on from the previous meeting.

She did look at me a bit curiously and ask, "You don't think he has found something with you, with your DNA? Oh God, don't let that be."

I reassured as best I could by repeating what little the doctor had told me told me during the phone call. "He said it's definitely nothing to do with my health."

"Mary's? No, not Catherine's!"

Fiona was now near panic, something that I had never seen before. I tried to reassure her as best I could. "Definitely not anything to do with Catherine, otherwise he would have insisted that you be there also. No, it's something to with Ian. Perhaps he didn't have Becker's MD at all, or perhaps something else with the Becker's. The only slight mystery now is why he was so adamant that Mary should not be told that I was seeing him."

Fiona calmed. She realised what I had said was logical, and logic was one of her driving characteristics.

--///

I arrived at Dr Barker's surgery as arranged. After welcoming me, the doctor got down to business straight away.

"Peter Schulz, your brother's consultant remember, is acting as a conduit for University College because the staff there are not involved in your family's medical affairs. They are just doing the research with your and Ian's DNA samples and reporting their findings. So because Peter was closely connected with Ian and his fight against MD and I was his family doctor, he has asked me to pass on what the College have discovered."

He paused for a moment, fiddling with a typed sheet of paper that lay in front of him. He was struggling to find the right words, and I was feeling a sense of dread.

"The University College team are a long way from any conclusions with their studies into siblings within families that suffer with genetic diseases. What they have done so far is to perform a preliminary screening of your and Ian's DNA, a coarse comparison if you like. They have repeated the test five times and there is no doubt about the results. Ian is, was, your half-brother and not your full sibling."

The temptation for me to break in, say something at the shock of this statement, was very great but I managed to resist.

"You share the same father but different mothers, that it why you didn't get MD. It had nothing to do with some one in four chance."

"But we were so alike, taken for twins when young. What

you have just said can't be true."

"There can be no doubt in this report," he said, waving the sheet of paper between us. You say that you were very similar to look at, but which of your parents did you both look like, your common father, or Mary?"

I pictured the photo of Colin on Mary's bedroom wall. "Like Colin, very like Colin," I conceded. "But equally that there is no doubt that I am Mary's child. I was born well after their marriage, eighteen months or so, and I have seen photos of me as a new-born in her arms."

"Then the only possible conclusion is that Mary did not give birth to Ian. He could have been adopted, I gather adoption procedures were pretty casual during the war, grandparents and aunts assuming responsibility for children without parents. You know, war time casualties or just parents who disappeared. Another test using a sample from Mary might shed some light, but I'm sure that would be out of the question?"

"Absolutely out of the question. But even that couldn't explain us having the same father."

"No, no it couldn't. That is a riddle that can only be solved by your family. Or ignored, which is probably what I would advise. Let sleeping, or dead, dogs lie. But you can now understand why I have chosen not to reveal anything to Mary, and nor will I ever."

There was really nothing more to be said. I thanked him and went back to The Courts where I told Fiona all about Dr Barker's information once we had gone to bed and Catherine was asleep.

Fiona listened carefully and asked a couple of questions to help clarify what I had been explaining.

"It absolutely unbelievable," she said in amazement. "Ian and you don't have the same mother. All this time he was adopted, or was he? And Mary never let on. Do you think she ever told Ian, even at the end?"

"No, I wouldn't think so. I'm positive that if Ian had ever found out that Mary was not his birth mother he would have told me. We were always so very close and had no secrets from each other, I'm sure."

"So why did she keep it to herself, and who was the mother and- Oh my God, I've got it! Ian's mother is Ingrid."

"But that's absurd. Why would Mary take in a child of Colin's born out of wedlock? I could perhaps begin to understand it if Ian had somehow turned up needing a home after Colin's death, but there are photos of me as an infant with him peering into my cradle. He was in this house before I was born."

"It's Ingrid, Ingrid," Fiona riposted forcibly. "Think of the timing. His recorded birthdate was early June 1941 which means he was conceived on or around the beginning September 1940, assuming of course, that he was materially neither premature nor late. We've been all through these numbers before, haven't we? When Colin left Arisaig and went to fly fighters in Liverpool, Ingrid must have been pregnant, although she wouldn't have realised it then. But by Christmas she would certainly have known that she was carrying Colin's child. So what was she to do? She probably knew about his marriage to Mary. Was she to turn up on the church steps and say that she had good reason for stopping the marriage? Or did she wait until the child was born and dump it on the doorstep of this house. It's no wonder that Ingrid was so guarded with us about her time in Scotland with, and after, Colin. There's a whole saga waiting to be told."

We stared at each other trying to disbelieve what we both realised was true.

Fiona's face took on a mixture of shock and sympathy. "Oh, the poor woman. She gave up her son to an absent father. The father died. The son died of a disease inherited that she would realise, by now, was inherited from her. A fling in the grass at Arisaig... look where it all led! Poor, poor Ingrid. Remember, we told her in Bodø that you had an elder brother; I thought that she seemed unduly taken aback by that. Up to then she must have thought that you were her son. Now she has lost that son twice!" Fiona was weeping openly.

I cuddled and comforted her. I had never seen her so upset, but while her sympathy lay principally towards Ingrid, mine was directed more towards my brother and my mother.

"There are only two people that know what happened, Mary and Ingrid," I reflected. "I'm not going to ask Mary, and if Ingrid were to break cover we could only get half a story from her. There are clearly good reasons why they have stayed silent. They don't want anyone to know what happened! Mary treated Ian completely as her own flesh. I don't think we should rock the boat just to satisfy our curiosity. What I've just found out diminishes my love not a jot for Ian. He was my brother and best friend. That should be all I need to know."

"But all the same?" Fiona said between sobs.

"But all the same I do need to know and so do you."

"Yes."

"The person who may have the answer is that policeman or whatever, Rupert Noakes, assuming that he is still alive. I'll phone Eugene tomorrow."

Eugene confirmed to me that Noakes was still going strong and, indeed, still seemed to be working on some advisory role in national security. He gave me a phone number in London.

I got hold of Noakes the same day. I wanted to be cautious in what I told him but I couldn't avoid telling him about Ian's death, which he hadn't known about, so I concocted a story that his death certificate had uncovered some muddle about his birth mother. I could almost sense Noakes' acute interest when I told him that it appeared that while I and Ian shared the same father, Colin, we had different mothers.

"Well," he said. "That's taken a long time to come out, although I had hoped it remain forever hidden."

"So, you know about it."

"Yes, I actually had a part in it... his adoption."

"Then his mother was Ingrid. And the relationship between her and Colin in Arisaig was very much more than she led us to believe when I and my wife, Fiona, who you met at Aldermaston, visited her in Bodø last year."

"Yes, your brother was Ingrid's son." Look, it will be

difficult to explain it all over the phone, could we meet?"

"I'm at the family home near Margate for a few days. I could easily get up to London from here by train."

"Come for lunch, and bring Fiona if she wishes. I live in a mews house near Sloan Square, there's a great little pub nearby, the Grenadier. Why don't we meet there for lunch, say midday Thursday?"

"That would be fine. I actually know where the Grenadier is. I'll ask Fiona to come too. We will have to get Catherine looked after, but my mother, my true mother, will willingly do that."

"Catherine? Who is that?"

"Our little girl, 6 months old now."

"Making her Colin's granddaughter. Congratulations. See you Thursday."

Fiona was enthusiastic to meet up again with Noakes and get the full story about Ingrid and Ian. I asked Mary if she would look after Catherine for a few hours while Fiona had a day off, the first in 6 months, sightseeing in London. She, of course, readily agreed. A day with the grandchild alone, heaven!

Chapter 22

Fiona and I walked out of Knightsbridge underground station and cut through some narrow streets, alleys really, until we reached the north side of Belgrave Square. We found Wilton Row, with is original stables now all turned into very expensive homes, and headed up the stairs leading to the small patio at the rear of the Grenadier. I had been there with Ian when he was still working in London. Ironically it was one of his favourite watering holes. We were a little late and Noakes was already sitting at one of the small wooden tables on the patio with a beer in hand. Having greeted him, Fiona and I went inside the archetypical 18th century pub, stuffed full of brown panelling, ancient looking furniture and hung with a myriad of pictures mainly displaying soldiers in uniform on horses

We purchased two small beers and returned to Noakes.

He raised his glass and said, "It's pretty obvious that the Grenadier has been, in many ways still is, a military pub. Of course it helps that the Horse Guards barracks are close by on the edge of Hyde Park, just across the way from Harrods. Did you know it used to be the Duke of Wellington's Officers Mess?"

"No," I admitted. "I came here a few times with my brother Ian when he was still working in London."

"Really! Or that is one of the most haunted places in London?"

"Nor that," I again conceded.

"Well, enough of the history. They do good food, menus are in the bar. Do you want to eat or discuss Ian first?

"Couldn't we do both at the same time?" suggested Fiona. "Order now, talk and drink our beers while we wait, then continue when the food's arrived."

"Fish and chips are very good here. That's what I'll have, and I'd like to treat you both as a slight token of regret in withholding what I know of the full story of Colin and Ingrid. We all settled for the fish and chips?"

Noakes went inside the pub to place our orders. He was back in just a few minutes bearing a bottle of white wine, cooling in a silver bucket of ice, in one hand and three glasses in the other.

"This can keep cold until either we finish our beer or the fish arrives. Now, have you actually seen or spoken to Ingrid?"

"Yes," replied Fiona. "I've met with her twice in Bodø, the second time with Martin last year. She enthralled us with the story of her trek up the coast of Norway in 1940, her meeting up with Ian in Bodø, their escape from the sinking of the Glorious, and their meeting up with you in Arisaig in June. After that it gets a bit vague."

"Ah yes, Arisaig, all that time ago," Noakes commented in a reflective manner.

I interrupted the start of his reverie. "We know about Ian getting a posting to fly fighters in Liverpool in early September 1940, and about Ingrid joining the SOE and eventually being parachuted back into Norway in 1944. Ingrid did admit to having a brief relationship with Ian during those weeks together in Scotland. She rather shrugged it off as one of those wartime things."

Fiona took over. "Ingrid was very short on details of that time spent with Ian and, not surprisingly, of what she actually did with the SOE. However, we do also know that Ian fudged his flying log book to show that he was flying Lysanders back with his original squadron at Ickenham while he had in fact been at Arisaig with Ingrid doing no flying at all. Martin's birthdate is June 1942 while Ian's supposedly was almost exactly a year earlier. We also know when Mary got married in January 1941, and we can count nine months in either direction."

Noakes was impressed. "Well, that's as good a brief as Eugene could have prepared for his political masters, he sends his regards by the way. He is in good health although bigger than ever. Now what I have to tell you is what I know of the Arisaig liaison and its end result."

We had finished out beers. Noakes opened the bottle of wine and put two thimblefuls into the bottom on his glass. "Pretty good, it's from Sancerre. I love its steely taste. Cuts through the fat of fish and chips."

Just as he had finished pouring all three of our glasses, the lunch arrived.

We sipped our wine and started on the meal before Noakes continued with his story. "I think you know that I met them both at Arisaig, in fact I was instrumental in getting them away from the Faroes, because I didn't want them getting mixed up with the rest of the survivors from the Glorious. Colin had played the role that I had given him at Ickenham so my professional interest in him was effectively at an end, but Ingrid was of great potential value. Remember that this was at a time when the SOE was being formed amongst considerable opposition from various established organisations who thought that it was their role to act covertly in enemy territory. She had shown herself full of initiative in transporting that barrel and displayed considerable guts too. She spoke ever-improving English and, of overwhelming importance, she had worked at Vemork. She knew the plant intimately, and was very familiar with the surrounding countryside. An ideal person, in fact, to help the preparations for the destruction of the heavy water plant, a project that had already been recognised all the way up to Churchill as being of high priority. I didn't want her name being publicised as a Glorious survivor any more than I wanted her pinched by one of SOE's rivals."

As Noakes paused to continue his meal, Fiona said, "Ingrid told us about the air raids and the ground expeditions against Vemork, the failures and the successes. She regards it lucky that her parents were not killed by the Allied bombs that took the lives of some of the locals."

"Yes, indeed," Noakes commented. "So, where was I? Oh yes, the doctor who had examined both Ingrid and Colin when they arrived at Arisaig told me that although she was physically improving after her ordeal, she was mentally exhausted. He advised that, because of what the two had experienced together, it would help both if they could support each other emotionally and thus should not be separated for a while. I took his advice and arranged for Colin to stay for a couple of weeks at Arisaig. I think the Air Ministry forgot about him in the turmoil of the withdrawal from France and then the lead up to the Battle of Britain. So, as you seem to know, the emotional support they gave each other had a practical side and they became lovers. I went back to London before the end of June and stayed there, busy with the birth pangs of the SOE, until well into August. It was a busy time for many people in the south of England as the air battle raged overhead and the knowledge became widespread that Hitler was building an invasion force on the French coastline. When I returned to Arisaig the whole surrounding district was beginning to turn into a major training area for SOE, Commandoes and the like. I was very surprised to find that Colin was still living there as, of course, was Ingrid. Seeing the two of them together, it was clear to me that they had an intimate relationship. It was clear to other people as well. The Adjutant, an infantry Captain, drew me aside and said that Ingrid was having difficulty settling down into her SOE role because of the distraction of Colin's presence. He recommended that the RAF take him back into operations and out of Arisaig. I had a small suspicion that the good Captain fancied

Ingrid himself and thought his chances better if Colin were removed. Nevertheless, it was clear to me that the liaison should be broken which is why, as I said earlier, I got onto the Air Ministry. I left for London again and didn't return to Arisaig for several more months."

Noakes stopped speaking to finish his meal and then polished off the remains of the wine.

"Is that it?" asked Fiona sounding a little aggrieved. "That's not much more than we already knew, or had guessed at least."

"Oh, no", he replied. "Now we come to the really interesting bit. As I say, it was months before I saw Ingrid again. April 1941 I think. I do remember the weather had been filthy and instead of managing to cadge a flight from my RAF friends, I had to make the whole journey from London by train which took nearly two days. I was in a pretty filthy mood by the time I got to Arisaig and was given a room. I cleaned up and went into the bar for a pre-dinner drink where I saw Ingrid sitting in a chair. She got up to greet me. Now, I remembered her as a well-built girl, not really fat but well-covered is perhaps the expression, pretty as well, but it was patently clear to me that she was pregnant. There was an SOE officer masquerading as a Major also in the little Arisaig bar. He caught me staring at Ingrid and beckoned for me and Ingrid to walk through the French doors onto a patio overlooking the garden. I remember his accent, Winchester and Oxford I guessed. It was clear that he was used to giving instructions and having them obeyed. Ingrid moved ahead, hanging her head low to avoid gazing at us. The Major told me that he was Ingrid's, he called her Miss Johansen, de-facto commanding officer.

'She is valued highly here,' he said. 'Her input into our little plans is invaluable and we would hate to lose her. Depending on how this war progresses there may be a role for her back in Norway, something that she says she is willing to take on. But, as you can see, she has an encumbrance, so to speak, although she has been so good at hiding the fact that it only became obvious a few days ago. When are you, eh… due,

Miss Johansen?'

'In June,' she mumbled in reply.

The Major dismissed Ingrid by suggesting that she now went to the dining room to have supper while he and I discussed what to do next.

It became clear that the Major was on the horns of a dilemma. He desperately wanted to keep Ingrid working for the SOE but she couldn't do so with a baby or a toddler in tow.

'There is no way she can be dropped into Norway with a young child back here, so I am afraid that I'm going to have to let her go.'

But the germ of an idea was forming in my mind.

How do think she would react if we, me perhaps, suggested adoption, I asked him.

'That would all depend on how badly she wanted the child. It's that Flight Lieutenant that accompanied her from Norway, he's the father I'm sure.'

And so was I. Ingrid was just finishing up her supper, alone, when I went into the dining room. I told her that we needed to have a serious chat about her future and that of the child. She accompanied me to a small office at one end of a corridor. I quizzed her about adoption. She was ambivalent. She knew that the baby would curtail her work with the SOE and that with a young child she would never be allowed to operate inside Norway, but she was also aware that she was likely to have a very strong bond with the child once it was delivered.

She admitted that Colin was the father. 'But that is all over now. He sent me a short letter before Christmas saying that he was getting married to an old sweetheart called Mary and wishing me success in my time at Arisaig. I received it just as I realised that I was pregnant. I never thought to tell him. I regarded it as my problem to sort out. There was no blame, there was no guilt. As of now, I think my inclination is to put my baby up for adoption, as you have just suggested. But who knows how I might feel about that in a few months' time. Even a woman in the SOE is sure to develop strong maternal instincts as the months tick by. I can't predict how I might feel when I first hold my baby in my arms. You are asking a terrible question of me which I cannot answer for certain right now. But I understand your logic. You are rather good at mind games aren't you and I know I have a duty to help my country. So it's a sort of conditional yes, but don't be surprised if I change my mind. In the meantime, I'll continue working on what I do here for as long as I can.'

I stayed for a few more days in Arisaig, seeing her several more times. She looked happier and I asked her to let me know as soon as the baby was born.

My plan was to confront Colin with his impending parenthood and ask him to adopt Ingrid's baby, with Mary's agreement of course. But his RAF service had moved him to Egypt I was told, and my proposition was not the sort of thing that I could commit to a signals pad. Instead, I decided to speak directly to Mary. The Air Ministry, with a little persuading, revealed that she was living in a rented flat in Wandsworth, south London.

I drove to Wandsworth and told her the whole story. Colin, Ingrid, Arisaig, the baby. Rather to my surprise, she agreed to adopt the child, if that was what Ingrid wanted she insisted. I think perhaps, with so many pilots being killed, she realised that she might never see Colin again. She could be left with nothing tangible to remember him by except for this unborn child who would act as a living memory. I asked myself that if and when he did return safely from Egypt, what sort of a conversation would they have? I don't really know what went on in her mind. How she would explain her reasoning to Colin? What pressure would she put on him? But the decision to adopt was what I wanted, and what my country needed. I was content with what I had done.

And that's really the end of it. In June a healthy boy was born, and in July he was in Mary's arms."

Noakes looked at his watch, exclaimed that he had to meet someone else, said that he hoped that his story had filled in the gaps in our knowledge, said the meal was all paid for and departed.

On the way back to Westgate, Fiona and I ran over what Noakes had told us. We agreed that it added nothing much materially to what we already knew or had guessed about the beginning and end of the story. Ian was Colin's child conceived in Arisaig in about late August 1940, and that the child ended up in Mary's home. What we didn't know is how Ian was passed off as her own baby, and how her decision affected her and Colin's relationship.

"But what about the grandparents, the mothers and fathers of Mary and Colin? Joan, Byron and the two that lived in London?" Fiona asked. "Surely they would have had to have been told? Mary could not pass Ian off as having been found under a gooseberry bush."

"You are right, they had to know, but maybe it was shame or guilt or whatever that persuaded them to go along with the deception, for both Colin's and Mary's sakes. I don't suppose that we will ever know and... it's not important. The only important thing is what we now say to Mary."

"Nothing," Fiona was adamant. "What would be gained by bringing it all back to her?"

"It's not Mary so much that I am thinking of, it's Ian. Do I owe him something? Do we owe Ingrid something? She gave up her child, one could argue, to help rid her country of the Nazis. She is a good woman. The pain must have been immense. The intervention by Noakes was near genius although a high risk strategy."

"We saw his birth certificate when we were making all the arrangements for his funeral. It clearly stated that Colin was his father and Mary his mother."

"A war time sleight of hand, I imagine," I suggested. "Probably arranged by Mr Fix-it Noakes."

"Yes," agreed Fiona. "Probably. I'm sure that he has had many secrets and fixed many things during his life. Perhaps the Ingrid and Colin story is the last of them. Perhaps we have done him a favour by allowing him to reveal it. I'm rather sorry that I regarded him as creepy. I rather like him now, or at least respect him. And it must have been him that set up the OBE award to Colin. But are you really thinking of confronting Mary about Ian's origins?"

"It's the idea of having such a fundamental secret closeted within me. I don't think families should have such secrets from each other."

"Do you have secrets from me?" Fiona asked.

"No, no I don't think that I do. And if you press me I'll get onto Meredith who, by the way, was extremely helpful to me when you went through the crotchety period of your pregnancy."

"Really! She told me that she had given you a right royal bollocking... secrets, you see." She leaned across the railway carriage and kissed me. "Do whatever you think, darling, but take your time to decide, and tell me first."

Chapter 23

*I*t's early evening on the 14th January 1983. Ingrid's plane for Norway has just taken off from London's Heathrow. She will arrive in Oslo late and will have to overnight there. Fortunately, she has hung onto to her aunt's apartment which was bequeathed to her on her death six months ago. She knows that she should sell it but cannot bring herself to sever this last link with her beloved aunt.

Today, however, she did sever a last link. That to her son Ian. 'Why did Fiona phone me immediately after his death? Does she know about his birth, his conception in those hilly moors surrounding Arisaig? No, surely not.'

Ingrid tries to rationalise why she attended the funeral service but deliberately avoided showing herself or talking to any of the family gathered in that hall. She was driving her rented car back towards Heathrow even before they came out into the sunshine.

'It had to be my private farewell,' she concludes. She had been so full of hope with that first phone call from Fiona when she claimed to be married to Colin's son, so eager to talk with her in Oslo. So happy to learn about her partner Martin, 'my son's name in Martin!' She had felt her heart skip a beat. She *had never given the baby a name during that short month when he was hers, she hadn't dared to unless the intimacy proved too hard to break.*

Her thoughts turn to that day in Bodø when she met Martin for the first time. 'I was gazing at my son, trying to control my excitement, looking to see if there was any resemblance to me, but seeing only Colin, wanting to reach out to hold his hand. Then the devastating blow. The discovery of the cruel truth that it was his older brother, Ian, who was really my son, and then the even crueller revelation that Ian was dying in England of Muscular Dystrophy.'

Then the day she arrived back in Bodø after the boat trip up to Kirkenes with Fiona and Martin. 'I went to my doctor and asked her about Muscular Dystrophy, and now I know that it was me that passed it on to Ian. It was me that was killing my son. So I had no choice but to attend his funeral and silently beg his forgiveness.'

'Arisaig,' she thinks. 'Arisaig... I can never go back there to relive those few short weeks with Colin or to confront the ghosts of all those that passed through there and on to their deaths. But I spent over three years at Arisaig and there are so many of the memories of the stone buildings, intimacy and people that are seared into my memory.'

She recalls how those first few days at Arisaig were for her filled with the strangeness and confusion of finding herself in the unfamiliar military environment, and not knowing what her future was to be. The house was imposing, almost overwhelming for a girl brought up in a small Norwegian village. It was sprawled over a large area and was high; five floors with the cellars. It had originally been built in the mid-eighteen hundreds from local stone as the centre piece of a hunting estate for a wealthy English industrialist. She was surprised at how pristine the interior looked, but was then told that the house had been completely burnt out about ten years previously, with rebuilding completed only in 1935. There was a sort of courtyard between the main building and its wings giving access to the main entrance. That was where the car with Noakes, Colin and her had pulled up when they first arrived from Mallaig. A tall clock tower, part of the main structure of the house, loomed over the courtyard and had internal steps winding to its top with small alcoves off.

'I used to go up that clock tower,' she thinks. 'When I sought solitude and peace from the other inhabitants of Arisaig. The room I was given was at the very top of the house. It was quite spacious and originally intended as the bedroom for a servant and, unlike other bedrooms on the lower floors, it had a bathroom right next door. There was an identical room adjoining it which was occupied by the nurse... Beryl, now I remember her name, who looked after me when I first arrived. She and I had shared the bathroom. We regarded ourselves as rather privileged. Being an officer, Colin was given a bedroom on the floor below mine, but with a long walk to his nearest bathroom which he had to share with half a dozen others

Apart from my signing the Official Secrets Act, attending some briefings explaining the purpose of the SOE, how the organisation was being built up and the setting of rules for the conduct between ourselves, the SOE staff and the local inhabitants, although Colin was excluded from all this because of the 'Need-to-Know principle, he didn't need to know, he and I were pretty free to do what we liked during our first couple of weeks at Arisaig.'

For a few minutes of her flight, Ingrid tries to avoid thinking about the time that Colin and she spent together, but then she realises that she cannot achieve closure for Ian until she addresses it as a kind of catharsis.

'I didn't get issued with a proper uniform for the first two weeks and spent my time using the collection of clothes provided to me when I first arrived. In the day time I used to wear that set of khaki overalls in which, with my hair still cut short and a service beret on my head, I looked like a young man. This stood me in good stead when Colin and I were on our own outside and trying to look inconspicuous.

I am not really sure that Arisaig had been officially taken over by the SOE in that June, although preparations to *regularise its occupation were certainly in progress, accompanied by a great many people coming and going and the installation of desks, filing cabinets and the like. Colin and I were not involved with any of this so we took the time to explore the surrounding area. We clambered down the steep terraced gardens of the house and strolled the two hundred metres through that broad meadow down to the sea shore. There we gazed over the Sound of Arisaig towards the south west and, if no one was around, held hands. There were two brick huts in the meadow that were full of farmyard junk when I first arrived. Later one was used as the ammunition dump for the SOE firearms and explosives training, while the other was fitted with iron bars at the windows and used to indoctrinate SOE agents with a taste of the prison conditions which would await them if captured by the Nazis. I was never subjected to that side of SOE training.*

A stream, or burn as it was called, ran behind those huts down to the sea. All that summer its water was crystal clear. Colin and I used to paddle in it to cool our feet when returning from those progressively longer hikes as our strength returned. Colin seemed to have been forgotten about by his RAF bosses and there was little more for me to do for many weeks except help set up offices and order stationary while a proper role was found for what, the SOE thought, were my native knowledge and talents. We had lots of spare time to ourselves. I think that the other SOE staff were happy that we kept out of their way. We explored the barns and stables around the house, all of which were eventually utilised for training and the like. We tramped the moorland hills and valleys that surrounded the house. We saw eagles, red deer and salmon making their way up rivers towards the lochs. And a few times we saw SOE instructors practising their explosive skills by blowing salmon out of the water for our meals.'

Ingrid now realises she must address the core of her memories of Colin if her catharsis is to be complete. She takes a few minutes to drink the large Scotch whisky that the cabin staff have just offered. Her mood changes as the spirit starts to *infuse her with a pugnacious glow. Her thoughts become a response to an unknown inquisitor, almost an excuse for her and Colin's behaviour.*

'We first made love at the end of our first week at Arisaig. I even remember the date; the 20th of June. I still really don't know how it happened. I wasn't what might be traditionally described as in love with him, neither he with me, I think. He was going to marry his girlfriend in the following year. He had told me that when trying to survive in those cold Norwegian waters. We did it because we were there together. We had survived against all odds but still felt somehow under threat because of the uncertainties then still clouding our futures. I think the defining moment for me was when we were told that the Gladiator pilot, Jack Falkson, had not escaped the Glorious sinking, I had spoken him several times in Bodø. He had an accent that he told me was South African and I somehow equated his death with Colin's survival, both young RAF pilots.

So we did it, as often as we could, in the woods, on the moors, clothing on, clothing off and it was nothing like I had ever experienced before, since losing my 16-year-old virginity my first month at technical school, or afterwards with Peter. Although I truly loved him, we really just went through the motions without any real passion. I think the capability for passion was lost to him while in prison. Sometimes Colin used the dreadful Government Issue condoms, supplied as much to provide waterproof sacks for SOE equipment as for personal enjoyment, but mainly he didn't, and we had no regard for the consequences. 'What will happen, will happen' was the creed of many people in those dark days of the Nazi war.

Then Colin departed. I knew that I would never see him again and I tried to put him out of my mind as my role in the initial planning for the destruction of Vemork began. I missed him for a while, of course, but I wasn't heartbroken. The needs of my little role in the war overrode the needs of my body, although for several weeks I would cuddle a pillow in my bed and think of him.

Arisaig House was fully up and running by December 1940 and the person in charge then was a Major Munn, but I seem to remember he was only there for about three months. The first people to enter training were a collection of Spaniards and Italians. I didn't have much to do with them and they soon moved onwards to one of the other large, rambling SOE houses dotted around the rural surroundings between Arisaig and Mallaig. One of these, Meoble Lodge, was particularly remote and hard to reach by a vehicle track which was little more than bush path. It was principally used for housing French agents, but there were also Norwegians so I found myself there often during the planning and work up for the various operations which culminated in the destruction of much of the Vemork facility in early 1943.

But shortly after that first Christmas, which had been quite 'jolly' as some of the Army staff described it, I confided in Beryl that I thought I was pregnant. She had a test performed by the Fort William hospital which provided the confirmation. I swore her to secrecy and tried to hide my expanding shape beneath ever more voluminous boiler suits. But by the beginning of April my pretence failed and not long afterwards Mr Noakes turned up. He made that outrageous suggestion that the baby, my baby, be adopted by Colin and his new wife so that I could continue in the SOE. But he was a difficult person to deny and he dangled the possibility of my operating in Norway as a kind of bribe, which I took. He arranged for me to move down to the south of England, Warnborough Manor, Guildford, where I could be useful in the selection process of SOE candidates and in June I gave birth, easily, to my baby boy in a Guildford nursing home. A month later I handed him over to the care of Mary and the absent Colin.'

The initial effects of the Scotch are wearing off and her train of thought has started to depress. She asks for another then flips through the airline's magazine for a few minutes, but Arisaig, even without Colin and the baby, will not leave her mind.

'I soon returned to Arisaig and found myself increasingly busy with Vemork, the training and befriending of SOE agents. At no time did anyone try to start an intimate relationship with me. I think the word got around that I was 'Off Limits' and, besides, I was one of those girls who didn't know how to avoid getting pregnant.

If I choose to dig deep there are so many memories of my time in Britain. I wasn't always in Scotland. Sometimes I had to go to the several other SOE establishments scattered throughout England but mainly centred on London. Sometimes I travelled by train, very tedious in wartime conditions and sometimes by air. I even flew in one of Colin's Lysanders at one time. But my abiding memories are those of the young men and women that I helped train and prepare for their trips to occupied Europe, often just one way. Many of them were so young, sometimes barely out of their teens, and the SOE was still in its infancy when the stories of their capture and dreadful fates started to filter back to us. Yet still they volunteered and still they went. I got to know many of the female agents quite closely. They went mainly to France and often got betrayed, were captured, tortured and then executed immediately afterwards or sent to concentration camps where, again, most died. Their full stories started to come out after the war was well over. Some of the executions in these camps, by lethal injection, gassing or shooting, took place in February 1945 at Ravensbruck when the Allies were already entering a collapsing Nazi regime and just a couple of months before capitulation. I discussed this with Peter after we had married, 'Why did the camp guards kill them when they knew the war was effectively over? Wouldn't have they realised that they would face retribution by the victors?' His reply was simple, 'They were Nazis and had not been told not to kill them, so they just carried on doing what they did.'

My repeated requests to become a proper SOE agent and be dropped into Norway eventually bore fruit. I was formally trained as a radio operator and was subjected to much of the standard SOE training. I knew what I might face if captured by *the Germans. I was scared I remember, but determined. I had had enough of seeing other SOE agents departing for who knows what fate, and I figured I could do the same. I had nothing really to lose, no Colin, no son... I could do it. I parachuted into the Lillehammer area soon after D-Day in 1944 where I flitted from place to place working as a radio operator.*

I remember my parents' faces when I crept in to their house for the first time late one night in September. I had six more months to survive to war's end and I did so without much excitement, compared with those poor girls that went to France. I never told my parents about Colin and my baby, but Peter could tell from my body that I had given birth so I spun him a fairly sanitised version of my Arisaig saga.

Oslo approaches.

'It's over, all over. Ian is dead. Now I must never revisit these memories again'.

Chapter 24

*C*atherine is nearly nine months old and it is three months since Mary last saw her. Martin and Fiona are bringing her here today, Saturday. They will stay the whole of the week, they say, so Catherine gets plenty of Grandma-time. Mary expects to see a big change in her, Fiona has proudly told her that she is crawling already. 'That's about right,' Mary thinks. 'Both Ian and Martin were crawling by the same age.'

She tells herself that she has pulled through the crisis of Ian's death. The emptiness of the house, much too large for me now, she thinks, no longer seems so threatening, and the emptiness in her heart, well, that is being filled by Catherine. With Martin and Fiona now working only part time, the child will grow up nurtured by both of them, and they have promised to bring her down to Westgate more often which is why, she supposes, she has put out of her mind any ideas of moving to a smaller place.

She realises what she has just thought, that she has re-placed Ian with Catherine, and scolds herself. Although there was nearly nothing to choose between Ian and Martin as characters or, indeed, in looks, they had both done her and

Colin proud, she has never really come to terms with the circumstances of Ian's birth. Not so much because of Ingrid herself but because of the disease she, unwittingly Mary knows, passed on.

Mary has known for years that Becker's MD comes from the mother and almost never affects girls and only then in a mild manner. Of course, Martin and Fiona will know that too. They will assume that she, Mary, is the carrier of a crippling, deadly disorder which Martin has been lucky to escape. And they are probably thankful that she never produced a daughter. Has she been selfish by never sharing the secret of Ian's birth with Martin? There have been times since Ian's death when she has felt a near overwhelming need to unburden herself. It is almost as if she will never let go of Ian, completely move on, until she shares the secret with Martin and Fiona. 'But what would their reaction be? Disappointment in her certainly,' she thinks. 'Anger perhaps, or some sort of sadness that Ian never knew who his true mother was?'

Yet, in her heart she knows she was right to adopt Ingrid Johansen's son. Right from the very beginning, there was never really any doubt in her mind that she had a responsibility for seeing that the child had the best upbringing she could provide.

--///

She remembers well the rather suave man knocking at her door that morning in April 1941. He is in civilian clothes, a dark suit. He has that air of being some sort of military officer or senior civil servant and there is a sly, furtive perhaps, manner about him that immediately sends a cold shiver down her spine. This, she imagines, is how you get told that you have lost your husband, killed somewhere in Egypt. Colin has been gone for over a month now. Four months of marriage and it's all over, she thinks.

The man introduces himself, "Noakes, Rupert Noakes from

the Air Ministry. May I come in?" He notices the look of horror on her face. No," he says. "It's not your husband Colin, but really it is I suppose, but he has not been killed or anything like that."

He comes into the lounge, sits when invited, and begins. Some things she knows already. Colin had told her about trying to build airfields in Norway, how he was ordered to accompany a Norwegian girl out of that country to Britain, how both of them had survived the sinking of a warship. She is astonished when Noakes tells her that the ship was the Glorious. She knows how very few had survived that catastrophe and that many RAF pilots had died in the sinking. She knows that Colin spent time up in Scotland recovering from his ordeal before taking up flying again in Liverpool in September. He had come to see her the weekend before and they had made plans for getting married in the New Year.

Noakes tells her about the house at Arisaig, and then tells her that Colin and the girl, Ingrid, had an affair while there. She is not too surprised at this. There had been something troubling Colin during that weekend which she had put down to the after effects of the ship sinking. But now she realises that it was probably guilt.

"Now Ingrid is pregnant, by Colin."

She remembers the exact words uttered by Noakes. Her feeling of forgiveness towards Colin turns into shock. Shock that he had pressed her to marry him just a few days after leaving that girl in Scotland.

"But he doesn't know that, he is in Egypt, isn't he?"

"Yes," she whispers. "I haven't heard from him since he left in March, a month ago."

"Now I know that this news will have come as a complete shock to you. Would you like to make a cup of tea while we consider what has to be done?"

"Why should I be considering anything other than how I will deal with Colin when he comes back... if he comes back? The child will just be another born out of wedlock, fathered by little more than a passing stranger. It's happening all the time

271

in this war; the men get to die and the women get sorrow and suffering. I don't need any tea."

"Let me put things in another context. Miss Johansen, Ingrid let's call her, is a highly valued member of a very secret and important government organisation. The work this organisation is doing is vital to the winning of the war, and Ingrid's knowledge and capabilities are a key part of plans now being made to bring the initiative in this conflict back to our side. It is only us against Germany at this time. The so-called Battle of Britain may be a turning point but is only the beginning of a long path to peace and the dismantling of the Nazi empire. Ingrid cannot continue her work if she is encumbered with an infant child. To be quite blunt, she wishes for it to be adopted, and by you and by Colin so it is brought up with its natural father."

Mary is completely nonplussed. She excuses herself and walks around the garden for ten minutes while she endeavours to bring some sort of sense into what she has just been asked. Suppose she takes this child on, who would she have to tell? Her own parents obviously, and those of Colin of course, but no one else surely because of the stigma that would attach to Colin. The child will have be treated as if she is the birth mother. It will have to be their child, not their adopted child, of both their flesh and blood. How about the neighbours here in Wandsworth? She can hardly produce a child from nowhere. She will have to move. The second house belonging to her parents in Westgate? It's got tenants in it now but they can be given notice. In the interim she can stay in the house opposite with Byron and Joan. She will have to time it exactly right. Be down there with the baby and claim it was born in London. But if she can get Byron and Joan on side it should work, although it's all a bit 'iffy'. Then there is Colin. Does she write to him in Egypt or present the child as a fait accompli on his return. And if he doesn't return? Then the child will be brought up by her alone. She has a plan of sorts, she will agree to take the child, but there will have to be some conditions.

She returns to Noakes. "When did you say that the baby is

due?"

"The beginning of June I understand."

"I will take the child and bring it up as mine."

A smile breaks across Noakes' face and he starts to speak, but is hushed by Mary holding up the flat palm of one hand, and continuing. "But I insist on the following conditions. The child comes with a valid birth certificate bearing my and Colin's names as the parents, the natural parents, there is to be no mention of adoption and if a girl her name is to be recorded as Joan after my mother, if a boy then Ian after Colin's father. After handing over the baby to me, Ingrid is to have no further contact with it, me or Colin and she is never to divulge to whom her child went and she is not to see the birth certificate with the child's name."

Noakes looks a little concerned on hearing Mary's stipulations, she sets to reassure him. "Mister Noakes, I believe that in your life you are involved in murky things that I have no wish to know about, thus I am sure that you know how to arrange what I have asked and if not, then you can find somebody that can. When you come back to me saying that all is agreed as I have requested then that is when you will receive my final agreement to take the baby, and not before then."

Noakes departs and Mary awaits his next contact. A few days after the beginning of June he phones Mary. "A healthy boy was born to Ingrid in a south of England nursing home. She has agreed for you and Colin to adopt him and also agreed to the personal stipulations you requested of her. I, for my part, have arranged everything else you asked. Congratulations, you have a baby son, Ian."

For a brief moment a voice inside Mary screams 'No!' She can't do this, she can't take this baby away from her mother, her loving and true mother. But the moment passes and the resolve that will help guide her through single-parenthood and her hidden love affairs takes charge. Mary confirms that she will take Ian and requests that he be weaned before the handover.

"There is just one request from Ingrid," Noakes replies.

"She would like to see you just once. She needs a face to identify as her baby's new mother. I thought I would bring them both down to you in a month's time."

"Yes, I accept that. We would meet here, then you can drive us down to his new home in Kent, Westgate on Sea. Remember, there is to be mention of his name in front of Ingrid"

--///

July 1941. Mary answers the knock on her front door that she has been expecting since lunchtime. She opens the door and there stands Noakes. By his side a tall, well-built woman in her early twenties. He is wearing his usual dark suit, she is dressed in a navy blue, two-piece boiler suit, clean and pressed. 'Nothing much in the way of clothes shops in Arisaig' thinks Mary. She smiles and advances to the woman to shake her hand. "Hello Ingrid, welcome to Wandsworth such as it is." She is trying to reduce the strain on Ingrid on this appallingly difficult day for her. She sees from Ingrid's eyes that she has been weeping.

"Hello Mary," Ingrid says.

Noakes breaks the ensuing strained silence. "Here we are all safe and sound. The baby is in a carrycot on the back seat of my car, asleep. I think that the sooner we get this over the better for everyone."

Ingrid is choking back sobs. "I want you to know Mary that I never wanted to steal Colin away from you, and I never wanted to get pregnant. Does he not know?"

"No," replies Mary. "I will await until I get news of his return from Egypt later this year. I will present the child as a done deal. He owes me that at least."

"I want to you to also know, Mary, that I promise not to come looking for him ever. He is yours and Colin's. He is a lovely baby. I've tucked a bottle, milk formula and some clothes that people at Arisaig have given me into his cot,

please take everything. But tell me, are you going to live here with him, with the German bombing? We saw lots of destroyed houses on our way here."

"No, I shall be taking him to a family house in Kent, by the sea, a long way from any bombing."

Noakes is beginning to feel left out of this conversation. "Right Ho! Then let us get the baby out of the car and into your place, then I'll drive Ingrid back to the Norwegian Club and in twenty minutes I'll be here to take you down to Westgate."

Ingrid gives the child one last kiss as the cot is carried through Mary's front door and laid at the foot of the narrow stairs by the side of two large suit cases. She turns one last time to Mary, "What will you call him?"

"I don't know yet", she lies. "I will discuss names with Colin when next I see him."

Ingrid heads straight to the front seat of Noake's car without saying another word.

--///

September. Noakes delivered Mary and Ian safely to her parents' house and handed her the birth certificate that names her and Colin as the parents. He confirms that Ingrid has not set eyes on it. Mother and child stayed with Joan and Byron for four weeks while the house opposite in the Courts was vacated, but they are now well settled into their new home. Byron and Joan fell for Ian straight away, and readily joined in the deception to their neighbours that Mary had recently given birth in London.

Two weeks ago, Mary received a telegram saying that Colin was on a ship sailing back to London from Egypt. She phoned a number in London for a message to be passed to him telling where his new home is.

--///

And now she waits for him. Ian is sleeping in the bedroom next to hers upstairs which has taken on the air of a nursery. Through the lounge windows she can see Colin climb out of a taxi and walk up the path to the front door.

She opens it. She has planned and rehearsed her next actions over and over again. She greets him with a welcoming smile, takes two steps and embraces him. He is carrying a large kit bag which he puts just inside the hallway and kisses her deeply. She leads him into the kitchen and puts the kettle on for tea, all the while asking the sort of things suiting the situation. How was the journey? How was Egypt? You are looking rather thin!

He answers her questions, they drink their tea, then, "Colin, I know about Ingrid."

He looks startled, then guilty.

"I know that you were lovers, and I know the circumstances. We weren't actually engaged then and you were recovering from an ordeal that put the two of you together in the most perilous circumstances. I am not blaming you, these things happen in wartime and I still love you."

He starts to apologise, she stops him. "That's enough Colin, no more apologies. They are not needed by me."

A muted child's cry is heard by them both.

"What? Who was that?" Colin asks.

"I'll take you to see." She leads him by the hand up the stairs. The cries become louder as they ascend. The bedroom door is ajar. She pushes it gently open, gathers up the baby who immediately stop's crying and grins broadly. "This is Ian, Colin. This is your half Norwegian son, now nearly three months old."

"Ingrid?" He asks incredulously.

"Yes, Ingrid's, but now our adopted child and to be treated at our natural offspring. His birth certificate gives us as the birth parents."

Colin is struck dumb for several moments. He gazes at the

child. Mary places it in his arms.

"My son," he says softly. "Ian?"

"After your father, of course and my decision."

Colin, still clasping Ian, follows Mary gingerly down the stairs back to the kitchen where she prepares a bottle. She takes back the baby and while feeding it tells Colin the whole story of her dealings with Noakes.

"Noakes, he always seems to be around. This all started with him sending me to Norway and ends with him presenting me with a son."

The return of Colin has gone better than Mary anticipated. He has just one week of leave before he must return to operations, taking Spitfires out to Malta he thinks. His support of her decision looks very promising for Ian's future but then, she considers, his equanimity, his niceness, have always been to her the more attractive aspects of his character. He has erred but is forgiven in her eyes. They must both, all three of them, move ahead. And she needs her own child, and soon. A sort of consolation for her while he is away, and a talisman should he not return.

Before they retire to bed Mary has one more demand of Colin. "Ingrid has undertaken to forget Ian. That's not a good word, she will never forget him, but she has given up any contact with him and with you. Noakes won't breathe a word, I'm sure he is good at keeping secrets, and now I want you to clear Ingrid from your mind. If Ian is to have no inclination, ever, that he is adopted, then your time at Arisaig must be forgotten, erased from your mind and your records. You have your flying log book which you will one day show to your child, or children. I want it to show that you were flying in England rather than holidaying, or whatever, in Scotland."

"I would have to rewrite my whole log book."

"Then so be it; that's what you must do. And let us not forget what Ingrid has chosen to do, giving up her child so that she can continue her struggle to free her country. I feel very sorry for her but we have to put her out of mind, out of our lives, out of Ian's life. Poor, poor Ingrid."

They make love that night while Ian sleeps in the adjacent bedroom, and every night during the remainder of Colin's stay in Westgate.

--///

She goes to answer the knock on her door. 'Here they are,' she thinks. 'They have made good time from the airport.'

Fiona and Martin are standing on the door step. Catherine is in a pushchair between them. Hovering behind them is a woman. Martin steps to one side. He extends a hand to the woman. "This is Ingrid, Mary."

Mary gazes at the woman for a moment. "Yes, Ingrid, welcome. We met once before." She embraces the woman, both have tears pouring down their cheeks.

Ingrid chokes, "I was so sorry that you lost your son Mary, and that it was my fault."

"There was no fault, Ingrid; he was the son to both of us."

The End

Glossary

- AA: Antiaircraft gun
- Ack-Ack: shells from antiaircraft guns
- Air Box: Air Ministry, London
- Bofors: Quick firing anti-aircraft gun – used by British Armed Services (and many others)
- Cruiser: Warship, larger than Destroyer
- Destroyer: Warship; fast, lightly armed,
- DFC: British medal, Distinguished Flying Cross
- FAA: Fleet Air Arm (British Navy)
- Funk hole: colloquialism, a place to take cover when under attack – hole in the ground
- GHQ: General Headquarters
- Gladiator: British Air Force; single engine biplane fighter – obsolete by the beginning of WW2.
- 'Groupy': Group Captain, RAF rank equivalent to full colonel, typical rank for airfield commander
- Heinkel-111 (He 111): German, twin-engine fast, medium bomber
- Heinkel-115 (He115): German, twin-engine float plane, torpedo-bomber.
- HMS: His Majesty's Ship (British Navy)
- Junkers 87 (Ju 87): German, single-engine dive bomber – the 'Stuka'
- Lysander: British Air Force, Single-engine reconnaissance aircraft
- Messerschmitt 110 (Me 110, Bf 110): German, twin-engine fighter-bomber
- NAAFI: 'Navy Army And Air Force', provided food, drink and social services for British Armed Services
- OBE: British award, Order of the British Empire
- RAF: British, Royal Air Force Skua: British Navy, Single-engine bomber and reconnaissance aircraft
- Rating: British Navy non-commissioned seamen
- Recce: Reconnaissance

- RN: British Royal Navy
- Scapa Flow: Major naval anchorage for the RN, North of mainland Scotland.
- Sunderland: British Air Force; large, four engine maritime reconnaissance and Anti- submarine flying boat.
- Wardroom: British Navy, social room for Commissioned Officers

Author's Notes

The inspiration for this story sprang from my father, Cedric's, WW2 diary. Chapters 3 & 4, Colin's Story, are near exact transcripts from the entries covering his time in Norway except for the addition of Ingrid who does not feature in them, and the naming of Noakes. Similarly, the leader of the RAF attempt to build the airfields was actually a Wing Commander Maxton, not Sexton, whose character is not intended to mirror that of Maxton in any way.

My father flew in combat for most of WW2, by the end of which he had reached the rank of Group Captain. Thankfully, he did not die in a plane crash but passed away peacefully in the year 2000. Like Colin, Cedric was awarded the OBE at the early age of 26, the reasons for which have never been made entirely clear. He also had a mysterious period away from flying duties about which nothing is known. His flying career is described in my book, 'An Average Pilot' which also chronicles his descent into Alzheimer's.

I have no brother (well, not known to me at least), but I did live in the house at Westgate during much of WW2.

The Norway and Scotland settings for the story are as accurate as I could make them.

The Norwegians from Namsos and Bodo, Harborg and Wick, are based on the real people, as are the three Gladiator pilots and sadly, their fates.

Arisaig House was purchased by Emma Weir in 2010 and is operated by her sister, Sarah Winnington-Ingram and husband as a very special hotel. My thanks to Sarah for the information she gave me about the house during a short stay there with my wife, Elizabeth, in 2017.

About the Author

Christopher Masterman was born in South London in 1942. His father was serving abroad with the British Royal Air Force; father and son did not meet until 1945. Christopher also joined the RAF where, with an MSc in aerospace technology, he served for 16 years as an Engineering Officer; at one time he was Prince Charles's personal aircraft engineer.

After leaving the RAF he worked for the European Space Agency in Austria before moving with his family to Canada where he joined a major aircraft manufacturing company where he rose to be an executive. In 1992 this company moved him back to the United Kingdom where he eventually retired. In 2006 he moved to Australia where he lives with his wife Elizabeth by the sea-side south of Perth.

An Average Pilot
An affectionate history of
Cedric Masterman OBE DFC

Cedric had recognised the sound of Hawker Harts, a sound he could not have heard since before World War Two. Yet if questioned, he wouldn't have remembered that he had ever been married, or had a son, or where he had ever lived.

'I entered a kind of denial. Cedric was suffering from a bad memory, nothing worse. He had never shown any frustration at being unable to recall events, places or people. Eventually I realised that this lack of concern was not because he couldn't remember them. Rather, in his mind they never existed and thus there was nothing to recall.'

But I had his flying log books and knew all of his extraordinary flying career.

Travelling to Tincup

'In June the trout of Tincup Lake can be taken on a dry fly.'

Simon Maitland was a passionate and expert angler. Tincup Lake in the Yukon Territory of Northern Canada was a fishing heaven to him, but his other obsession, that of intelligence gathering in the age of the Cold War, led him into situations beyond his control.

'Size (of Russian weapons) could often be determined from shadow lengths: comparing the shadows of known objects in the photo, people, doorways, vehicles, with those of the missile and perhaps the vehicle carrying it. Internal dispositions could be deduced from visible skin joints, intakes, access panels, antennae covers and aerodynamic configuration'

This obsession started when he lived in Prague in the 1950s as the son of a British diplomat.

'Simon could hardly believe what was happening to him. He was in a car, travelling through an Iron Curtain country and being tailed by secret police. Just two days before he had been in the normality of his grandparents' London flat. His school friends would never believe him, but then he knew that they were never to be told.'

Along his life's journey to Tincup, Simon works in Austria and falls for a local girl who may not be quite as she seems. And his eventual savage death in the Yukon wilderness may not be as straightforward as it first appears.

Deathly Confessions

Charles Carrington lays suffering from the terminal effects of cancer in an English hospice. His audience is part-time journalist Tony Mansfield who has been researching the internal combustion 'Discus' engine invented by Charles in the 1970s and which is now having a renaissance as a potential power plant for American military drones.

Tony discovers that two Americans believed by Charles to have stolen his design have recently been shot dead in similar circumstances in two different countries. He suspects that Charles is somehow connected with these deaths and contacts Charles' sister, Mary, for permission to visit him. During Tony's visits Charles gradually reveals the secrets of his past and the ingenuity behind them.

Almost by accident Tony becomes the possessor of dangerous knowledge; he seeks to discover why Charles did the things he did and why he has been chosen as the holder of the secrets. But did Charles' murderous tendencies start with the theft of his engine design or has he had sinister inclinations since childhood? And how much does Mary really know?

The Bridge at Braunau-am-Inn

May 1945: Adolf Hitler has been dead for two days and the war in Europe is ending.

US Army Officer Paul Strobel, twenty-two years old, of German parentage and Jewish background, stands on the German side of the River Inn looking at a partially destroyed iron bridge that forms the gateway to the Austrian town of Braunau. He reflects that this broken link mirrors the collapse of the seven-year, Nazi-inspired Anschluss between Germany and Austria.

He expects to pick his way across the wrecked structure with his fellow soldiers and spend the night in the Braunau house in which Adolf Hitler was born. Instead, he suddenly receives orders to travel immediately to Dachau.

His experiences as a member of the American legal team investigating the extraordinary crimes committed at Dachau and other Nazi death camps affect him severely for several years and stunt his ability to function normally in society.

Paul achieves a level of contentment in later life through a loving relationship with a strong woman, but the political elevation in Europe of a one-time Nazi officer resurrects his Dachau demons. It seems that they can only be completely excised by one more visit to the bridge at Braunau-am-Inn.

Lightning Source UK Ltd.
Milton Keynes UK
UKOW04f0311251117
313273UK00001B/173/P